BEYOND THE STARS

THE TALES OF THE SELYENTO: BOOK TWO

ERIS MARRIOTT

This book is dedicated to my grandfather, whose soul is now among the stars and heavens.
Thank you for giving me my fire. Alti'ya.

AUTHOR BIOGRAPHY

Eris Marriott is a graduate student working to pursue her Ph.D. in economics. When not contemplating the quandaries of supply and demand, she spends her time riding her horse, Andy, playing with her dog, Cuddles, and writing.

Her love of writing stems from her love of reading, naturally. Her favorite genres are fantasy, horror, and mystery, all of which she draws inspiration from when she crafts her own worlds and characters.

She likes her coffee black and her days warm and sunny. Nothing makes her happier than to get outside and enjoy life while it lasts.

CONTENTS

1. Tyrladan — 1
2. Shadow Storm — 21
3. The Neylka Seeks — 29
4. Hunted — 39
5. Leyun — 49
6. Vengeance — 59
7. Kreyuhl — 67
8. Connection — 81
9. Reckless — 95
10. Confessions — 103
11. Guilt and Vengeance — 125
12. Fate — 139
13. Partners in Crime — 155
14. Uncovering the Past — 161
15. Reflections — 171
16. Into the Shadows — 187
17. Unicorn — 199
18. Praises Be — 211
19. Reborn — 221

THE END — 227
The Current Mansalo Codex — 229
Acknowledgments — 233
Author's Note — 235

TYRLADAN

Clarisse

*D*ying, as it turns out, is as simple as breathing. At least to Clarisse it is. She feels a warm hum kick up in her veins, urging her toward the infamous light at the end of the tunnel. Her heart is full when she looks down and sees Death still beside her, a steadfast companion whom she no longer fears.

The light begins to subside; her eyes greet some all-too-familiar twinkling beings in the sky. *Stars.* They're everywhere, littering the night with lights far brighter than anything in Ashville.

Her feet, now bare, find purchase in the blades of cool, damp grass of a new world – the mystical Tyrladan she's heard so much about. The night paints them an odd, cerulean blue and Clarisse wonders what it must look like when brushed by the kiss of dawn. *And what does the sun look like here?*

Her thoughts are cut short at the sound of Death's melodious chuckling. She turns to him, finding his eyes a bit misty and a grin firmly fixed on his wolfish features.

"I don't think I've seen you this calm… or happy."

Clarisse can hardly swallow the lump filling her throat. Tears blur her vision. "I feel different. More alive… even if I'm not." She twines her fingers together in a nervous habit, but stows them at her sides when she realizes he's still watching her.

Death sighs. "It's a shame, at your age, that you should feel that way. John, Deborah, and Arthur must all pay for their transgressions. Magic or not, abusing a child and milking them for profit is vile. I despise those people. Were there not laws about interfering with fate and timelines to follow, I'd have long since destroyed their souls in Kohlu."

Her heart lurches at the mention of magic. "Am… am I in trouble? For using magic?"

Death's eyes widen and he seems startled by the question. "Why would you think that?"

Tingles creep along Clarisse's skin. She starts picking at her nails again and her teeth nibble on the insides of her cheeks. She only lets go when she decides what to say next.

"Because you said if I used magic and altered my timeline, I could be damned like Terrence." Her voice cracks and embarrassment warms her cheeks.

Death nods. "Depending on how you use it. If Terrence had influenced you to do the things he did when he was still mortal… or if you'd gotten carried away with freedom, things might have ended that way."

Clarisse holds up a hand. "Are you saying there's a proper way to use magic? One that doesn't alter my timeline and cause me to become damned?"

Death pauses. "Yes and no. Using magic always comes at a price. Terrence failed to teach you how you were paying, let alone how to consume energy and use less of it per spell."

Clarisse huffs and her heart races as the memories of her stars and all the pain that came with them rushes through her mind. Her gaze lands on a vibrant purple tree in the distance. She rests her gaze there to avoid Death's penetrating stare.

"Are you saying all of this could have been avoided if I knew how to use magic the right way?"

Clucking his tongue, Death follows her gaze to the purple tree. He shuffles in front of her path of vision, blocking out the strange, dark world that lies just out of view. Clarisse stifles the urge to go explore… for now, at least.

Anywhere but this conversation would be good right about now. I can't… I can't handle a betrayal from Terrence. If he knew how to free me all this time and chose not to…

Death's voice interrupts her spiraling thoughts. "How long did it take you to really know your stars? And, if I may, do you truly understand what they are and how to use them? Certainly by now, you realize they aren't balls of hot gas from outer space."

At this last statement, Clarisse giggles—she can't help herself. She blurts, "You're full of stars!"

Death's constellations become tinged with a light pink. His expression changes from one of seriousness to one of humor. A deep laugh rumbles in his chest, the hilarity winning him over. "Smart ass. You know what I meant! Seriously, what do you know about your stars?"

Stopping to catch her breath, a stitch still pulling at her sides, Clarisse smiles as she thinks of all the times she summoned her stars. Emotions drove them most of the time. Intense feelings—happiness, anger, sadness, jealousy… Their colors were random, but always vibrant.

A thought strikes her. "They whisper things to me. I hear my stars in English, but they were speaking… Mansalo. Did I pronounce that right? Your language."

Death doesn't speak, but the spark in his eyes and the yellowish tinge to his stars betray his excitement. This reminds Clarisse of a question she's been harboring.

"Do your stars reveal your emotions?"

Death takes a step back, his ears pinned against his head. "How do you… how do you know that?" His stars turn a strange shade of orange and seem to pulsate as Clarisse continues to stare at him.

"I may not be as worldly as you, Death, but I'm able to figure *some* things out. It's pretty obvious that they change depending on your mood. They always seem to match your eyes."

He clears his throat, shuffling his paws and looking elsewhere. *Is he… embarrassed?*

"Back to the subject at hand," Death says stiffly, straightening his head. "Did you say the 'stars' spoke to you?"

Making a note to push him on the subject of emotions later, Clarisse returns to the memories of her magic. "They would occasionally murmur things. I never really understood them, though. Sometimes I thought I could make out what they meant, but I can't remember specifics now. My memory from before is fuzzy in places."

Death hums. "That's curious."

Silence ensues. Clarisse resumes picking at her fingers. Her eyes, for the first time, trail to the robes draped along her body. To her horror, they look almost sheer. *When did these get put on me?*

Snapping her fingers, she fashions a thicker fabric to obscure her nude form. She doesn't think twice about the action until she's already done it, but before she can ponder it, Death's voice distracts her.

"How did you do that?"

Jerking, Clarisse meets Death's gaze and feels the heat in her cheeks return. "That's not important right now. We'll figure that out later. What I'm more curious about is why you thought it was okay to just stand and stare at me when I was practically nude and not say anything to me!"

Death's stars turn dark pink.

So it is emotions! Clarisse stifles the thought, but she's excited to know she's right.

"That's how everyone arrives!" Death's voice cracks a bit on the end as he rushes to his defense.

Scoffing, Clarisse tries to focus on other things to alleviate her embarrassment. Just then, a strange, glittering white figure draws her attention in the distance.

"Death?" she starts.

He scowls. "Don't keep changing the subject. What are you so keen on hiding, anyway? Is that why you aren't willing to answer my questions?"

The accusation slaps her attention back to him, a ringing fresh in her ears. She feels tears prick at her eyes. When she looks for the strange creature, it's gone. She whirls back to face Death with her fists clenched.

"I'm not changing the subject to hide things, Death. You should know better than that. To be fair, this is a lot for me to take in. I just *died* and it's my first time in Tyrladan. I don't know what I'm supposed to do here, and I know at some point you'll have to leave me and get back to your duties. So I'm trying to figure things out just as much as you!"

Now a hint of blue casts over his stars and he has the decency to look embarrassed. "Listen, I wasn't really paying attention to what you were wearing. It's custom for newly arrived souls to be clothed in such garb—sometimes they arrive without any coverings at all. I wasn't ogling you. Why would you think that, anyway?" He shakes his head. "But I am sorry. I should know better than to accuse you of trying to keep secrets from me. We're past that, I think, now that you know my true aim is to help you."

Clarisse feels herself start to calm, but she's still irritated with him. "I didn't accuse you of ogling, Death. At least I didn't mean to. I just freaked out, okay? And why would your mind immediately go to me keeping secrets in the first place? It's not like... Ugh, just whatever, okay? I don't even know what to say now."

Before he can answer or she has the opportunity to decipher how she feels, she turns her back to him and takes a deep breath.

The moon, now a glimmering orb of sliver, shines brighter over Tyrladan. A cool breeze glides over her skin and she wraps her arms around her middle for warmth. Closing her eyes, she inhales the loamy scent of dirt and the sickly-sweet smell of flowers. Roses. The same flowers her mother held a fondness for and would plant around the house. These smelled even stronger than Mom's.

I hate roses.

Her stomach churns at the sight of the wretched, thorny things when she opens her eyes and spots them. They sit a short distance away, nestled among various other flowers she doesn't recognize. As vibrant as they are, they fill her mind with poisonous, murderous thoughts. Clutching her fists, she imagines them burning. In the next blink, she gleefully watches them go up in ravenous flames, one by one.

Death rushes up beside her. "What are you *doing*?" His voice is clipped and his stars are a mesmerizing swirl of red, yellow, and orange. They blink at her, a frantic symphony screaming for her to stop.

Clarisse chooses to ignore their caution.

Instead, she turns her nose to the sky, catching the faintest hint of a familiar smell amidst the smoke that now curls through the darkness. *Is that water?*

A violent urge to submerge—even drown—consumes her. She doesn't register when her feet pick up into a run, carrying her at breakneck speeds in the direction she thinks she might find her source of absolution.

"Clarisse!"

She wonders if it's the wind speaking to her rather than Death. The way it echoes in her ears makes her head feel close to bursting.

Her lungs scream for air as she gallops across unfamiliar terrain, her feet sliced by the blades of grass with every desperate stride. Startled, she realizes her blood appears gold in the strange Tyrladan light. The gilded blood spilling from her veins almost makes her stop —almost.

The sound of the river's whispers slowly erupt into an angry roar. She's about to find purchase in the silvery rapids just out of reach when the Reaper eclipses her. His blur of stars comes hurtling at her before she can even think to dive.

His teeth puncture her not-so-sheer robe, gently grazing the skin beneath. Then they both tumble, rolling and scraping against the dirt before skidding to a halt on the pebbled riverbank.

She blinks up at him as sanity slowly returns to her. Clarisse feels a deep, aching shame well up in her chest that quickly bubbles over into tears that pour faster than she can think to speak. An incoherent mess is all that tumbles from her lips as Death pulls back.

His eyes rove over her with urgency, filled with concern. It's an unsettling image that burns into Clarisse's memory where she knows it will haunt her forever — just like all her other memories.

"What's gotten into you?" Death's voice, as calm as it sounds, trembles a bit. Is he scared?

"I... I don't know." Her throat is full of hot gravel. She turns to the river and the dryness in her mouth threatens to unravel her rapidly fraying mind.

Death rises and steps aside so she can brush the dirt off her robe. Instead, she dunks her head into the river.

"What are you doing?" he shrieks.

Death's voice is frantic, but Clarisse doesn't worry about what he's saying while she takes her fill. The cool, refreshing water tumbles down her throat. The liquid spreads through her chest and trickles into her veins, invigorating her.

"You probably shouldn't make a habit of drinking just anywhere in Tyrladan. This is the Afterlife, you idiot!" Death snaps.

Clarisse laughs. "What could possibly happen? Will I die again?"

Rolling his eyes, Death snorts. "No, but you can still suffer consequences. You're safe here, but you should always ask, just in case. Yehta is built for souls who have passed on. The rest of the Afterlife... not so much."

Sighing, Clarisse nods. The concern on his face is enough to keep her from arguing. *It's nice that I feel safe enough with him to argue.* The thought lingers and she can't help but smile.

Death clears his throat. "So, are you going to explain what happened back there?"

She picks at her fingers again, refusing to look back up at him. Shame courses through her and she struggles to find an answer. "I don't even know how I did that," she whispers. "My mom used to plant roses... I saw them and I just got so angry I couldn't help myself. I've never been able to set things on fire before. Lights, sure. And the house... But Terrence had to help me. You remember that."

Death laughs. "I don't know. At *that* display, I'm beginning to wonder how much he actually had to help."

"Now that I'm dead, will my powers be more intense?"

Cocking his head to the side, Death hums. "It will, but being able to set specific flowers on fire from a distance without formal training... That begs the question as to how far your powers might have stretched, even while you were still mortal."

"What a classic thing for a man to focus on," a third voice calls.

Clarisse jumps and instinctively tumbles back towards Death. To her surprise, he doesn't seem startled. Instead, he groans.

"Bast, what are *you* doing here?"

Death's tone reminds Clarisse of the many times she'd been forced to answer a teacher's question in school when she did something wrong.

"Why do you frown, child?"

Clarisse squeaks as the source of the voice emerges from tall blades of grass surrounding the riverbed. A slender, jet-black panther emerges. Her teeth are on display in something that resembles a grin.

"Don't be frightened. As delightful as fear smells on you, I don't think you want anything else to catch a whiff of that." The panther—Bast—laughs.

Clarisse clutches her shoulders to try and suppress a shudder. Death nudges her with his snout to reassure her, but the cold from his stars end up shocking her even more.

"Sorry," he whispers.

"It's okay," she manages to answer through her clacking teeth.

"Who are you?" Bast settles down not far from where Clarisse stands.

"Bast, this is Clarisse. I trust you'll forgive her torching your roses... and drinking from your sacred river. She's newly arrived, you see. Doesn't know the rules yet," Death hurriedly explains.

Clarisse's heart jolts. "Th-those were your roses?"

Bast swipes a paw in the air, waving off the offense with a laugh. "My dear, I know you're new. And quite frankly, I'm honored someone as powerful as yourself would take a drink here. You're more than welcome. However, I must ask... why burn the roses? What crime did they commit?" Purring, Bast's eyes sparkle with anticipation at what Clarisse might answer next.

Clarisse looks to Death and he nods. "My mother used to grow them in her garden. She... um... she abused me... a lot."

It's hard for Clarisse to form the words, let alone swallow them. Being free of her parents' clutches is difficult to comprehend. The ghost of their lashings and hate still grip her, and her chest hurts every time a memory struggles to the surface.

Frowning, Bast growls. Clarisse takes a step back.

"What did they do to you, child?" the panther asks.

It's harder for Clarisse to breathe all of a sudden. She can't see through the haze of her pain. Stepping forward, she holds out a hand to Bast. Her hand shows an ethereal, white glow that pulses. Before she can ask what's happening, Bast accepts the extended hand with her massive paw. The instant they connect, Bast's silvery eyes go blank. Clarisse steps back and Death starts shouting.

"What did you do? How did you… *What did you do?*"

Clarisse turns to him and sees that he's back in his human form. Why does he have to look so good when he's upset?

Death groans. "Stop ogling me and pay attention!" His golden eyes are alight with panic and his tanned skin ripples over taut muscles as he paces back and forth, running hands through his ebony hair. "You have to think before you act," he scolds.

"I—she wanted to know what I went through, and I just thought I'd show her instead of explaining! I couldn't bear the thought of saying it all out loud," Clarisse protests. "I didn't even know I could do that!"

Death stops. "Then how are you doing it? You just think about what you want to do, and it simply happens?"

Clarisse shrugs as hot tears return. *I'm still a freak. After all this time…*

Before she can stop it, a heavy sob escapes her chest. Death freezes, recognition passing over his face. His wide eyes go soft and he clucks his tongue. "Clarisse, I'm not trying to frighten you or make you feel alien," he offers kindly. "I just... I've never met a soul like yours. And you must imagine I've met quite a few souls during my long existence."

"And yet you have the nerve to treat strange ones like science experiments, you emotionless dolt!" Bast hisses.

Clarisse whirls back to face her and finds that silver tears have drenched Bast's face. She pounces, enveloping Clarisse in a human hug. When she pulls back, Clarisse finds herself face to face with the most beautiful goddess she's ever seen. Her delicate black braids are adorned with gold hair cuffs. Her deep, ebony skin reflects the moonlight and shines off her ample curves and angled face.

Imagining how much lovelier she might look when her vision isn't blurred by tears makes Clarisse's head spin.

"You have suffered too much, child, and *this* idiot is the one who came to save you?" Bast clenches her fists. "Why was I not informed? It is my sworn duty to protect children!"

Death avoids her gaze.

Bast growls, the sound low and menacing. "You knew about her and didn't tell me? You knew she had power and you let her suffer these tragedies?"

"The timeline cannot be interrupted for every child, Bast. You know this!" Death hisses. "I thought everything would be amended. That it would be under control."

His voice is laden with sadness. Clarisse could swear his voice broke a bit, but that's impossible. As Death, he is incapable of feeling emotions like that.

"That's a foolish excuse." The thunder in Bast's voice makes Clarisse flinch. "Come here, child." Bast extends her hands and Clarisse is compelled to take them. Her hands are soft, but firm. "Listen: you do not have to be afraid anymore. You have already proven yourself more powerful than most Selben I know. I didn't even know mortals like yourself could wield such power. You may not understand yourself yet, but you will. I will help you and so will Death."

Death scoffs. "Teaching people is *your* department, Bast. You know I'm not good at that."

Bast's nostrils flare. "Do you seriously have the audacity to tell me what to do?"

Rolling his eyes, Death shakes his head. "No, but Bast, I have several important things to attend to."

Clarisse's heart lurches. "You mean you're leaving me?"

"Clarisse, I can stop by for visits, but I can't stay here indefinitely. What do you think I do all day?"

"He certainly causes more problems than he's worth," Bast huffs.

While the two of them bicker, Clarisse dissolves into a painful state of reflection. She's still unsure of where she is—or why. Being dead is weird.

The river still calls to her, but she avoids it now that she knows it belongs to Bast. It's puzzling how someone can own a river, but she's not about to overstay her welcome by asking impertinent questions.

Kicking the grass around with her toe, she pays attention to her surroundings for the first time. The trees all have different colored foliage here. By the soft light of the moon, she makes out leaves in muted shades of purple, blue, and even the odd orange or yellow-neon. The leaves are folded into odd shapes. It's reminiscent of a child's painting in some ways, but with the artistry of a master's application.

In the distance, she can see the silhouette of a strange, smallish willow. Its leaves are silver and gold with a few odd colors dashed here and there, but they're shaped like... wind chimes?

By now, Bast and Death are hurling insults at each other in a language she doesn't understand—Mansalo, most likely. Their attention diverted, Clarisse wanders off toward the tree. As she gets closer, a strange tinkling sound of chimes brings a smile to her face. Weary, she slumps against the willow's golden bark and curls up amidst the roots that break the soil's surface.

Her hands pluck at the strange, vibrant grass and she watches as the pieces tumble through her fingers, littering them about like confetti. Sighing, she rests her head against the tree. Closing her eyes, she lets the strange music from the chime leaves lull her into a trance of her own making.

Her mind returns to Earth. She can practically see Terrence standing in front of her in the strange house they built together. He's standing over her body, screaming for her to wake up.

But I'm not there anymore.

A rustling in the grass snaps her eyelids open. Part of Clarisse wonders if Death was wrong. Maybe something lives in Yehta that can hurt her, after all.

The ominous feeling of being watched creeps along with the goosebumps forming on her arms and legs. "Who's there?" she calls aloud in the hopes that Death or Bast might hear her.

The same flash of silvery white she saw earlier kicks her heart into overdrive. If she were still alive, she'd worry about having a heart attack.

"Hello?" she calls again.

When nothing answers except for rustles that gradually inch closer, she urges herself to stand. Fear makes her legs feel like jelly, but she plants them firmly on the ground and backs up against the tree to protect herself where she can't see. She softens her vision so she can see from all angles, relying on her peripheral vision to try and get a read on what might be approaching. Still—nothing.

"Clarisse?"

Death is running to her. She breathes a sigh of relief. *Finally... he noticed I was gone.*

The rustling goes away. When Death gets close enough, she sprints to him. Without thinking, she slams into him for a hug. He catches her awkwardly, caging her with his arms rather than hugging back.

"What are you doing over by the Selyento?" his voice rumbles above her head.

Clarisse blinks and looks up at him. "Where have I heard that term before?"

"Clarisse, that's the tree of Fate. It's where all the strings for living souls are tied."

Clapping a horrified hand over her mouth, Clarisse turns back to glance at the tree with fresh eyes. With its gnarled roots and smooth bark, it seems unassuming for something so important. For the first time, Clarisse notices the odd glow that sparks between the branches.

"I didn't... I didn't know. It looked like a nice place to sit," she stammers.

Death scrutinizes her like she might be a wild animal. "You sat on the Selyento?" He frantically turns her around and starts examining her. "Are you hurt?"

Clarisse, now panicking, pulls away. "I thought you said Yehta was safe!"

"It is! No one typically sits on the Selyento, though. She's picky about those kinds of things!"

She?

"Well, *she* didn't seem to mind! And it's not like you told me!" Clarisse fumes.

Bast comes running up behind Death. "You didn't show her the Selyento? What is *wrong* with you?" Upon seeing Clarisse's terrified expression, the panther goddess laughs. "Well, if it's any consolation, if she let you get that close, she definitely likes you!"

Clarisse gasps. "You're saying this tree is alive?"

Death and Bast both nod, Death looking almost aghast that she asked such a silly question.

Bast cuts her eyes at him. "Don't be foolish, Death. The girl doesn't know. How do you expect her to learn? Not even the Selyento takes offense. She let her find refuge beneath her branches."

Death grumbles something in response, but Clarisse doesn't understand him.

Bast narrows her eyes. "It is also rude to speak in a different language and confuse our *guest*, Death."

Seeing the two of them bickering reminds Clarisse of an old couple. Her heart twinges, full of emotions she can't name. She hesitantly asks, "Are you two married?"

Bast pauses before bursting into a high-pitched laugh. "To this idiot? No. He's like a sibling to me."

Death huffs. "I'd rather take a dip in the Neylka before I'd marry this harpy."

Clarisse is startled. He hardly ever shows emotion and it's unsettling to hear him say something so brash.

"No, my dear, my heart is set on another," Bast says. "And this one here will probably never settle down with anyone. He's had plenty of admirers, but he's too dense to understand how to properly care for anyone. Take you, for instance. Imagine having *him* for a husband!"

Bast shudders, but Clarisse feels her cheeks burn. She chooses not to imagine what it would feel like to call Death hers. *That would be too much.* Instead of meeting Death's eyes, she refocuses on the strange noise she heard by the tree.

"Are there other souls nearby?"

Bast shakes her head. "Most souls are far from here by now. When souls arrive here, Death typically ushers them to their home here in Yehta. Why you're all the way upstream is puzzling. This is where particularly troublesome souls are judged. He had no business letting you come this far."

Death throws up his hands. "Who says I let her? She's the one who set fire to your roses and ran!"

Bast chuckles. "It's so easy to upset you, you fragile thing."

Before Death can say anything else, Clarisse holds up her hands. "Are you saying I have a home here?"

"You're supposed to," Bast answers. "Death and I would be happy to escort you."

Death doesn't protest, but Clarisse has the feeling he'd be much happier letting Bast take her back on her own instead. He probably has more important things to do.

Bast nudges her shoulder. "Come on. Why don't we start walking there and you can enlighten us as to what happened while you were under the tree. Then you can tell me more about yourself, since Death has been stingy with the details." Bast sneers at him as if daring him to argue.

Death stays quiet, his eyes lost in distant, troubled thoughts. His eyebrows are knitted together in a way that Clarisse has learned means he'll be ruminating on them for quite some time.

She nods at Bast and smiles. "Lead the way, then."

"So, why don't you tell me about these stars of yours...?"

Haltingly at first, Clarisse tells Bast everything. About the stars. The Church of Light. Father Simmons. And... about Terrence. Just thinking of him makes her heart hurt.

As they walk along, she feels Death's hand reach out for hers.

"I'm sorry," he whispers inside her mind.

She snaps up to look at him, but he makes no motion to acknowledge having spoken to her in such an intimate way. Instead, she's jolted to attention by Bast's sudden shriek.

"Whose blood is this?" She's stopped just short of a golden pool that's gathered in the grass a few hundred yards from the river.

Clarisse remembers the sharp grass slicing her bare feet as she ran to the river. Clearing her throat, she offers, "I believe that's mine."

Bast whirls around. The rage in her eyes threatens to scorch her, so she stumbles back. Death catches Clarisse before she can fall. Bast marches toward her without a word, her face a mask of righteous indignation. Her hand arches back and Clarisse closes her eyes, waiting for the slap.

Instead, Bast's hand makes contact with something else. Death's face.

"Why didn't you tell me she was a Selben?" the woman shrieks.

Death reels back from the impact and almost drops Clarisse, whose eyes are still closed. She prays he'll continue holding her. Suddenly, she's too dizzy to stand on her own. When Death doesn't let go, Clarisse focuses on taking deep breaths.

"Why did you have to hit me so hard?" Death rubs his cheek.

"What does having gold blood mean?" Clarisse feels her voice crack as fear creeps up her neck.

"Have you ever heard of ichor, Clarisse? Here, we call it Liadan. Life water. Blood. Specifically, ichor is the blood of the gods."

Clarisse scratches her head, her memory of mythology fuzzy. She remembers a few things about golden blood and how it poured from the gods. *But why is mine gold? Aren't I a mortal?* Simmering rage bubbles up in her chest. *There are still secrets about me that even I don't know… Why does everyone else know so much about me?*

"How much more about her are you going to keep hidden from me, Death?" Bast's voice is sharp, her blade landing squarely within his court.

He scoffs, "It's not like it was intentional. Her blood was *red* back on Earth. Everything about her was mortal. Everything. Do you really think I don't care for her? That it didn't crush me every time I had to leave her? My job dictates that I don't intervene. How much chaos would I have caused if I always stepped in to save her, Bast? She's not the first magical human and she certainly won't be the last. But it always leads to trouble—*always*. If they don't become corrupted, the world's corrupt nature consumes them. How many like her have been burned at the stake? Drowned? Beaten to death? I knew her life would be filled with pain, but there was nothing I could do. That's not my responsibility, Bast. The truth of the matter is that sometimes, life sucks. Why else do you think I exist?"

Clarisse is stunned. She swears she sees a tear or two forming in his eyes. She reaches for his hands and clasps them firmly. They're icy cold and filled with raw power; the crackling shocks her a bit, but she doesn't let go. *He needs someone to ground him.*

"You don't have to help me," he whispers.

Again, she's startled to hear his thoughts in her head. He doesn't acknowledge her, and she wonders if he knows she can hear him.

"Death," Bast starts.

"Don't 'Death' me. You know how hard this job is for me! I care deeply for Clarisse, despite having known her for only a short time. I never would have willingly left her unless I had no other choice, which I didn't. And I *did* intervene the moment I felt her magic would lead her to more trouble. If I was one of my own Reapers, I would have punished them for such a transgression. Perhaps even dismissed them. I broke my own laws for her." Death's voice is raw with pain.

Clarisse looks up at him and smiles. "I don't blame you for anything, Death. You came and got me. You tried to help. No one could fix my situation. Terrence tried, even if it was the wrong way, and it still wasn't enough. Magic can't fix everything."

Bast laughs. "It's always so cruel to see how wise the most abused people become. And look at you—you have the Grim Reaper revealing feelings I never knew he possessed. But, my dear, do you have any idea how you've become a Selbeno?"

Clarisse furrows her brows. "I take it Selbeno means..."

"Goddess," Bast answers.

Clarisse swallows. "No, I don't. Nobody knew what I was. Not even me. They called me demon. Monster. Witch..." Her voice trails off and she winces as memories of the exorcisms surface. "Has... has this ever happened before?" Death's hands grip hers tighter.

"We've had people approach Selben-type levels before," Bast explains. "Demigods, as you know them. Perseus. Hercules. And those are just two from Greece and Rome. I would have to get you a very long list if you wanted to know them all. But to ascend to true godhood upon dying? No."

Clarisse glances up into Death's face. He's clenching his jaw so tightly, and she fears he might shatter the bones in her hands if he grips them any tighter. But she doesn't complain.

He's scared.

The idea of the Grim Reaper being scared is unsettling at best. Something terrible brews in the pit of her gut, but she can't place what the unnerving emotion is.

"Okay, so we clearly have some work cut out for us, then. And I'm not sure Yehta is the right place for you," Bast muses.

It strikes Clarisse as odd that she can be so calm after hearing such a strange revelation.

"Maybe the blood is a fluke. Are we sure it's not just the way the light falls on it that makes it look gold?" Clarisse knows it's a stupid hypothetical question, but she asks it anyway.

Bast stalks up to her and pulls out a dagger. "Hold out your palm," she orders. There's a suddenness and authority that compels to Clarisse to obey… almost, anyway.

Death releases her right hand to block Bast. "That won't be necessary."

He procures a light—a star—on the tip of his finger. It floats before landing on Clarisse's open palm before disappearing within it. The glow from it pulsates inside her skin. Clarisse remembers plenty of times on Earth where the redness in her palm would fascinate her if she brought her own stars out to see her blood flow just beneath her skin.

I miss my stars.

On command, they reappear. They chatter with excitement as they watch Death and Bast examine Clarisse's hand.

"That looks like a golden glow to me," Death says firmly. "We need not resort to violent measures to have all our answers, do we Bast?"

Bast looks a little homicidal at Death's quip, but Clarisse chooses not to approach the subject. Instead, she continues to stare at the way her hand looks golden beneath the surface.

"Clarisse, I think it's best if we take you to see Fal. They might be able to assist in interpreting your Falme so we can trace your steps and figure out where and how this happened," Bast says.

Clarisse feels more confused than ever. "Who is Fal? And what is a Falme?"

Death answers, "Bast is saying we need to bring you to see Fate. Her name is Fal. Falme refers to the 'string' that holds the record of who you were in life." Death holds out a hand again, leaving Clarisse's right hand somehow colder. *When did he even grab it again?* "But before we get into all that, I think it's wise to see what her home here looks like first. One, she needs rest. Two, it will give her time to regroup and retrace her steps with us. I doubt the Falme will have much to offer," Death argues. "My list is rarely wrong when it comes to someone's manner and time of death."

Stunned, Clarisse looks over her shoulder at him. Her neck is getting tired having to crane backwards to see him, so she turns and faces him. "You *knew*? You're telling me you knew when I was going to die? If you knew that much, then why didn't you know I was a goddess?"

Death sighs. "Yes and no. As for the goddess thing, this is news to me as much as it is to you and Bast. Can you trust me enough to take a rain check on this conversation and explain later? I'm a little offended if you think I did all that work to save you for show."

At this, Clarisse laughs. He looks startled at the response. "No, I don't. You seem genuine. But you *do* owe me an explanation." Clarisse musters the bravery to stick her tongue out at him.

He rolls his eyes. "How juvenile. Sometimes I forget you are only eighteen on Earth."

Bast, clearly irritated, snaps, "We are taking her to Fal!"

The temperature plummets and Death strides in front of Clarisse before Bast can close in. "This is *my* soul to guide. We will follow protocol."

"Nothing about this is protocol now, Death!" Bast argues.

As much as she wants to pipe up, Clarisse decides now isn't a good time. Instead, she huddles closer to Death. As much as she likes Bast, she's still not sure if she trusts the panther goddess's motives. Granted, she's unsure why she trusts Death so readily. Especially when he's worked so hard to keep her a secret. At least according to Bast's accusations.

But he made so many valid points. And who am I to judge him for simply doing his job?

The strain of her conflicted emotions is exhausting. Clarisse just wants to sleep and recharge. Her chest and eyelids are heavy.

"Death?" She hasn't been paying attention to a word either of them has said. Her head is fuzzy. "I don't feel too well. I don't care if my home here is the right place or not. I'd like to go there now, even if it's not going to be my home forever. I know you've already broken a lot of rules for me, but I'd really like you to stay."

Death sighs heavily. "I can't abandon you now. Your soul is at risk."

His words puzzle Clarisse, but she's too tired to worry about those kinds of things.

"Clarisse, I know you're tired, but we need to figure out where you got your powers. It's incredibly urgent information to parse through," Bast argues.

Throwing up her hands, Clarisse lets exhaustion guide her frustrations. "I mean, we have eternity now, don't we? There's no time clock. No deadline. I'm not going anywhere. Let Death take me home. I don't mean any disrespect to you or your hospitality, but I'm dog-tired. Everything aches."

Bast's expression softens. "I understand. Forgive me; I'm just eager to help."

Clarisse stumbles out from behind Death and walks over to her. "I know." She holds out her hands. "I appreciate that. We can go see Fal, just not right away. I want to sleep." Clarisse's eyes water when Bast pulls her in for a hug.

"You'll be alright. Let's take you home. As a matter of fact, why don't I go get Fal and have her come to you, instead? I'm sure a newly discovered Selben can coax them out." Bast releases Clarisse from her embrace to glare with stern authority at Death. "Can I trust you to look after her in my absence?"

Clarisse feels her veins freeze in the frigid light of Death's stare.

"Why would you ever insinuate that I can't look after her?" he replies in a deadly calm voice.

Bast takes a step back. The silence between them is icy. Clarisse shivers, shattering the tension just enough for Death to speak.

"I will take her. You go and find Fal. I will ensure that any more mishaps are handled."

Bast nods. She's unreadable as she shifts back into an inky black panther, her muscles rippling with power as she darts back in the direction they came.

"Clarisse," Death starts.

"Yes?"

"Try not to set anything else on fire on the way to your home, okay?"

Clarisse starts to defend herself when she sees the ghost of a smirk on his face. "Okay," she giggles.

"Shall we?" He loosens his grip on her shoulders and offers his hand instead. She takes it, glad for once for the cold grip of his fingers in hers.

SHADOW STORM

Clarisse

larisse aches. They've been walking for ages and there's still no sign of her Tyrladan home. Certain it's a myth, she can't suppress the tired groan that escapes. She claps a hand over her mouth, refusing to make eye contact with Death as he turns to her.

His golden eyes glitter with mischief and he grins, revealing just how sharp his teeth are in the waning moonlight. "We're not wimping out, are we?"

Clarisse laughs, taken aback by how... *cheery* he is. "What's got you in such a good mood?"

He shrugs. "I got Bast off our case and I enjoy spending time with you, of course. I'm almost sad our time will come to an end soon."

Stopping, Clarisse can't hide the panic in her voice. "You still plan to leave me?"

Death's smile drops. "My dear, you know I can't stay with you forever. I'm just pleased I can help you end one chapter and embark on the next. Of course I'll visit from time to time, but you must know how busy I am."

Tears threaten to spill, but Clarisse manages to stifle them. Her heart seems to ice over colder than his stars. *He'll leave me just like everyone else did. Just like he did the first time.*

She swears she sees him flinch, but she shakes it off. Affecting a brave face, she blusters, "That's okay. I need to learn to be more independent anyway."

Death looks hurt, but Clarisse refuses to say anything else and give in to the anger brewing within her. *Why do I care so much anyway? Terrence is the one who got me out, not him.* Grief at losing her shadow friend starts to trickle into her tough veneer. Her lungs and veins burn with pent-up rage, indignant when she considers how much she's lost. How she never stood up for herself until the bitter end.

I bet my parents are living their dream life now that I'm gone.

A fire builds within her. Fearing another incident like the garden roses, she quiets it... at least for now.

She realizes she's gotten far ahead of him in her chaotic state. She wipes her sweaty palms on her robe and wills herself to let go of any trace of the way his hand felt in hers.

He can leave and never come back, for all I care! It's not like he's going to visit me, anyway. I'm just another soul he's ferrying over.

"Is that what you think?"

Whirling to face him, Clarisse finds that he's not far behind. His eyes seem... Misty? "Are you crying? What's wrong?" she asks.

He reaches for her hands. Begrudgingly, she offers them.

"Wait... Do you hear my thoughts?" Clarisse whispers. *And why can't I hear his? Or... can I?*

Death blinks, and a glistening tear tracks down his cheek. He moves to take his hand away and swipe it away, but Clarisse grips his wrist and pulls him back.

"Answer me."

"Yes," he sighs. "I can. And you can hear mine... just not all the time. You still guess my emotions, but if I didn't keep a guard up, you'd hear me."

She ticks her head back in surprise. "But why? I don't hear Bast. How is it that I can hear you?"

He gave a slight eye roll. "You heard Terrence in your head all the time, Clarisse."

"Yes, because he let me. I don't think you mean to let me hear. And

I'm certainly not trying to let you hear my thoughts. Besides, I mastered that trick—keeping people out, I mean," Clarisse argues. "Why are your thoughts slipping out? And mine?"

Death sighs. "I suppose one of your gifts is mind reading. No one else has been able to intuit what I'm feeling like you have."

"Why couldn't I hear Bast, then?"

He huffs. "Why are you so full of questions today?"

The sun—three suns, rather—are now peeking above the horizon, dousing Death's form in an ethereal, golden glow. His black hair appears more mahogany in the early morning light, and his eyes look like stars are trapped within their golden depths.

The sight of his otherworldly beauty causes Clarisse to lose the ability to speak. Instead of providing an artful response, she stammers.

Death chuckles. "Cat got your tongue? Bast is gone."

His mood swings are giving Clarisse whiplash! With great effort, she regains her equilibrium. "For your information, I made it a point when I talked to Terrence in my head to erect walls. When I wanted him to hear me, I let him in. I'm *not* letting you in, which means you must be doing it on your own. Why are you poking around in my head?"

Death shrugs. "You looked upset and I wanted to help. So why were *you* poking around?"

Suddenly embarrassed, she offers, "I don't mean to."

A shadow passes over Death's face. "Did you really mean it when you said you don't want me to visit anymore?"

Clarisse swears he looks more angel than Reaper in this light. It's heartbreaking to see him so sad. "No. I'm just… lonely. And selfish. Plus, I miss Terrence, even though I know he can't be here. And even if he could, I still want you here, too. You're my… friend. If I can even call you that."

Death finally reaches up to wipe his tears away. "Clarisse, I'm hurt that you would think I was only leaving because I didn't want to be here. And of course I'm your friend. I… I'm rather fond of you."

Clarisse blushes. "I'm sorry. To be fair, there's a reason those were thoughts and not words. I never would've spoken them out loud. I'm just scared. I don't *feel* like a Selben. Frankly, I don't even know what that means! And I like Bast, but I trust you more. I don't know how I'm going to navigate being dead and trying to figure out how I became the way I am."

Death reaches out and tousles her hair. In spite of all the awkwardness between them and the fear she feels for the unknown, she laughs.

"You'll figure it out," Death offers kindly. "I'll try to arrange something with Bast so we can teach you more about all this. It's unfair of us to assume that you'll just catch on to everything without the proper guidance. Terrence always was a better teacher."

"Where is he, by the way?"

Death shrugs. "Free. I let him go as you requested and removed all the orders to capture him. He still can't enter Tyrladan, but maybe someday he'll re-earn the right."

Clarisse smiles at the thought of seeing Terrence again.

I hope you'll tell me later why he was really damned. Like, really *explain. I'd like to know, if that's okay.*

Laughing, Death grabs her hand again. "In time, Clarisse."

Terrence

*B*ack on Earth, Terrence remains steadfast by the spot where Clarisse died… on the floor in front of the couch.

Moving is hard. Breathing even more so. As soon as he received word that he was no longer being hunted, he returned to where she once lived and doused their home in shadows.

He blinks and forces his mind to play back memories of her over and over. Guilt consumes him.

"She's just a dumb human," he whispers.

One you befriended. One who trusted you. One you betrayed and destroyed. And for what?

Terrence winces as one word tumbles through his mind over and over… Why? Why did he do it? Why did he make her practice magic so recklessly? She was a beacon, one who shone brighter than any star she could form.

He closes his eyes and tries his best to make sad remnants of her stars dance behind his eyelids. Anything to remember her.

Heat rises from his body, and in seconds, thick walls of smoke coat everything. Before long, the house will go up in flames if he doesn't rein in his despair.

Months have passed in her absence.

I can't keep sitting here like this.

For the first time in what feels like eons, Terrence feels his legs twitch with something like… purpose.

Groaning, he pulls himself up.

He's not sure where he finds the strength to or why, but suddenly he's overwhelmed by the need to start walking.

"I miss you, Clarisse."

His voice is below a whisper—an affront to the unbearable silence he's been awash in since she died.

Terrence finds his paws leading him to the kitchen. The pantry door swings wide and he chokes at the sight of all the cereal boxes.

What was I thinking?

He doesn't understand what his motives were. *I just wanted to help. Why did I push her so far? Why didn't I listen to Death? Was it pride? Envy?*

He pours cereal into a bowl, unsurprised that it's stale. He doesn't use milk. She teased him about that once. The porcelain bowl is chilly against his tongue as he forces himself to take one bite. Then another. And another.

Eternity passes and half the bowl still remains.

Setting it down on the table, he sighs. The sugar isn't nearly as sweet as the memory of her.

A feverish desire to seek revenge for the ills inflicted upon Clarisse festers in his chest. Saliva wets his teeth at the mere thought of tearing into Father Simmons, Arthur, or Deborah.

All three at once would be preferable.

He wonders what kind of progress has been made on the abuse case that was levied against those monsters. They were arrested, after all. Father Simmons was slammed with several allegations of financial crimes, along with child abuse. Clarisse's broken, battered body served as excellent evidence for the state to prosecute. Terrence wonders why the healing magic didn't last. *Does that mean all that healed skin was merely an illusion?*

Something about that still doesn't add up, but he's grateful her scars could serve some purpose beyond the grave.

He wanders back to the couch, though this time he wills himself not to sit and weep or stare mournfully into space. The acceptance stage of grief seems to be approaching and, finally, he's ready to welcome it.

His eyes flick to the television remote. He doesn't understand how she managed to get it to work. They never paid a cable company to come out and service them, yet it sat at the ready and played a show or two during their brief time together.

Another magical quandary I'll never solve. He settles upon the idea that Clarisse was a supernatural mystery beyond anything he's seen in his time as a Reaper and an outcast.

He blinks and the button to turn on the television is pressed. There's no sense using his paws when it takes so long to get his claws to land on the right button. Pleased, he sees the local news channel is already playing. He's not going to question how he still has a signal. Examining the validity of her lingering magic can wait until later, though he doubts it will make sense without its creator.

The sound of her name pulls his attention back to the screen and his heart sinks.

While the newscaster speaks, the ticker across the bottom screen reads in bold letters: *MONROE FAMILY AND FATHER SIMMONS ACQUITTED OF ALL CHARGES.*

He blinks and the off button is aggressively jammed.

At first, he's only aware of his beating heart. It drums so hard he fears it may make him deaf. He's certain he'll be the first case of hearing loss from the rage that starts to drown him.

He feels it—a deep, angry tidal wave that rises within him.

The flames that engulf the television go unnoticed, as do the ones catching onto the couch upon which he sits. He is numb to the power of his own flames.

"How?" his voice thunders.

The flames creep higher and he slinks from the couch, an ever-growing shadow losing its wolf shape with every breath. Before long, he eclipses the living room and the walls are encased in smoke, crumbling to ash in his wake.

Only a few minutes pass before the entire house is consumed.

The swirling darkness whirls into the sky; the only visible remnants of life are the red eyes that gleam from the middle of a dark cloak that devours everything in its path.

He doesn't care if Death is called down to deal with him. He doesn't care if Reapers are summoned.

I will avenge her.

THE NEYLKA SEEKS

Clarisse

She shuffles her feet between the blades of tall grass that slide along her toes. Her robe is tangled with weeds, leaves, and twigs where she's trudged through the hillside as she and Death trod along through Yehta.

"How much longer until we get there?"

Death stops with a groan. "I don't know, Clarisse. I've already told you. I'm following the traces of your magic. We'll know when we get there."

Clarisse sighs. If she was still alive, she's certain her feet would be hurting if she'd walked all this way on Earth. A comfortable silence stretches between her and Death, which she prefers to their earlier bickering. Just then, thunderous rumbles quake below the ground. Clarisse holds her arms out in an attempt to stay steady.

"Death?" Her voice is pinched with fear.

In an instant, he's beside her, curling her into his arms. "Don't move."

The rumbling only worsens. She's ashamed by how greedily she clutches Death for support, and heat rises to her cheeks. Thankfully his focus is elsewhere. She follows his gaze when his eyes widen and manages to swallow a strangled scream. The tall grass surrounding them has begun to catch fire.

"We have to go!" Clarisse gasps. "I thought you said this wasn't Hell!"

"It's not!" Death stammers. He clasps Clarisse's hand and forces her to face him. "I won't let you go there. Don't run just yet. This is a magic I've yet to see, but it may simply be an illusion. Remember: *you can't die here.*"

His words do little to slow the quickening pace of her heart, but Clarisse manages a curt nod. Hot tears slide down her cheeks, though she can't remember when she started crying.

"Clarisse, look at me," Death whispers. "I don't sense any immediate danger. We just need to stay back."

Wiping her eyes, Clarisse nods. She stays close to him; together they watch as a dark plume of smoke curls up through the grass and spirals high into the sky. The flames, Clarisse realizes, are such a dark black they're almost indistinguishable from the smoke.

"Look!" Death gasps.

Clarisse's eyes dart in the direction of his outstretched finger to see a foundation has caught fire. The foundation to a house. *Her* house.

"Death!" Clarisse races toward it, her heart in tatters at the sight of her beautiful home in flames. The one she made. With… *Terrence.*

Her instincts tell her to turn and look for him. She cranes her neck in every direction, hoping—praying—that she'll see him. Death is hot on her heels, calling out to her.

"Terrence!" she cries out.

The smoke travels higher and faster, revealing more of the house engulfed in flames. She reaches the front door, prepared to feel the stinging burn when she touches the handle. Instead, her skin is greeted with cold metal. She shrieks at the shocking sensation and pulls her hand back. Looking up, she sees that the column of smoke has disappeared. In its stead stands the house. Swallowing, she looks back at the doorknob. Her heart drops into her stomach and she wonders… *Is it okay to go inside?*

"Just because I said it's safe to watch doesn't mean it's safe to approach!" Death chides as he pulls up beside her. For once, though, his eyes are focused on the house and not on her. Before she can reach for the door, his own curiosity gets the better of him. He opens the door and puts a finger to his lips, shushing her. "I'm going in first," he whispers.

Clarisse rolls her eyes but lets him go ahead. She does, however, follow straight after him, refusing to wait on the porch while he investigates.

The smell hits her first. Acrid and stale with grief. Terrence's grief. While Death heads toward the living room, Clarisse makes a beeline to the kitchen. She opens the fridge, not surprised to find it bare. The pantry, on the other hand, is littered with a few things, namely an assortment of cereal boxes in disarray. She turns around and sees a bowl full of cereal crumbs on the kitchen table.

"He's been here," she mutters.

"Terrence?" Death calls out to him, which surprises Clarisse.

They didn't part on the best of terms. Worry creeps up her neck and shoulders. "Will he be in trouble if he's here?" she asks timidly.

Death holds up a hand before calling to him again, artfully dodging her question.

"Death," she continues. "Will he be in trouble?"

Sighing, Death turns to her from where he stands in the middle of the living room. "No, Clarisse. But I do need to know why he's here. Just because I pardoned him doesn't mean he's welcome to come and go through Tyrladan as he pleases."

Crossing her arms, she studies the ceiling. Everything looks the same as she left it. As fresh as the sadness is in this place, she doesn't feel Terrence's shadowy presence.

"Death, I don't think he's here," she says softly. "I think he was fairly recently, but not now. How did the house get here, anyway?"

Deep in thought, Death taps a finger against his temple, but he doesn't answer. His preoccupation leaves her to look around the rest of her house alone.

Without waiting for him to catch up, she investigates the space more closely. Dust has gathered on the railing of the stairs that lead to her bedroom. The doors to the ballroom are ajar and she wanders there first, to the place where Death collected her soul.

Staring up at the ornate chandeliers, she's struck with the memory of being chased by the fearsome creature Ralun. Shuddering, she shoves the memory of the spider centaur into a crevice in her mind where he can't crawl back out to get her—at least she hopes he can't. Nightmares are tricky beasts, after all.

Plodding about, she stares through the windows and into the land beyond. The three suns are high above, illuminating the glass and leaving bright prisms of light scattered across the ballroom floor.

"Terrence?" Her voice is feeble. She knows he's no longer there, but some part of her wishes he would answer anyway. That she would see some sign of him. In the window, she catches a flicker of something white and gold. The image flashes faster than she can register it, bringing her back to that moment in Kreyuhl when she saw something by the Selyento tree.

What is that thing?

"Death? Are you there?"

"Yes, Clarisse?" He's by her side faster than she can think.

"I… I saw something outside the window."

Death walks over to peer through the elegant panes in search of anything strange. "What did you see?"

She struggles to articulate the flash of white that frightened her more than it should. "Something… white. And gold? It looks like what I saw by the Selyento."

Death stops. "You saw something by the Selyento?"

Clarisse nods. "I thought I told you about it. Remember when I asked if there were any other souls in Yehta?"

Death shakes his head. "I remember you asking that question, but you never mentioned seeing anything. Did it have a shape? Any distinctive features?"

Before she can answer, the sound of footsteps echoes through the house. Clarisse jumps, a prickle of unease prickling across her skin as she tries to remember what she saw.

"I think I may have an idea of what she saw," Bast calls from the hallway. Her silver eyes are alight with curiosity and… *panic?* "Clarisse, things have changed. I don't know if it's safe for you to stay here in Yehta. I need you to come outside and meet Fal."

Death's hand lands on Clarisse's shoulder, where he squeezes it with soft reassurance. "She will go nowhere without me," he commands authoritatively.

Rolling her eyes, Bast motions for them both to follow her. "That's fine, but eventually we'll have to discuss what it means for you to be separated from your post for so long. Please follow me. We have much to discuss. Fal doesn't have much time, and I need to impress upon you the danger in which you're embroiled."

Several questions bubble to the forefront of Clarisse's mind as Death puts his arm around her shoulders to escort her from the ballroom. She peers back behind her, hoping to catch a glimpse of whatever she saw outside the window. But the windowpanes are empty of anything but sun, trees, and vividly painted grass.

Outside, Clarisse finds herself face to face... or *faces*... with the most unusual being she's ever seen.

The creature Fal stands before her. Her skin looks to be woven from the forest itself. Earthy browns, stark whites, leafy greens, and even crystalline blues stretch across her flesh like the embodiment of planet Earth. Silver and gold mismatched eyes sit fixed in three heads that share the same body; their long, glossy silver hair falls down their back like a silvery waterfall.

"H-hi," Clarisse stammers. "I'm... Clarisse. Are... are you Fate?"

Fal laughs, three voices interlacing with one another in a startling fashion. It's somehow both soothing and terrifying.

"Fate is not to be trifled with, Clarisse. Don't let her calm demeanor trick you. And make sure to call her by her proper name—Fal."

Clarisse reaches out and grabs Death's hand. He doesn't shy away, instead clutching her fingers between his and distractedly playing with the small ring on her index finger. *When did that get there, anyway?* She decides to ask about it later.

"It's a pleasure to meet you, Ms. Monroe," Fal says, her warm tone deceptively welcoming.

"Fal, I think Clarisse is partly aware of what you're about to tell her." Bast's voice is shaky, confirming the panic Clarisse thought she sensed earlier.

A frown fixes itself on all three of Fal's faces. "Little one, your time here in Yehta, while earned, has not been secured. I have some startling news. I'm afraid it's not as optimistic as we hoped."

"Cut to the chase, Fal," Death warns, his voice becoming more like rolling thunder than the usual, melancholy tone to which she's become accustomed. Clarisse doesn't pull away, but she makes a mental note to remember that Death is not human, as much as she'd like to believe he is.

Fal's six eyes spark with something that resembles rage, but Bast puts out a hand to calm the powerful Selbeno. Fal offers, "My dear, I'm afraid there's not much to go on when it comes to your Falme."

Confused, Clarisse tries to think of something to ask, falling short of words and intimidated of the powerful creature Fal. "What... what is a Falme again?"

"I believe she needs you to elaborate," Death huffs. "She is newly dead, you know. Not everything has been explained to her."

Bast arches an eyebrow. "I wonder whose fault *that* is?"

Fal smiles and pointedly ignores their bickering. "A Falme is a string that's tied to our sacred Siralto's tree, the Selyento, which you met upon your arrival. Her roots are comprised of strings that are connected to every living soul that passes through Earth and, sometimes, beyond. Since you lived, I am supposed to be able to read to the string and play it back to get a sense of who you truly are."

Before Death can retort, Clarisse finally thinks of something to say. "Is there anything in my Falme to give me a clue as to who I might be? Or... what my responsibilities are as a Selben?"

Fal's eyes glitter. "That's just it, dear. I pulled what is supposed to be your Falme, and it's blank."

Death's grip on Clarisse's shoulders becomes so intense that she winces from the pain. *"Sorry."*

She pats his hands to reassure him that she's okay.

He composes himself with great effort. "How can you say that? Every living soul has a string, Fal. I know the rules and so do you. Are you sure there's absolutely *nothing*?"

"Listen," Fal sighs, "I know you're content to dictate your job to everyone else, but who are you to talk, ye who has abandoned your post?"

Death grunts. "I beg your pardon, but Clarisse is a special soul. My job is guidance as much as it is retrieval."

Clarisse doesn't want to think about what happens when she no longer needs his guidance. She clutches his fingers and tries not to let the weight of being an unknown goddess crush her. A wave of dizziness clouds her vision and she stumbles, clutching Death's hand tighter.

"Are you okay?" Death faces her, closing her off from the others.

"I just—there's a lot going on. I just died. And now… all this?" Her voice wavers, her heart consumed by a litany of emotions she can't name.

Death runs a gentle finger through Clarisse's hair, his expression softer now that he's focused on her. "My dear, this is a lot to take in. It's quite alright if you want to ask questions or take a break from it all. You're entitled to do so."

"Death, we don't have time for breaks!" Bast interrupts, her voice an urgent hiss.

Death's eyes glow. "Bast, I will destroy anything that gets in her way while she's still processing her new existence."

Clarisse can't help but wonder why he's become so protective. Not long ago, he insisted she had to go through the pain of living with her parents and under Father Simmons' thumb. But she's not about to question him in front of the others. Instead, she leans into his hands so he can run them through her hair more fully. Her tears fall freely now and she doesn't try to hide them.

"Truthfully, I'm just tired. I thought you got to rest when you died. Now I'm in danger and we don't even know who I am!"

Her chest, tight with grief, threatens to run away from her. Death holds her tight, closing her off from the stares she feels at her back. All her life, she's felt like a zoo animal, caged and subject to gawking bystanders. Now it seems she'll be one for eternity.

"You are not an oddity."

Death's voice, though in her mind, helps still her spiraling thoughts. She pulls back so she can look up at him, though he's blurred by her tears. "What does it mean if I don't have a Falme?" Her voice trembles, threatening to shatter like glass in an earthquake.

"Clarisse, why don't we go back inside and sit down on the couch?

I'm sure you've got a stack of blankets stored someplace. We can talk about all this over a mug of hot tea, rather than out in the open." Death glares at Fal and Bast, daring them to protest.

Surprisingly, smiles flit across Fal's faces and she throws her hands out wide. "I have a great recipe for tea I've been meaning to try!"

Impatient, Bast rolls her eyes but dutifully follows Fal as they march into the house. Before Clarisse can take a step, Death cradles her in his arms. Too weak to fight, she allows him to usher her into the house. The familiar scent of Terrence—though stale—threatens to send her careening over the edge once more.

"How did he get the house here?" she whispers.

Death chuckles. "I believe he burned it in his grief. He was here, but he's not now. I suppose your magic carried on into the afterlife. Your home wasn't here in the beginning because it hadn't arrived yet. But now it's here right on time."

While Death seems amused at this, Clarisse's heart lurches at the thought of Terrence grieving her back on Earth. *I hope he can move on. He deserves to find happiness of his own.*

As much as she would like to ask Death the big "why" questions— Why her? Why now? Why did Terrence feel the need to push her so hard until she burned herself away?—she doesn't think badly of Terrence. In fact, she still loves him like the friend he was.

Death frowns at her, but he remains quiet. Her cheeks flush as she remembers he can still hear her thoughts. He places her on the couch and holds a finger up to her face.

"Wait here," he orders. "I'll get you some blankets. Then, we're going to sit here and discuss the parameters of the dangers you're in and what it means to lack a Falme."

Fal, busy in the kitchen, turns her three heads fully around to smile at Clarisse. It's a startling image. Clarisse gets a bit nauseous.

"Do you take honey in your tea?" she asks solicitously.

Clarisse nods.

The clinking of mugs is unsettling. Especially because Fal's fathomless eyes never leave Clarisse's.

How can she possibly stir the tea without looking?

"She drinks a lot of tea," Death answers with a chuckle in her head. Death's eyes glimmer and they share an inward laugh.

Fal drifts over to her. Idly, Clarisse wonders if anyone else has been served tea by the enigmatic being. With a sigh, Bast grabs a mug and settles into a lounge chair perched across from the couch. Fal remains standing.

"Where to start on discussing a missing Falme..." Fal distractedly runs her fingers along the rim of her mug.

"Fal, we don't have time for this. I need an explanation and I need it *now*," Death huffs.

"For starters, no one truly exists without a Falme, Death," Fal begins.

Clarisse feels sweat break out across her forehead. "Are you telling me I don't exist?"

"No, child, you exist. But you are not Clarisse Monroe. At least... you weren't always."

Clutching the blanket Death tucked around her, sudden shivers wrack her frame. "Are you telling me I'm someone else?"

Death paces in the living room. "How can that be?"

Fal clears her throat. "Death... Clarisse is a recycled soul. She escaped the Neylka."

HUNTED

Clarisse

Struck numb by Fal's cryptic proclamation, Clarisse's ears feel stuffed with cotton. She's aware that Death and Fal are speaking. Arguing, in fact. Bast remains seated, her silver eyes glazed over with turmoil. Clarisse isn't sure exactly what it means to be from the Neylka, but the idea of being recycled is a terrifying thought.

I'm not who I am?

The idea is enough to send her into a comatose stupor. She languishes on the couch as Death stomps across the rug, only semi-aware of tugging the blanket closer around her chin.

Death comes to stand over her, his golden eyes haunted by worry. Without his skull mask, his face is an open book—at least to Clarisse. His soul is on display for her, raw and wretched. She wants to reach out and hold his face in her hands. To feel his bitterly cold soul engulf her. As the stale scent of Terrence's fur wafts to her nose from the couch, everything becomes blurred by her tears again.

Why am I so weak? she thinks miserably.

Shuddering, Clarisse pulls the blanket entirely over her face, fully intending to stay there forever. She can't fathom getting up after learning her whole life was a lie. All the pain and suffering was for nothing. It doesn't make sense.

Why choose to be reborn only to live a life as terrible as that one? What would I possibly have to gain from living through that? Why subject myself to such torment? Did I hate myself? Do I hate myself now?

Suddenly the blanket is tugged off her face and she finds Death's nose just beyond the tip of hers.

"Clarisse," he whispers, "do not hide from me. Not now. You need help. You need assurance. Do not hide."

His breath tingles her skin and goosebumps slither up her arms. She could get lost in him if she isn't careful. She shakes herself internally, cursing for letting him bewitch her like this.

"Are you hexing me or something?" she accuses.

He blinks. "No, but my magic does have a calming effect on people. It helps me usher souls into the afterlife. It's quite shocking when people die. Without that influence, people might not be so willing to follow me into the unknown."

It hurts a little knowing she only feels drawn to him due to magic, but she's also relieved to know she's not the only person in history who's been swayed by his charms.

She casts her tear-stricken face up toward his. "Death, I want to disappear. I want to go home. Who am I?" *And what is the Neylka?* she adds silently.

Fal hums. "That's just it. *Someone* knows who you are, but that's where the danger lies."

Bast leaps to her feet, her eyes boring into Clarisse's. "Now is not the time to engage in self-pity!" she scolds. "Who cares about the Clarisse you were before? She's gone. You are only who you are *now*. We have time to figure out your past, but one thing is clear: your past self chose to be reborn. There must be a reason for that. The problem now is convincing the Neylka to let you stay who you are. If you start giving in to the notion of trying to find your past self, you'll make yourself an easy target."

Death blinks. "Did you say who *cares*?"

Clarisse is overcome by another dizzy spell. She tugs the blankets up and tries to cover her head again, but Death is quicker. He rips it from the couch and hoists her up in one smooth motion. Pulling her into his arms, he whispers in her ear. "Don't hide. We are here to help."

Bast stares at him, her jaw agape. "Don't tell me you care for this girl *that* much!" she snorts derisively. "What the hell has gotten into you?"

Death rolls his eyes. "I don't care to be analyzed right now, thank you very much. Besides that, this is a lot for a newly-passed soul to carry. We need to learn how a soul can come back. Don't you think that's enough to concern me?"

So, I'm just a job?

Death glares at her. *"No. You will never be just a job."*

Before she can prod him for more answers, Fal interrupts.

"Death, there are many things about Clarisse that aren't common. We've known of souls that were recycled before, but this one's energy signature is… unique. That said, the Neylka wants it back. Every time I look for clues about who she is, the Neylka chases me. Clarisse, can you describe what you've been seeing?"

With her head spinning, it's hard to find the right words, but Clarisse tries her best. "Something… white, but there are also flashes of gold. It's never been close enough for me… for me to…" She stumbles over her words, unsure how to articulate the inexplicable fear she feels every time she catches a flash of gold from her periphery. Even though she knows Fal is simply searching for answers, she feels they're going out of order.

I want to know who I was instead of spending time talking about a creature that may or may not be following me. Why can't I be curious about my past?

"You can, Clarisse. I will help you."

His silent promise brings her some peace, but not nearly enough to stomach everything she's been told. She turns to him. "Death, I need to lie down. I can't… I can't keep doing this. I'm running on empty and I need time to process everything that's happened. What is the Neylka? Should I be concerned that it's hunting me? I know you want me to tell you what I know, but I need answers to my own questions first." Hands balled into fists, her head throbs.

"I will explain everything I know about the Neylka," Death soothes her. He toys with the ends of her hair.

The motion is soothing and hypnotic, and it takes everything in her not to fall asleep. Clarisse sighs. "I want to lie down. In my bed. Is that alright with everyone?" Death nods. Bast and Fal seem weary themselves. Clarisse points to the staircase in the foyer. "Listen, I know there are more rooms in this house. I made it myself. Why don't you each grab one and get comfortable? Feel free to make my home yours. I wish I was stronger and could give you the answers you need. I just don't know enough."

Fal glides over and places her hands on Clarisse's shoulders. Being face to face with three other faces is startling, but Clarisse is getting used to it. Thankfully, she doesn't fall apart. *The pressure must be getting to me.*

"Stay calm, Clarisse."

Clarisse almost says something aloud in response. Instead, she settles for glaring at her dark-robed friend.

"Clarisse, I need you to understand one very important thing," Fal begins earnestly. "You don't have to know everything right away. We're simply worried because this is uncharted territory for us. There are forces at work here that we've never dealt with in this capacity."

A shuddering breath finally makes its way through Clarisse's chest. "I don't understand what's happening. You're saying all these things, and I'm struggling to make sense of it all. I'm still trying to wrap my head around the fact that I'm dead."

Fal gives a firm nod with one head while the other two peer at her with kind eyes. "As you should! I think a night's rest is in order. It may be a little early to turn in, but there's nothing wrong with taking a break. I think you should go upstairs, lie down, and get some space. I worry, though. I don't want to leave you alone, in case…"

Death perks up. "Are you saying the danger you sense is imminent?"

When Fal hesitates, Clarisse feels her heart try to stop. *I can't die again, can I?*

"No, you cannot," Death answers firmly in her head.

Clarisse isn't reassured. The Neylka presents a clear threat, even if the threat doesn't include dying again. She suddenly remembers one of her conversations with Terrence. "Terrence mentioned the Neylka a few times. He said the gods can… regenerate themselves. Do I remember that correctly?"

Death sighs. "Yes, though I doubt talking about this right before you lie down will help you get a sleep worthy of helping you heal."

Waving off his concern, Clarisse wobbles to her feet. Rolling her shoulders releases a few stiff snaps in her spine.

"You deserve to know what hunts you," Fal says. "The Neylka is considered the world 'in between'. It's like the fabric that makes up our universe—our existence. Tryta and Siralto built it to perform as the glue that holds everything together."

"I'm not going to pretend I know what you mean by that, but that *does* help. So how does the Neylka hunt me? And why?"

"People don't come back from the Neylka the way you have," Bast interjects. "When something is recycled, it becomes a part of everything else. But you… you're intact in every way except for your memories. We've learned the Neylka sent one of its Aiyeliu to hunt you down. It wants you back because it didn't do its job right."

Clarisse raises an eyebrow. "How do you know this, Bast? I thought Fal was the one who dealt with this kind of stuff."

"You think she didn't fill me in?" Bast laughs. "I am here to protect you now, even if I couldn't while you were on Earth. I protect children."

Clarisse glowers. "I'm *not* a child."

Bast laughs, a light, tinkling sound. "Do you know how old I am?"

Clarisse crosses her arms. "Okay, but just because you're old doesn't make everyone else a child," she argues, anticipating Bast's next statement.

To her surprise, Bast giggles.

"We're getting off topic." Fal grabs Clarisse's shoulders again, though not hard enough to bruise her. "You must be careful. Death can explain only so much of how this world works, and it will take a long time to learn what you need to know. You must use caution, ask questions, and stay close to those you trust—and give your trust sparingly. As much as I appreciate your offer to stay here, I must attend to my duties. But know this: *I am an ally*. If you need my help, you need only summon me."

Clarisse blinks, briefly aware that a handful of tears betray her emotion. "How do I summon you?"

All three of Fal's heads smile. "For you? All you have to do is think of needing me. Call to me with your mind like you've been speaking with Death. I may not hear your thoughts as clearly as he does, but if you let me in, I'll know."

Clarisse blushes.

Bast gasps. "Wait a minute. You two have been talking with your minds?" Bast looks furious, so Clarisse wisely remains silent. "You'll answer to me about that later, Death." Bast jabs a finger at him, but he doesn't respond.

Clarisse ignores them both. "Thanks, Fal." She steps forward and gives the unique being a hug. Death and Bast immediately stiffen, worried what Fal will do, but Fal returns her embrace eagerly.

"You are bright, Clarisse. I have no idea who you once were, but whoever she was, she was strong enough to return. I hope you find the answers you seek. When you do, tell me. I'd love to chat with you about it." With those parting words, Fal turns on her heel and strides out the front door.

It all happens so fast, Clarisse hardly has time to register that she's gone. "How does she move that fast?" she marvels.

Death chuckles. "None of us here are human, Clarisse. We don't operate by mortal rules."

Outside, the suns are still high overhead. Back on Earth, Clarisse would struggle to fall asleep when it was daylight, but her muscles ache and her mind is full to the brim with new information. Worry threatens to swallow her whole.

"I need that sleep, Death."

Bast taps her foot and narrows her eyes at me, then Death. "You're seriously not going to answer me about the mind-speaking?"

Glaring, Death huffs. "Yes, Bast. It's totally normal. We can all speak with our minds."

"Did she let you in?" she asks shrewdly.

Clarisse holds up her hands. "You guys, I can't handle any more weird revelations today. Yes, he's in my head. Yes, he's been in my head since I got here. I used to talk to Terrence the same way. Make of that what you will, but I need to get some sleep! Bast, are you staying here or not?"

Bast looks surprised, but nods.

"There's an empty room for you to the left of mine. Let's head upstairs. Death, you have a lot of explaining to do, but I'm tired. If you stay in the library and I leave the door open, will that suffice for not being left alone?"

Laughing, Death walks over to her. "So, you're telling me all it takes for you to take charge and be confident is to be tired?"

Sticking out her tongue, Clarisse waves him off. "I want sleep. I *need* it. I need a break from all the crap that's been hurled at me. You're all talking about this like it's second nature, but you seem to forget that I just got here. I'm being hunted by… the *glue?* A fricken glue stick is hunting me because it thinks I'm still supposed to be in there. How does any of this make sense?" Snorting, Clarisse suppresses the urge to break into maniacal laughter. Her mind is strained so far, she fears it might snap. "You know what? It sounded crazy in my head, but it's even more ridiculous when I say it out loud! I can't deal with this right now. I'm going to sleep, and we can figure this out later. And you both need to find a better way of explaining this to me if I'm truly in danger."

Bast laughs. "You are very entertaining, dear. I have a feeling you and I will be close friends after we get things sorted out."

The cool, crisp embrace of white cotton sheets almost causes Clarisse to collapse into the arms of unconsciousness straight away. Then it occurs to her that none of them *need* to sleep. If they're dead, what's the point? She wonders what Bast and Death will do if they're not actually tired.

Clarisse doesn't care if sleep is a frivolity left over from her human existence. Her mind needs a break, and her soul needs a chance to take a breath and walk away. Her new friends, though lovely, aren't the best teachers when it comes to helping her understand the Afterlife. Where is Tyrladan in relation to Earth? How does the Neylka work? And how can an inanimate object *chase* her?

She's partly tempted to go rifling through the library for answers, but she knows if she starts reading, she'll never stop. At least not in time to rest so she can escape whatever creature has been summoned by the Neylka to chase her.

And what's to say it won't find me when I go to sleep now?

As if on cue, Death peeks his head in the doorway from the library. "They won't get you, Clarisse. I won't let them."

Clarisse rolls her eyes. "You should be more careful about poking around in my head since according to Bast, it's *not* normal."

Death waves her concern away like a wisp of smoke. "Don't let the silly cat goddess get your head riled up with ideas. Besides, I've known you long enough to make that sort of connection. We've been over this. Now, do you want me to explain the Neylka in greater detail?"

While it's tempting to push back, Clarisse knows it's more important to understand what she's up against. "Okay, tell me about the Neylka."

With a flourish of his long, slender fingers, he conjures a chair out of thin air. He drags it up to Clarisse's bedside and clasps his hands together, his eyebrows knitted together as he thinks of what to say. "You already know of Tryta and Siralto," he begins.

Clarisse nods. "But that story doesn't make sense. Terrence and I don't buy it."

Death rolls his eyes. "Must you bring Terrence into this? Anyway, Tryta and Siralto created the Neylka a long time ago in order to serve as the framework of the universe. In its purest sense, it absorbs energy and pushes it back out again. It recycles what isn't being used or is truly dead in a way that is unretrievable and puts it to use elsewhere." He pauses. "It goes back to how matter and energy cannot be destroyed—only converted."

"So, you're telling me the universe is a physics lesson even when you're dead?"

Laughing, Death sits back in his chair. It's odd seeing him so comfortable, basking in the glow of knowledge that Clarisse can only hope to fathom someday, let alone grasp.

"Sort of. In any case, you know how Siralto ultimately ended."

"I thought Tryta murdered her?" she asked hesitantly.

Death shrugs. "Yes, but also no. A god cannot truly be killed unless they *will* themselves to be. They must put their energy away. Siralto had to be willing to give up her energy for the Neylka to receive it. By doing so, she created the first permanent death for the gods. Her energy was eaten and redistributed in Tyrladan to be used by everything else."

Shivering, Clarisse pulls the covers up around her shoulders. Her heart aches for Siralto and the unimaginable pain she must have endured.

"So, what does that have to do with me?"

"Somehow, Clarisse, you escaped in one piece. I guess the Neylka didn't recycle you properly, so it didn't get to receive you as it should've. I've never heard of a situation like this in all my eons of life. Partially whole gods and goddesses have returned, but a whole one? And without her memories, no less? It's inconceivable."

Swallowing thickly, Clarisse's nausea returns. "Death, I don't think I can escape my fate if the Neylka is everywhere. But what I don't understand is what it wants with me. Does it want to restart me again? Recycle me? Am I going to die?"

Reaching out, Death grabs her chin. "Not on my watch. We will get this sorted out. I'm sure there's a loophole in some way, shape, or form. Besides that, it can't receive you if you aren't willing to be recycled, and I'm not sure that's its aim, anyway. The more concerning matter is why it sent an Aiyeliu to hunt you. I need more time to figure out what it's after before we allow you anywhere near it."

She peers up at him with eyes that blaze with undisguised fear. "But I can't be recycled unless I want to be, right, Death?"

Death nods. "In a sense. It would take quite a lot of effort for someone to be forced into that position, and that's an issue of murder. But one does not walk into Neylka and simply become recycled. It is dangerous and it will try to deceive you into wanting to go, but that's a separate issue. I would never let you go alone, anyway."

"Could—could *you* die in there?" The question hurts to ask, but she blurts it out before she can stop it and then curses herself for being so nosy.

Death ponders for a moment. "I suppose I could, but my nature is unique. I'm not like other gods and goddesses. I was created to be an ending and a beginning for souls who wander into the Afterlife. Even if I were to give up my post, my nature is something different. In fact, I'm not truly alive like everyone else. I know you've teased me about this before, but my soul is different. So… it's an odd question, and one I've never pondered. It's not in my nature to worry about living or not, as it's not something I've ever done."

Clarisse can't help her jaw from dropping. "What… does that even mean?"

Shrugging, Death stares at the ceiling. "It wasn't really explained to me all that well. It's just what I know myself to be. It's how I was created. Unfortunately, the details of that were lost with my Creator."

"Do you mean Siralto?"

Death hums, though he doesn't answer. His eyes are closed. She wonders if he's tired, too. *Maybe he needs sleep.*

Cracking an eye open, he grins. "Don't you worry about me, Ms. Monroe. I can survive without sleep, which is fortunate because you need someone to guard you while you rest. If you think I'm going to let you sleep without a protector, you're wrong. And while Bast doesn't need sleep either, cats get cranky without their naps."

Giggling, Clarisse squirms down into the warmth of her blankets. "What happens when you have to leave, though? Will I have to deal with a cranky cat alone?"

Death doesn't answer, and Clarisse is too tired to ask again. Instead, she rolls over, enjoying the feeling of her warm fleece pajamas. It's not cold in Tyrladan, but the comfort of something so familiar is too good to resist. Finding them in her dresser was a relief. With her head engulfed in the pillow, her eyelids droop.

"Death?"

"Yes?"

"I have more questions, but I'm too tired to ask them." She manages a tired smile and he matches it.

"I'm not going anywhere right away. You can ask me more when you wake. I agree with you—you need rest. It's imperative you give yourself time to decompress."

Clarisse lacks the strength to argue. Instead, she sinks into the sleep that's been seeking to devour her and lets it swallow her whole.

LEYUN

ack on Earth, Clarisse's feet are bare in the blades of grass that provide a soft pathway to her home. It's still summer. Crickets call from the underbrush and a chorus of frogs can be heard from all directions. A small breeze whispers through the trees and into the clearing, draping itself about Clarisse's shoulders.

She wears a pair of jean shorts and a t-shirt. The fabric is a comfort compared to the strange cloaks and robes she's donned in Tyrladan. In this moment, Tyrladan seems like a distant nightmare. Here, she is safe—home. Away from the burden of gods and goddesses who scrutinize her every move, she stretches her arms high into the air and sighs.

The fresh air fills her lungs, invigorating her. In the distance, she spots her house. It's back where it belongs, as though it never left. The flames of grief have yet to claim it. Smiling, she wonders if maybe Tyrladan was a nightmare after all.

"Maybe... it was just a bad dream?" The nonsensical situation in Tyrladan would make far more sense if it was a dream, rather than reality.

She thinks about Terrence and swallows. The business with Terrence still hasn't been solved. There are so many questions she wants to ask him. Did he help her because he truly cared, or was there some grander scheme at play? He'd repeatedly insisted he was there to help, but so many things didn't add up.

Is Death still hunting him, then? *she wonders.*

Just the thought of the Reaper sends chills down her spine. But this time, she wonders if the chills are because he's not there. She's been having so much fun with Death lately. Learning from him. Journeying with him. Her heart pangs at the thought of losing him again. That somehow, their friendship was just a dream.

She tries to set those troubling thoughts aside and convince herself that if she can talk to him, she can get everything sorted.

Looking around, she tries to find Terrence, but he's nowhere to be found. Not even a trace or echo of his magic can be felt in the night air. She realizes how empty this place feels without him. No longer is her home full of the welcoming energy she gave it when she first created the house.

Something is wrong, but she can't quite place what it is. Instinctively, she flicks her hand and summons a star to her side. She's missed her stars. "I don't talk to you guys enough, do I?" she says out loud.

The biggest star hums in agreement before zipping around her head like a startled dragonfly.

"You all stay close. Something is wrong. We must find Terrence."

Her gut tells her he's not there, but she's not willing to let go of her delusions just yet. She points to one star. "Go look for traces of him. He might've gone out shopping or into town to investigate. Come back to me when you can." The star zips away into the night, a dutiful pet. "Are you all pets? Are you sentient?" Shaking her head, Clarisse forces herself to focus. The rest of her stars remain, celestial sentries on guard against whatever strange darkness has begun to slink about, sucking her in.

She continues trudging toward the door. The house looks more ominous now. The high roof looms over her, casting more shadows in its wake than the light from its windows can make up for.

Before she can set her hand on the doorknob, the door creaks open and the lights inside flicker like in a low budget horror film. With a shudder, she tries to turn and run, but her feet are glued to the floor. The only way she can move them is forward. Swallowing, she flicks her hands about, summoning a strange, crackling energy between her fingers.

Rather than Terrence's heat, she feels a steady, cool breeze whipping up from within the house. One of her stars volunteers itself, zipping up high to replace the flickering light in the living room.

Once the light is steadied, she can proceed without feeling dizzy from the flashing. Her head is pounding. She doesn't know when the headache started, but it's a full hurricane of pain and discomfort. She must squint to keep her eyes open at all, which greatly narrows her field of vision.

Sweat beads along her forehead and her stomach grows queasier by the minute. Nothing shows itself, but she's certain that something is sharing the space here in her home. Something is lurking—waiting.

Clenching her fists, she holds them up in a weak imitation of someone ready to fight. "I'm not going down that easily!" she calls out. "Your magic won't stop me."

But what is trying to stop her? And why? These thoughts poke a hole in whatever resolve she has left. Tears form in her eyes and she yearns for the comfort of Death's presence. Even Terrence would be a happy sight right about now.

Clarisse is unsurprised when her feet lure her to the ballroom of their own volition. "Why does everything magical seem to be centered there?" Her breath is labored, and she has to fight to keep it coming. Her lungs feel like they're being jackhammered by the air around her, rather than taking the air in. "Hello?" She stumbles, slapping a hand against the wall beside her to try and stay steady.

Nothing answers, but she knows something heard her. A jolt of powerful magic laces through the air, grabbing hold of her hands and pulling her forward, almost knocking her over. Bile rises in her throat and she wants to be anywhere but here. Still, her feet will only move forward.

"Hello?"

She knows the lurking creature can hear her. Rounding the corner, she watches in terror as the ballroom doors open on their own. The source of the breeze blows strongest from the center of the ballroom. Still, her eyes can discern nothing unique.

Something breathes within the darkness. Summoning all her strength, Clarisse turns up the brightness, her stars whirling around in a blinding tornado. That's when she catches a flash of white.

Its razor-sharp teeth are on full display within a maw stretched wide, ready to devour her. Silver-white eyes gaze upon her with intense, predatory rage. Its golden mane stretches down its neck, a small, matching leonine tuft flicking back and forth at the tip of its tail.

"A... unicorn?" she gasps.

Just then, it lunges. Clarisse screams and tries to take a step back, but her feet won't move. Its teeth sink into her skin, pulling her back with it into the center of the dance floor. She pulls and tugs, but it won't let go.

"Please! Stop!"

Clarisse wails for help, hoping to somehow convince the beast to release her from its clutches. She tugs as hard as she can, tearing her skin in the process. Her blood, now gold, spills all over the place, staining her shorts and the unicorn's snowy white fur.

Without warning, it releases her and hurls its head back. Its teeth are outstretched again, but this time, they grip her shirt and hoist her up onto its back with a mighty swing of its head.

Her arms feel glued to this strange beast as it rears up. She knows she should scramble off its back. She doesn't know how to ride a horse, let alone a raging unicorn. But no matter how hard she tries, she can't let go.

"Let me go! Please!"

Her blood-soaked arms have painted the creature's entire back and neck with golden splotches. The beast starts to run, carrying Clarisse out of the ballroom and through the front door of the house. With every stride, the world she knows becomes smaller and smaller. When she turns to see where it's taking her, she's greeted by nothing but darkness.

"Where are we going?"

When it doesn't answer, Clarisse realizes it probably can't speak. Tugging with all her might, she manages to release her arms from its neck. Her numb legs start to regain feeling, first with tingling, then with stabbing pinpricks. Throwing caution to the wind, she flings herself from the creature's back. Dropping to the ground with a bone-jarring thud, she pinches herself as hard as she can.

"This must be a dream. Wake up, Clarisse! Wake UP!"

Clarisse shoots up in bed, screaming so hard her lungs feel like they might explode. Death comes sprinting into the room and barrels onto the bed, grabbing her in his arms and holding her close as the terror from her dream turns into frantic sobs.

"Death! Death!"

He clutches her tighter, desperately trying to tell her to calm down so she can say what's wrong. Bast bursts into the room with a glowing spear clutched in her hands and her rage evident in the piercing glare that surveys the room.

"I know," Clarisse gasps, "what's chasing me!" Sitting back, Death slackens his grip so Clarisse can catch her breath. Her tear-soaked cheeks are red with embarrassment. Frustrated, she does her best to wipe at them. "I saw it," she huffs.

Death fashions a tissue for her and she doesn't hesitate to wipe her eyes and blow her nose. Clarisse wishes she could disappear into it to avoid the watchful stares of her two friends.

"I'm—I'm sorry. It felt so real," she stutters. "I… I know what it is, though."

"Tell us, Clarisse," Death commands.

The authority in his voice makes her flinch for a moment. He looks hurt by this but says nothing as Clarisse takes a few more shuddering breaths. Clutching the blankets about her chest, she looks at Bast. "Is the Aiyeliu thing a unicorn?"

Bast's eyes widen. "It sent Leyun?"

Death's fists curl so hard his knuckles go bone white. Clarisse swears she sees a spark of flames in his eyes. A stern look from Death keeps her from asking him about it.

"Who's Leyun?" she asks instead.

"Not a typical Aiyeliu, I'm afraid," Bast answers.

"Okay, but that doesn't help much since I don't even know what an Aiyeliu is!" Clarisse's frustration slips into her tone, but she doesn't care. She's tired of not having answers or only being given half answers that lead to more confusion. She gives them both an accusatory glare. "You need to start explaining things better! I'm beyond confused, and it sounds like my Afterlife is on the line here. I don't want to go into this weird eternal recycling plant or whatever the heck it is. I'm *done* not having answers! What is an Aiyeliu, and how is Leyun special? I take it they're not unicorns, then? And how did I manage to see it in my dreams?"

To Clarisse's surprise, neither Bast nor Death look stunned by her outburst. Instead, Death nods and Bast clears her throat.

"Aiyeliu," Bast starts, "are a creature unique to Tyrladan." The cat goddess stretches out her fingers, producing a light between them. Bast's power allows her to create a projection in the air. The image of strange, warped-looking creatures flit across the image. They take various shapes, though all are slender with long, pointed ears. Leyun's, while shorter than most of the Aiyeliu Clarisse sees, still have the same slender, pointed arch to them.

To Clarisse, they almost look like a dog-deer hybrid. Most have razor sharp teeth and eyes similar to Death's—void of pupils.

They run around on the "screen" Bast created and Clarisse shudders as the memory of Leyun sinking her teeth into her flesh becomes clearer in her mind. She absentmindedly rubs her unblemished arm. "Are there other Aiyeliu like Leyun? Unicorns, I mean?"

Bast shakes her head. "She's not a unicorn, strictly speaking. I mean, she *is*, but not really. There are true unicorns, and then there is Leyun. She was created by the Neylka itself, not by Siralto and Tryta. She is an anomaly that operates solely on the Neylka's whims."

Raising an eyebrow, Clarisse can't help but be skeptical. "You're telling me that not only can the Neylka try and capture what it loses, but it can also give commands and *create* new life? Wouldn't it have to recycle something to create Leyun?"

"Sharp observation, Ms. Monroe," Death interrupts, his sharp grin making her melt a bit.

She almost pinches herself. *Almost.*

"You see, she is a recycled creature, but she is the first *independent* recycled creature, I suppose. One capable of the level of thought you see," Death explains. "Instead of parts and pieces being returned to what already exists or sprouting in plants, rivers, or other less obvious things, Leyun is a creature all her own—capable of unique, sentient thought. In a way, that's what you are. But you're not bound to the Neylka's whims and are different in that you were not successfully recycled, as I've come to understand it."

Realization sets in. "So the Neylka sent the one other creature like me to catch me?"

"Yes," Death sighs. "As for how you saw her in your dreams... my guess is that she feels some connection to you. She's been stalking you for some time, based on the flashes of white and gold you've been seeing. Those are her colors, so I imagine she will start taunting you, now that you've seen her. She won't strike in the open. Her goal will be to make you *want* to go. Remember, you can't be recycled unwillingly. Not truly. Someone must be incredibly powerful to force you through such a change."

Clarisse feels her palms get damp with nerves. She presses her nails into them and tries to force herself to think of other things. "Why would I ever willingly give myself up to be recycled?"

Death ponders this. "Hard to say. You're a stubborn thing who was pretty hell-bent on living. And you clearly didn't fall for what she tried in your dreams."

"Stubborn?"

Death doesn't answer.

"So… what do we do now? If she won't strike out in the open, what should we do from here?"

"Well, she's dangerous and she may try to harm you," Death answers.

His voice is too devoid of emotion for Clarisse to fathom. *How can he be so calm?*

"I assure you, I am not calm," he answers in her mind.

His eyes lock on hers and she feels as though she's under a microscope. Nothing escapes him. But for once, she senses an uneasiness in his demeanor. He seems afraid.

Death looks to Bast. "Fal never did get around to explaining the consequences of 'abandoning' my post."

Bast rolls her eyes. "We *did* get a little sidetracked, but it's not like you're going to leave your post anyway… are you?"

An uncomfortable silence stretches between them. Death shakes his head. "I really can't afford to…"

Clarisse's heart lurches. "You're… you're going to *leave*?"

"No, no, not yet," he answers hastily. "I just need to figure out how long I can have a leave of absence before there are consequences."

As much as Clarisse hates this answer, she knows it's logical. *How can I expect Death to give up his job?* The thought of being alone sits in her gut, simmering. Putting on a brave face is hard. She looks away from Bast and Death, choosing to focus on her twiddling thumbs.

"Well, now that we know Leyun can't really get me, why don't you return to your post?" Clarisse winces. "You can always come visit." When she looks up, she sees hurt in Death's eyes and a frown tugging at his lips. Before he can say anything, Clarisse holds up her hand. "No, Death, you're right. I love having you here. You're one of the only friends I've ever had, but you have a job to do. I mean, how long have you been gone from Earth now? You escorted me to my house, but what I'm going through now is beyond your purview. You don't have to look after me anymore. It's okay. Just promise me you'll visit."

Sighing, Death takes a few moments. Bast glances between them, her face unreadable. Finally, he speaks.

"Clarisse, stop. Listen, you're right. I *do* need to get back to my job, but there's something else going on. I think our souls are bonded."

"I knew it!" Bast shrieks, jabbing her finger in the air triumphantly.

Clarisse furrows her brows. "Bonded? What the heck does that mean? You can't tell me vague things like that and not explain, Death!"

Death pinches the bridge of his nose and lets out a frustrated growl. "This part is difficult to explain. Basically, as normal as it is to be able to hear another god or goddess' thoughts, it shouldn't be *this* easy and instantaneous all the time. You were at least aware when Terrence was listening, yes?"

"Not at first." Clarisse puzzles over this, trying to remember how it all started. "Honestly, everything is a blur to me, but I did have control."

Bast, whose grin is now more like a feral panther in the flesh, steps towards her. "Now, ask yourself, Clarisse, do you have control over your interactions with our friend Death, here?"

"Bast, stop," Death snaps. "I've already admitted there's an issue. I realize something is wrong. I feel *compelled* to stay here. It's more than simply *wanting* to stay with Clarisse. I feel as though I must."

The glitter in Bast's eyes is unsettling.

"Bast, it just means that fate—in the broader sense—brought us together. It doesn't mean anything more than that, so don't get too excited."

A flush of embarrassment settles in Clarisse's cheeks. "Does—does she think you and I are…?"

Bast giggles. "Deny it all you want, big guy, but I'm hedging bets. I know there's no point in arguing with either of you, but this at least proves my theory that something is there."

Wishing she was anywhere but in the middle of this conversation,

Clarisse wonders if there's somewhere she could go for therapy in the Afterlife. Somewhere where she can unload and sort through all her emotions.

She shakes her head. "Guys, this is too much for me to process. So, am I in danger or not? And Death, are you staying or leaving?"

Death sighs. Through the window, Clarisse sees the suns peeking over the horizon.

"Clarisse, I am staying."

She turns to face him. His gaze, though deep in thought, is still fixed on her. She tries not to think about Bast's theory, whatever it might ultimately imply. "So, does that mean I'm in danger?"

"Perhaps. The Neylka is crafty, but I'll be here to help you navigate this," he promises. "We will help you learn to harness your powers and possibly even discover who you are. I don't think Fal and Bast are right."

Bast starts to argue, but Death holds up a hand. "Part of why the Neylka is seeking her is to recycle her properly, because the forgetting part was not completed. That means somewhere in her memories, Clarisse knows who she is. And I think the Neylka might be inclined to leave her alone if she's able to figure that out for herself."

"Actually… I agree with that, Death," Bast concedes. "I think if Leyun is chasing her in her dreams first, that's a sign that it wants to break her from the inside. To beat her to the chase, maybe?"

Death nods. "We can beat the Neylka and Leyun at their own game by helping Clarisse figure out who she was the first time. It's the only thing I can think of to protect her from the ultimate end, which is either Leyun trying to force her into the Neylka, or the Neylka using Leyun to convince Clarisse it's her only path forward."

Clarisse lets the magic she felt in her dreams crackle to life in her hands. "I don't intend to go willingly."

The bright stars between her fingers start to swirl and engulf everyone in the room. Some seem to shine brighter than the very suns in the window, leaving blind spots in Clarisse's vision.

"Settle down," she whispers to her stars. They hum, bringing their harsh light down a few notches so she can steady herself. Clarisse straightens her spine. "As long as you're both staying, we should come up with a plan to ensure I don't bend to the Neylka's whims."

Smiling, Death reaches out to hold her hand. "I think that's an excellent plan."

For once, Clarisse feels herself relax. She takes one last look at her arms, her stars hovering around to try and search for any signs of Leyun's toothy grip. Not a scar remains.

VENGEANCE

Terrence

Several days have passed. Terrence, finally calming from his fit of rage, reduces himself back to normal size. All over Ashville, the news stations have been in a flurry trying to explain the swirling black mass of thunder and the resulting heat wave that followed in the wake of his display of uncontrolled power.

Discussions of things like global warming, climate change, and apocalyptic catastrophe have floated around. Scientists have begun to congregate, trying to trace the reason for the very localized weather changes.

Terrence chuckles, knowing full well that he's the reason for the change. *If only the mortals knew.*

His time in the storm of his own making left him with the space necessary to plan. Father Simmons and the Monroes cannot escape from their crimes, even if the human justice system thinks they can. This is always where Terrence and Death disagreed. Death was content to let Fal weave her strings and let free will fall and create the plans for when someone would meet their end.

Terrence, on the other hand, was a fan of pushing things along for people who deserved it. *Those bastards are more than deserving of punishment.*

He struggles, though, to understand his connection to Clarisse... *Why go to such great lengths to avenge her?* It's an uncomfortable thought, so he stores it away to process later. Right now, he only cares to see justice carried out.

He stands tall, declaring, "I may not be a Reaper anymore, but I know what justice looks like. And I can still make good on it."

Grinning, his wolfish teeth click against each other as he grits them to swallow another wave of rage. He can't afford to be a swirling storm of doom. There's already far too much attention on the town to make it tricky to get away with his plans to "take care" of Simmons and the Monroes.

Still, he grows giddy with the thought of sinking his razor-sharp teeth into their flesh.

And why shouldn't I? They deserve it.

Terrence realizes he's not quite sure where he is, although he knows he's still in Asheville. His rage-filled steps landed him in the middle of a large, open field. In the distance, he spies the shadow of the barn where he first met Clarisse. His rage led him to the very place where he hopes to seek vengeance against Mr. and Mrs. Monroe.

His mind is a blur as it fashions together several different scenarios as to how he might punish them. He knows Kohlu is the only fitting place for souls such as theirs, but his actions against them on Earth are limited by what he can get away with before Death comes after him again.

A part of him is, for the first time, tempted to stop. Clarisse wiped his slate clean. If he walks away now, he can be a free soul. Perhaps he'll never be *whole* again in the way he wants, but he could take advantage of this freedom and forge a new path for himself.

I wonder what it would be like to be free? A soul not bound to any duty.

But he knows the nagging guilt of having those who harmed Clarisse roaming the world free would follow him with every step. A far worse fate than dying would be the knowledge that he betrayed his friend and never found a way to settle his debt.

Her brown eyes still follow him wherever he goes. Her trusting smile. The warmth and light she exuded, though long gone, haunt his very breath.

"These fools must pay for their crimes," he whispers aloud.

A frigid winter wind passes through him. His hackles raise and he half expects to turn and find Death standing nearby, judging him for the heinous crimes he's thinking.

Terrence knows it's not time to strike yet. He needs to wait until the fervor surrounding his shadow storm has died down. When the humans aren't expecting oddities, it's easier to erase the memories of the occasional bystander who might be attuned to glimpsing acts of the supernatural.

I don't need Jack Frost on my case, either.

If Death catches wind of Terrence's plans, he'll no doubt trek to Earth to subdue a wayward ex-Reaper. The punishment will be severe.

I need to be more careful about this.

Still, his eyes linger on the house that looms just beyond the old barn. He puts his nose to the air, hoping to catch the scent of his soon-to-be prey. Wandering through the dried, crunchy grass, his paws squelch in the mud from recently melted snow. It came early this year while he was still swirling around in an angry fervor.

When the door to the barn creaks open, he realizes he's been muttering to himself and lost in a completely different set of thoughts, all while still walking toward the structure. Dust kicks up from within the door frame and little bits of hay and leaves float in the air, caught in beams of moonlight as they move to settle on the ground. He looks up, appreciating the soft light. He closes his eyes and lets the cool rays settle on his eyelids, lighting the dancing memories of meeting her from the back of his mind.

All at once, he's transported to that moment again. She was afraid of who she was. Her power frightened her. She believed he was a monster—a myth. Something her mind conjured up to punish itself for daring to imagine a life better than this one.

Terrence misses the smell of the summer breeze as it danced between her stars when they first met. He misses following her back to her home and helping her find that spark of imagination that made life so much more magical when she saw what *could* be, instead of what *was*.

She had a chance to be something where he failed. To chart out a destiny separate from that which befell them both in the end. As much as it was his fault for not heeding the warnings, it was also the fault of the people who raised her.

Death was content to follow the rules and leave her to live or die as it was fated. But Terrence disagreed. Even if it was wrong, he knew a few months of freedom were better than a lifetime of torture.

For the first time in months, the boulder of guilt in his heart starts to lift. His nostrils flare, truly smelling the crisp winter air that lurks in the shadows of the old barn.

She may be gone, but her spark isn't. Her memory floods his being, a sparkling banner that represents everything for which he stands. A reminder of why he rebelled is coated in every strand that wove the tapestry of his and Clarisse's brief story.

The rules truly are meant to be broken.

He would damn himself again before he'd ever let anyone go through what she did.

His resolve burns white hot in his chest. Smoke curls in his mouth and unfurls from between his teeth like a dragon. The village is doomed now, and he's lost the capacity to care about drawing unwanted attention or unsettling the humans. Who cares if people see? Perhaps it's time to let them know what happens when they violate others for personal gain.

Actions have consequences, just like Death always said.

I am the consequences.

A low rumble starts in his throat. He swallows a howl, worried he might alert the Monroes to his presence and give them time to think about leaving. He tips his head to the air and breathes in their scent.

Human souls have a spiritual signature, each one laced with a distinctive scent. It's no coincidence that Reapers all take the form of the Grim. They are bloodhounds—built to hunt, find, and capture.

And now to tear them apart.

Terrence licks his lips and imagines what he'll do to each of them. But why stop there? The cravings he used to have for the powers he yearned for in life are returning.

If I'm to be damned for being myself, then so be it.

His body is wracked with excitement, and a horrid grin splits his face. Were a stranger to walk in, they'd faint at the sight of his shadow, its mouth caked with foam and its gleaming red eyes alight with homicidal desire.

"They'll pay for their sins," he whispers, his voice a crackling flame. He slinks toward her parents' house, deciding how he might torture them for the horrible crimes they inflicted upon their only child. "Shall I let them see me and have fun before I ferry them to Kohlu?"

Any attempts at feigning sanity are pointless. Speaking aloud is the only normal thing he has left in his repertoire of mad dealings.

It takes him a moment to realize he's sitting on the front porch. His heart flutters. In a flash of clarity, he fears he might falter.

It's not too late to think this through.

He almost sneers at the ramblings of his conscience. *How can it be more selfish to do this than to walk away?*

As Terrence debates his next steps, he doesn't notice the curtains slide open before it's too late.

Deborah's scream almost shatters the glass in the windowpanes. He hears her shouting for her husband, then the sounds of her feet scrambling over the entryway carpet and crashing when she slips and hits the wall.

Even though he's not inside yet, he has the floor plan memorized from his brief time with Clarisse before they ran away. Chuckling, he decides to let them do this the hard way.

Storming in now would be quick—painless. Kohlu, as eternal as it is, is an old trick. Why not drive them insane first? Peer behind curtains and let them catch glimpses of him. Appear to one and not the other and have them argue over whether he's an apparition or the manifestation of whatever guilt they might bear.

He hears Arthur's lumbering frame move through the house. The man isn't graceful, his loud plodding a signal that it's time to leave... for now.

Terrence decides he wants to be a real-life horror movie for them. The demon in the closet everyone fears. And why not? Why not have some fun and make them suffer as they did Clarisse?

Prowling out to the tree line, he waits. When Arthur opens the door and sees nothing there, Terrence forces himself not to laugh and give away his position as the shouting starts. The man's scowl as he turns to berate his wife gives the wolf a burst of glee.

Give it time, my friends. You will regret your very existence before long.

A certain church comes to mind as a good place to stay while waiting for the Monroes to fall apart at the seams. It's only fair that John Simmons pays for his sins, too.

Isn't that what the Great Light would want?

At this, he allows himself a laugh. He knows it's pointless to pretend now. He's a shadow with a vendetta and he's going to make good on his promises, no matter the cost.

He knows it won't be long before Tyrladan's forces come knocking to try and understand the disturbances on Earth. Shadow storms and hauntings can be explained away by humans all day, but the Afterlife knows better. Death will know it's him long before the official reports are ever penned.

When they come for him, memories will be erased and he'll be sentenced to the Neylka. Death is one of the few gods that can make good on those threats. Why anyone granted him the power to murder gods along with collecting souls is a mystery to Terrence, but he can't find it within him to be concerned.

Let them come and punish me. What does it matter, anyway? It's no different from what I've already suffered…

Terrence feels he has nothing left to care for. Taking up arms in memory of the one friend he had is enough fuel to carry on, but for how long?

Suddenly, it occurs to him that he can probably find her in the Afterlife. Breaking in through Kohlu is an option. He grins at the thought of seeing her again, but he knows she'll have questions. Why? How? When? All the most horrible questions await him beyond the veil. He knows she's forgiven him—that much was clear as she passed on. But how could she ever let him go without explaining himself first?

With a shudder, he decides that vengeance is best served by a loose cannon in the guise of a wolf made of darkness. For now, he's content to honor her memory by being her sword of wrath rather than finding her.

Breaking into Kohlu would surely land him in trouble. He'd be hunted by Aiyeliu and brought to Death to stand trial for violating even more laws than he already has. With a firm nod, he decides his job is to set things right on Earth.

He smiles as he creeps up to the Monroes' bedroom window. Darting up to peer through the glass, he waits until Deborah sees him one more time before slinking away. Delighted by the sound of her shrieks, he sets off toward the church, aware that none of this will end well.

Not if Death gets involved, that's for sure.

But that's a problem for future Terrence to solve. For now, he's going to enjoy this. Thoroughly.

It's time for the damned to receive their just desserts.

KREYUHL

Clarisse

Clarisse stands outside her home. The tall grass sways in the wind and she wonders if it's safe to sit here and ponder a place that might have been hers.

If I weren't being hunted.

She plucks a few blades between her fingers, not caring that a few slice her delicate skin. Golden blood pools in small beads and she stares, fascinated.

Death and Bast speak in hushed whispers from within the house. They don't think she can hear them talking, but fragments of their words carry on the wind, even though she can't decipher what's being said.

Her mind replays the moment when Leyun bit her in her dream. It's disconcerting that her only kindred spirit is a monster she can't escape, even when she closes her eyes and turns her face to the light.

Aren't they worried she'll find me out here by myself?

Somehow, she knows whatever bond she shares with Death would alert him immediately to any danger in which she found herself. The churning in her stomach kicks up at the thought of their bond.

What does that mean, anyway? Why would Fal bind me to Death like this?

Death's voice whispers in her mind. *"She didn't—not strictly speaking. It's deeper than that. We must explore it to find the true cause."*

A sigh escapes her lips. Of course he can still hear her. It occurs to her that their mental conversations are mostly one-sided. Death clearly has more experience keeping his thoughts closed off from strangers, no matter how bound their souls might be.

Clarisse lowers down to the soft green grass and luxuriates in its embrace. Staring up at the sun isn't wise, but she doesn't care. Her stars are dulled in the bright light. For once, she wishes for the night sky. She wonders if Death would let her release her stars in his constellations.

Surely he has room.

She turns, though doesn't sit up, when she senses his presence. Death peeks out the door with a scowl on his face.

"Remind me not to leave you unaccompanied for more than ten minutes. You have strange thoughts when I'm not present."

Clarisse giggles as she lowers back to the ground. Death disappears back inside the house and the mirth in her soul recedes. As much as he was probably joking, she wishes her swirling thoughts would disappear. It's not wise to be left alone with them right now.

For one thing, how can she possibly figure out who she once was if there's no trace of her former self? Wracking her mind has proven useless. She can't quite put a finger on a nagging thought in the back of her consciousness—something dark that slips along the edges. So far, her only clue is that she's been partially recycled. Sort of like Leyun, but not…whatever *that* means. For another thing, if she's in so much danger, then why haven't they left? Why aren't they exploring Tyrladan to find clues?

Granted, she realizes it doesn't help to start off on an adventure when you don't know where to start, but all this sitting around seems pointless. She rolls over, finding that the grass is thick enough to have already started leaving imprints on her skin. A glance back at the house shows that Bast and Death are still busy talking. The river is too far away to explore, and the flowers around her house aren't nearly as pretty as the ones blooming near Kreyuhl.

Deciding to have some fun, she snaps her fingers and begins to imagine. Her conjuring skills, though wild and unstructured, are enough to summon flowers of wildly different sizes and shapes. Blues, pinks, and purples dominate the scene.

She loves asters the most, which resemble small purple daisies. Without flowers or landscaping, her Victorian house resembles a haunted one from the movie stills she saw while walking through the mall. Though it's not dilapidated, her house has a sad, antiquated presence that exudes mystery. The arched windowpanes even look aged, despite being new.

Yes, color is needed here.

Once she settles on purple asters, she weaves them in and around her house, not caring if they clash with the muted gray siding. As riotous pops of lavender edge along the house, it seems to come to life. No longer a sad, moody Victorian, but a respite from a long day and an even longer Afterlife.

She hears Death sigh in the back of her mind. Using magic without guidance will be the reason for their arguments—she can tell.

Some things never change... not even when you die.

Clasping her fingers together, she lets her magic fall back, receding into her body like a wave. When it crashes down, the world around her stills to an uncomfortable degree.

Suddenly, it feels like Death's icy powers are creeping up through the ground, except it's a different kind of cold. The sensation isn't comforting like Death's embrace, but eerily reminiscent of the void. The alarm bells going off in her head do nothing to alert Death. She sees his silhouette and Bast's through the kitchen window, blissfully unaware of what's going on outside.

Her arms freeze at her sides. She can't wave at them. She can't make a sound. A strange, violet haze settles over her. Her stomach twists in on itself so violently, she tries not to pitch forward and vomit. The ground beneath her back vibrates. Vertigo settles and shakes the outer corners of her vision.

"Clarisse..."

The soft whisper in her mind, though just as loud as Death's, is not his. Something else is inside her mind. Stumbling to her feet, she tries to center herself and find the source of it.

"L-Leyun?" Her voice finally breaks through whatever barrier was holding it back, though it's too soft for Death or Bast to hear.

"I am not Leyun," it answers.

Her head is on a swivel as she tries to locate the origin of the voice. In the distance, she sees a shadow emerge from the swirling gray. Pale, pearly white skin ripples over a strange, almost equine-like body. At first glance, she wonders if she's staring at another unicorn. Maybe one of the true ones that Bast mentioned before.

Then her eyes rest on its head and her mouth stretches into a silent scream.

An Aiyeliu!

The creature has a long, slender face that's a mix between a dog, horse, and maybe a bit of deer. Long, slender ears are affixed atop its head; they point to the sky, listening for anything Clarisse may have to say. Its eyes are milky white, just like the rest of its body. Clarisse wonders if it might be blind, but she's too frightened to ask.

Its stilt-like legs make no sound and leave no marks as it walks gracefully toward her, its ears tilting to the side, along with its strange head. A thin tail wags from side to side. It looks like an alien, a dog, and a horse all got smashed together in a factory of spare parts. The results are terrifying.

Clarisse stumbles back.

"Why do you back away from me?"

Startled, Clarisse registers the hurt in the creature's voice. While the haze of purple and gray doesn't disappear, in a blink, her fear starts to subside. She is fueled by curiosity, though she realizes how foolish it is to be lulled into calmness by a creature she doesn't know. She is easy prey if this thing wants to mangle her. She remembers Death's warnings, but she shoves them away. Warmth blossoms in her chest. "I… I've never seen… Who are you?"

The creature extends its neck proudly. "I am Kreyuhl."

Clarisse frowns. "Isn't that where the Selyento lives?"

It giggles. "I stole the name. I didn't have one before. I saw you there before Leyun showed up." Its voice is so soft, Clarisse almost doesn't hear it.

A hum erupts in the ground between them. The twinkling chimes of the Selyento's leaves weaves through her, making her shiver. Her power rushes to the surface, calming her even more and giving her curiosity permission to run the floor.

"Did Leyun chase you off?"

"No." The creature laughs. "I chased *her* off!"

It stretches its maw wide, showing off its teeth to make a point. Shuddering, Clarisse rubs her arms to try and flatten out the goosebumps that emerge as she continues to converse with this strange beast. She can't decide if she's frightened or not.

"Why? And how?"

It licks its lips, a serpentine, dark tongue darting out to give Clarisse several more reasons to have nightmares should she ever choose to sleep again. *Never going to get that sight out of my head.*

The creature flinches. *"I don't mean to frighten you. I'm sorry you find me repulsive."*

Clarisse feels horrible for hurting its feelings. "I don't mean it like that. I'm sorry… You just frightened me. I don't know who you are. I've been chased by Leyun since I got here, and I don't know who to trust."

The creature blinks, though the look of hurt is gone from its face. It settles down on its haunches and Clarisse wonders how it goes from looking like a terrifying cryptid to something that more closely resembles a weird looking greyhound.

It sniffs the air and Clarisse is almost embarrassed as she realizes she's trying to catch the scent of whatever it's picked up.

"I am Kreyuhl. It is where I met you. I am your familiar," it purrs.

Clarisse wonders how much more she can take before all these bits of information drive her insane. Her brain can't keep processing all these strange facts.

The creature seems to sense her distress. Before Clarisse can react, he closes the distance between them, slinking to her like a cat rather than a dog. It's baffling to behold, but Clarisse is somewhat charmed by him. Kreyuhl seems pleased that she is becoming more receptive to it.

With a start, she notices the calming sensation is back. Tears form in her eyes as something awakens inside her. Holding out a hand, she lets it sniff her palm. When it places its muzzle within her fingers, a jolt of energy passes through Clarisse's veins and the Aiyeliu makes a series of bizarre chirping noises. It sounds like a dinosaur in those fake science channel shows where they hypothesize how the beasts might've sounded.

Like a giant bird.

A chuckle echoes in Clarisse's thoughts and she realizes she's made the Aiyeliu laugh.

The purple haze surrounding them starts to diminish, but the Aiyeliu does not curl away as the smoke does. The grayness dissipates. All that's left is the two of them, her hand still outstretched, and its eyes closed as it receives the arc of energy that thrums between them. She can't see it, but she knows it's there. Her whole body receives information from the Aiyeliu. He's new—freshly created. He arrived in Tyrladan the moment she stepped foot in it.

He's bound to her and her magic. No one has to tell her this—it's ingrained in her. That explains why she's both terrified and drawn to it, her mind a cacophony of thoughts. Smiling, she strokes his muzzle and holds his face in her hands. He nuzzles her unflinchingly as she runs her hands down his slender neck. A silver mane stretches down to what Clarisse imagines might be called withers. *If you consider this thing a horse... what is an Aiyeliu?*

Clarisse recalls the image Bast showed her, but this one isn't quite like the rest. It looks even more lethal, if that's possible.

Somewhere in the distance, she hears Bast scream. When a massive black panther comes hurtling out of the house, Clarisse barely manages to throw herself in front of Kreyuhl in time. The cat slides, screeches to a halt, and snarls. Bast swipes a paw through the air, her eyes demanding that Clarisse step aside.

Death sprints out the door and into the yard, his eyes alight with terror as he realizes that Clarisse is no longer alone. "How did this happen and I didn't know?" he demands. When he crosses his arms, Clarisse swears she glimpses fire in his eyes.

Again? For a creature made of ice, it's strange to see flames in his eyes.

Death glares at her, daring her to say something aloud, but she wisely shuts her mouth before saying anything to get her in more trouble.

"How did this happen?" Death demands again, tapping his foot like a scolding parent.

Bast whirls on him. "You're more concerned with the why instead of trying to rescue Clarisse? This thing has her! And she's already been stupefied by its presence! She won't move aside so I can kill it!"

Clarisse holds her hands out placatingly. "Bast, he's my familiar. His name is Kreyuhl. We just met, but he's been chasing off Leyun."

At the mention of Leyun, Kreyuhl hisses and curls his body in a defensive position around Clarisse. The fact that it can bend itself like a pretzel leaves Clarisse with more questions than she started with.

"I know I don't know him, but deep down, I do. He's connected to my magic, Death," Clarisse explains. "I don't understand what a familiar is or what it does, but I know he's supposed to be here with me. I realize it was dangerous to interact with him without asking you first, but somehow he was able to tell me he meant no harm. I could tell he wasn't lying."

With a defeated groan, Bast shifts back into her human form. Her teeth are gritted and her fists clenched. "You must take more care to be protective of yourself, Clarisse!"

Clarisse flinches at the authority in Bast's tone. Kreyuhl lets out a soft growl, his teeth bared.

The fierce feline snaps her eyes at the strange creature. "Don't you speak to your elder that way, Kreyuhl! I'll not have you acting like you are superior in defending her. We're all after the same goal," Bast chastises the creature.

He pins his ears down and lowers his head in shame, though he doesn't uncurl his body from its protective embrace around Clarisse.

"You can trust us, Kreyuhl," Death adds. "I appreciate that you are looking after her with so much passion."

Kreyuhl blinks, his strange, statuesque figure relaxing as he reaches the conclusion that Clarisse is, for now, safe.

Clarisse smiles. "He's not going to hurt me, Death." Her chest no longer feels tight, and the confusion jumbled up in her mind is not quite the labyrinth it was a few hours ago. The Minotaur-sized lump in her throat, though not gone, seems to have entered a slumber. Kreyuhl must be the cause. His teeth peer out from behind his lips in something like a smile.

Kreyuhl finally releases Clarisse from his self-made cage. When she reaches out to pat him on the neck, he doesn't refuse the action.

Instead, he seems rather content to sit back and watch as Death and Bast collect themselves. Bast looks like she might hurl herself at Kreyuhl at any moment.

"Why do I have a familiar? I thought only witches had those." Clarisse feels small again as she raises another question. It's hard being new. Kreyuhl chirrups at this sentiment. Unlike Death, his presence in her mind doesn't feel wholly separate. He seems to belong there, like an extension of her.

Death is the first to answer. "Any magical being can have a familiar. They usually arise when someone has a significant amount of power that they need help channeling, though they can choose someone regardless of their level. It doesn't surprise me that you've gotten one. My only concern is that it arrived so soon. Is he new or old?" Death's fingers rise to rest on his chin. He taps at his face, deep in thought.

"He's new. He arrived when I arrived, according to what he told me." Clarisse looks up at him and realizes for the first time how tall Kreyuhl is. His nostrils flare and he rests his angled muzzle in her hair.

While Bast seems to have relaxed some, Clarisse takes note of how her eyes dart back and forth, searching for anything that might alert her to oncoming threats. Clarisse is grateful to have such protective and caring friends.

Her fingers conjure a star; she brings it to her lips and blows it toward Bast. It hovers in the air, a strange song following in its wake. It lands on Bast's nose and winks before disappearing. Bast smiles, though it's hollow—she's still unconvinced.

"As happy as I am that you have Kreyuhl, you must understand that we must proceed with heavy caution, yes?" Death ventures. "Your mind is clouded by the familiar bond, but Bast and I will be on high alert to ensure he's not an agent of the Neylka."

Kreyuhl's ears flatten and he huffs. *"Your friends must not linger on their worries over me. There are much more frightening things out there."*

Death freezes. *"I heard that."*

Kreyuhl turns to Death and walks over to him on his strange stilt legs. He silently hovers over Death. They stare at each other for a long time before Kreyuhl relents and walks back over to Clarisse.

"Uh, what was that about?" she asks quizzically.

"I was examining your bond with Death. It's curious..."

Perplexed, Clarisse pushes him for more information.

"It's not my place to explain. I don't think it's well-defined yet, anyway. All I can do is help you navigate the discovery."

Clarisse's shoulders slump. She wonders when the confusion will end—when the Afterlife might start to make sense. The glimmer in Kreyuhl's eyes doesn't promise an easy adventure. He leans over her, offering his warmth and strength.

How do you know everything when you just got here?

Kreyuhl answers, *"I am mapped to you. Undoubtedly, some part of your magic remembers me. You can consider your knowledge my memory."*

The thudding in her chest is so loud that Clarisse wonders if anyone else can hear it. Perspiration builds on her forehead. She wipes her hands on her clothes to dry them, but the sweat is replaced as soon as she does. Muttering under her breath, Clarisse wonders what else the day might bring. The thought of more problems and puzzles to solve makes her nauseous. Before she doubles over to retch, she clutches her stomach and closes her eyes.

So, my magic remembers who I am? How can my magic remember but I can't?

"That's part of the mystery," Death answers.

Before he can continue, Bast speaks up. "Can we all stop with the weird mind speaking and actually have conversations out loud? You can translate for Kreyuhl, but you two," she points to Clarisse and Death, "need to make it clearer what you're up to. I want to be able to help, too."

Clarisse's cheeks redden. "Sorry, Bast. I got lost in my thoughts again. This is a lot to take in, but you've been so helpful. Are you sure you want to be a part of this? I'm asking sincerely. This is a lot more than what I thought I'd be facing."

The throbbing in Clarisse's head picks up. Being sick isn't something she enjoys, let alone as an immortal soul. She knows a fever has settled in, which is odd, considering she can't die.

Bast approaches and takes Clarisse's face in her hands. "My powers revolve around helping young people find their strength in adversity. You are a young goddess facing horrible challenges that I wouldn't dare let you face alone. If I can lend my powers to mortals, the least I can do is lend some to you. I do not mind. You are a fellow Selbeno.

That alone is enough for me to help you. Your soul is worth the investment." She lifts her palm to feel Clarisse's forehead and sighs. "I do believe you have taxed yourself, Clarisse. My recommendation is to cease using magic until you learn to channel it. While I cannot stay for the whole journey, I will make it a point to instruct you in how to use magic while I am here. In exchange, I'll teach you how to lend me some of your powers. I would love to learn to make stars."

Death's face twists in surprise. "Why haven't you asked *me* before? I could teach you."

Bast holds out a finger to him but does not turn to face him. "You bore me. Hush."

Clarisse hears a thousand insults rushing around in Death's mind, but he quiets them when he realizes she's listening. The word "flekerleke" pops up again—she knows that one is particularly vulgar, but the definition eludes her.

The feline goddess rolls her eyes at him. "Since Death has decided to stay for the time being, I will return to my post by the river. However, should he need to leave your side, I will return and look after you myself. I want to spend some time searching through my tomes for information on how to help someone such as yourself channel powers like what you possess. Yours are unique, and I don't want to steer you wrong. Try to keep magic at a minimum in my absence, okay?"

Nodding, Clarisse is relieved as the nausea starts to dissipate. Her throat is no longer tight, and her head doesn't have an angry hammer going off every second like a strike on an anvil. "I'll be careful," Clarisse whispers. "Are my stars considered extensive magic? And what about when my magic comes without me calling it? Right now it feels out of control."

Bast smiles. "I understand that. It's hard. Your emotions are all over the place and you have two people trying to teach you who aren't really suited to teaching. But we will both try our best. You need to work on controlling your feelings more and recognizing where the magic reaches. How far does it extend before you're casting spells? How angry must you be? How sad? How happy? All these things are important. I suspect some meditation and relaxation exercises are in order."

Clarisse blinks. "Are you telling me to do stuff like yoga? Stretching?"

Bast inclines her head. "It's either that, or you hurl your innards everywhere you go and constantly need sleep and time to recharge. That makes you an easy target. Do you want others to think you're weak?"

A small amount of rage bubbles in Clarisse's stomach. *Weak? Me?* Memories of the torture she received in Father Simmons' church threaten to cloud her vision. They're so real that it's hard to remember without reliving the abuse. The beatings and exorcisms tingle beneath her skin, the scars fresh and vibrant, even if they're only visible to Clarisse.

Kreyuhl snarls, though at no one in particular. Bast jumps. "Keep that thing on a leash!" she commands.

Clarisse rolls her eyes. "He sees my memories, Bast. He's just mad because he can see what I went through."

Bast's eyes darken. "I take it he's seeing what happened to you at the Church of Light?"

It's hard to speak about what happened. Even her nightmares skirt around the edges. Darkness deeper than Terrence's shadows swim within the crevices of her memories. Her daydreams are filled with flashes of the past; she can't escape them forever.

"I won't be gone long," Bast promises. "I know you'll need as much instruction as possible. I'll reach out to those I know I can trust to come and assist. In the meantime, I regret to inform you that I'll be leaving you with Death." She jerks her head in his direction, still refusing to face him.

They remind Clarisse of how siblings act, at least the ones she had the pleasure of knowing during her time in the Church of Light.

Clarisse is sad to see the panther goddess go. "I'm really glad to have met you, Bast. I can't wait to learn from you and share what I can."

Bast smiles. "I know." She finally turns to face Death and holds out a hand. "I'll see you in a short while. Try not to get our mutual friend murdered. Not that she can die," she adds hurriedly, casting a glance back at Clarisse.

Death begrudgingly shakes her hand, but he refuses to answer her.

"So you're not worried about Kreyuhl then, Bast?" Clarisse teases. She's surprised she feels brave enough to tease Bast, but right now it's the only thing keeping her from going insane.

Bast shakes her head. "No, if he's tied to you in a way that Death can actually hear what's happening, I'm not as concerned. When I return and take over your tutelage full time, then I'll be more concerned since I cannot hear that connection. You'll have to learn to let me in."

Before Clarisse can utter a response, Bast shifts into her panther form again. In a flash, her sleek, shadowy form disappears.

The silence that ensues threatens to swallow her whole. Death has yet to look at her, his face turned to where Bast disappeared. Picking at her cuticles, she wonders if he'll leave her now, or what will happen if he stays too long and neglects his duties. Her eyes water; she wipes away the errant tears and finds solace in holding on to Kreyuhl's neck. Kreyuhl doesn't move, allowing her this moment of respite.

A cool breeze passes over her shoulders, alerting her to Death's presence beside her. Eyeing Kreyuhl warily, he puts an arm around her. "Clarisse, we will figure this out. Remember that you can't die here, and very few gods have the strength to force someone into the Neylka. Soon, your powers will begin to make sense, okay?"

His eyes, warm for once, are brighter than his stars. Seeing them glow, while unsettling, reminds Clarisse just how much power he has to keep her safe. As selfish as it is, she wants to bottle up this feeling and keep him with her forever if it means she never has to be afraid again.

He doesn't have time to protest before she barrels into him and wraps him in a hug. She squeezes tight for several minutes to hide the fact that more tears have started to break through.

Why am I such a mess?

His fingers run through her hair soothingly. *"You just died, Clarisse. You're a victim of horrible trauma. You just learned that you lived before and inherited powers that no one understands. On top of that, you found out there's an ancient entity chasing you. Why not give yourself some credit? I think you're holding up fairly well, all things considered."*

Clarisse pulls back, and a broken smile sneaks across her face. Her lips are cracked and dry, but she doesn't care. "I don't know what I'd do without you," she whispers.

"You'd carry on, just like you did before I arrived."

His answer is so matter-of-fact that Clarisse pauses to consider his words.

"No. You tried to save me multiple times, even though I was stupid and didn't listen and now you're staying with me... and you shouldn't. You have more important things to do than babysit me here while I find my way. You still have time to change your mind and go. Kreyuhl will keep me safe."

Kreyuhl makes a sound akin to radio static, his feeble attempt at speaking aloud to agree.

But Death is not swayed. "No, Clarisse. Even if I left, I'd still be able to hear your every thought. This is personal for me now. I have an army of Reapers for a reason, and they will ensure things are taken care of in my absence. I can still ensure my leadership duties are not abandoned—I'm not leaving my post without a word, nor am I giving up my job. I'm just... working remotely, I guess you would say."

"Right, 'cause the Grim Reaper can do that," Clarisse teases, though the guilt of having him stay with her squirms around in her veins.

He winks. "Yes, he can. I don't think you realize how many connections I have. Now stop worrying about me. We need to focus on you. As much as I *adore* Bast," he says, layering sarcasm in his voice, "I don't know that I want her watching you alone. I have no problem with you teaching her things, but being bound to a deity is no joke. You deserve to strike out on your own before making such a decision."

Clarisse ponders his explanation. *It would be nice to be able to figure out who I am before having to share.*

Death puts a finger under her chin. "I'm going to make sure you have that chance. Whatever bond you have with me, know it's not one where I expect anything in return. You must understand Clarisse, there are people who want to help you without wanting something back. I don't think Bast is manipulating you or has ulterior motives, but you deserve to make these decisions armed with the knowledge that you have friends who don't expect anything in return. Terrence didn't let you have that. Your parents didn't. Father Simmons didn't. And I regret that I left you in those situations. So now let me help you."

Clarisse's heart hammers faster than ever. Kreyuhl stays silent, but his eyes are fixed on Death with something like… suspicion? Jealousy?

Death releases her and motions for her to follow him. "Let's get you in the house and start sorting through the books I left in your library. I think you'll find them rather informative."

The sudden change of pace and intensity leaves Clarisse breathless as she tries to sort through her feelings. She wishes she could cloak her mind as she does her body and keep it hidden from him. Sometimes, it's nice to have privacy. She knows that Death isn't listening now—at least not fully. But she worries he might hear something she's not ready to admit.

Looking at Kreyuhl, they share a knowing look before following Death into the house.

CONNECTION

Death

Clarisse sits in the kitchen, sifting through a bowl of cereal. She conjured it along with the milk, though he doubts she realizes it. Bast's warning to her not to use magic wasn't taken lightly, but he understands she doesn't grasp the depth of her abilities.

The spoon clinks against the bowl, which will drive him mad if she doesn't stop.

Sensing his discomfort, she looks up at him and cringes. "Sorry," she offers. "I didn't realize it was so loud."

He sighs. "That's quite alright. You had no way of knowing I have an aversion to the sound of metal ringing on ceramic bowls. Tell me, how long have you been able to create food for yourself?" The blush that spills along her cheeks confirms his suspicions.

She winces. "I did it again, didn't I?"

Death doesn't answer, instead choosing to sit by her at the table. "You needn't apologize, you know. You're still learning, just like the rest of us are trying to figure you out. We can't ask for perfection if we don't even know what we're asking for."

Clarisse doesn't answer. She sets the spoon down by her bowl and buries her head in her arms. He yearns to comfort her, but stops himself from reaching out.

Why do I desire to help her like this? Emotions are not something I like dealing in.

Indeed, these constant, warm feelings in his chest are growing tiresome. He wonders why they won't go away.

He's no fool, though. He knows what they might be, but he ushers away the thought before he can ponder them further. His primary goal is to help Clarisse so he can get back to work. *Surely the bond will lessen once she's on solid footing. This is just an extended mission to help one soul cross over. It stands to reason that a soul such as hers would require extra help.*

When she looks up at him, he hopes she didn't hear him. Her face betrays nothing, and the strange, almost string-like magic that ties them together doesn't give anything away.

He turns his attention to the strange creature Kreyuhl. The damned beast has his face deep in his own cereal bowl. It's his fifth serving. He must know she's using magic to conjure the food, yet he can't stop asking for more.

He was born yesterday, in a manner of speaking.

This, though, he doesn't believe.

Kreyuhl's power feels raw—ancient. If he's truly "new," as he claims, then it stands to reason that he's a recycled creature himself. There's no other way to explain him.

A third data point.

He won't tell Clarisse what he suspects—not yet, anyway. He's surprised she hasn't asked how new life can form without Siralto and Tryta around to cultivate it. While new gods pop up periodically, they're never intact like this. They are typically created naturally through procreation or arise through freak forces of nature. New gods are not common, and new familiars are even less common.

She is a curiosity that may never be solved.

"Are we ready to adjourn to the library?" Death eyes the sixth bowl Kreyuhl has started on and sneers. He notices Clarisse's bowl is mostly full. "Not hungry?" He raises an eyebrow, trying his best to lighten the mood.

"I am, but I'm still queasy, to be honest. I thought cereal would be a safe bet, but maybe not. Let's head to the library before I try anything else. I want to start getting some answers before my head gets away from me. I have a feeling that may help me feel less sick."

Death isn't sure knowledge will cure her sickness, but he nods his acquiescence. Her skin looks paler than normal under the dining room light.

Gods can't get sick. So why is she under so much pressure?

Frowning, he decides to do some secret research to find out why she is getting ill.

Bast seemed confident that her struggles were normal, but Death can't help but worry. She's not bound by mortal constraints anymore… so why are they still holding her captive? Why does she feel so weak?

"Are you alright, Death?"

Clarisse's question snaps him back into focus. He realizes he's frowning and staring out the kitchen window. He wipes his face to an expressionless neutral. "Yes, sorry, just lost in thought. Is Kreyuhl finished?"

The wretched beast huffs and pushes his bowl away. Death hopes it isn't a seventh.

Together, they ascend to her room, the wooden stairs creaking beneath their feet as though they're hundreds of years old and not months. Death wishes Clarisse had a better grasp of her magic. He'd love to ask her why she gave the house such a variety of features such as these.

The ballroom is most curious as well. It seems more at home in a castle than a Victorian mansion.

Kreyuhl's icy breath down his neck makes Death stop to look behind him. The creature is right on their heels. He looks confused as to why they've stopped, and it takes all of Death's patience not to say something. He turns back around and continues toward the library. Clarisse keeps up with his pace better than she did yesterday, and she doesn't seem quite as tired as she did in the kitchen.

Thank Tryta for small favors.

When they reach her room, Death pulls the appropriate book from the shelf and it swings open, granting them entry to the hidden library. He fears Kreyuhl's mammoth size might cramp the room in the same way he does when he assumes the form of the Grim.

The Aiyeliu seems to sense this and hangs back in Clarisse's room, peering in through the small entryway to keep an eye on his charge.

Clarisse is already scanning the books, running her fingers over the spines of the different volumes Death hand-selected for her. In retrospect, he's not sure why he chose so many for her when he was certain she would fall for Terrence's tricks and die early, which is exactly what happened.

Since when am I ever optimistic?

Sighing, he starts to rummage through a shelf that contains books that might cover ailments of the immortal variety. Even though he's been through most, if not all, of these books before, he wants to ensure he's up to date. A second glance with a different intention always reveals new secrets.

He finds one — *BarulatyeAhksen* — translating to *Book of Ailments*, and gingerly leafs through its pages. He can tell the book has been recently read, which surprises him. When the pages fall open to the story of Tryta and Siralto, he stifles a chuckle. *What an odd choice.*

He leaves Clarisse in a cozy corner to read a volume she selected and remains nose deep in his own studies, reading about how Selben have become ill in the past. *Uhnten.* The word sparks a memory in him. He remembers hearing it mentioned a few times with gods of the past that he hasn't seen in a long time. *Exhaustion.* When a soul is taxed by different stresses, their power can be diminished, especially if they don't have control over their magic.

The remedies vary wildly in the accounts he reads. Strict bed rest. Odd potions here and there. Activities he'd rather not repeat. There's nothing here that gives a solid answer, and some of the potential solutions seem barbaric and unnecessary.

He snaps the book shut, deciding it's time to look for another. As he does, he reviews her ailments and realizes Clarisse doesn't have anything *new* ailing her. He searches through the books again to see if anything on Uhnten pops up anywhere.

"Hey, Death?"

Her voice calls him back from the trenches of his thoughts.

"I still don't understand why Tryta killed Siralto, and how creating Earth led to that outcome. Can you explain again?"

The soft sparkle in her brown eyes makes him cave. Normally, he doesn't care to relive that part of the past. For one, he emerged as a result of Earth's creation, and it wasn't long after that Siralto was erased—a quandary no one understands.

"Firstly, you must understand that there's debate there, Clarisse. Did she erase herself or did Tryta force her? Or was it both? The account is very brief, as you'll note. Not many were around when it happened, and Tryta disappeared not long after. Many wonder if he erased himself in grief."

Frowning, Clarisse's thumbs pick at the corners of the page, which very nearly drives Death insane until she halts, her finger sliding back up and down the words.

"How can I read these books when they're written in Mansalo? I don't understand why I have that power, either. I hear it and don't understand what's being said, But when I read it, it makes sense."

Death laughs. "The text is enchanted. Your magic likely interacts with it and translates it. Hearing things is far different than seeing them. You're likely more of a visual learner. You'll come to understand Mansalo being spoken in time."

After sitting next to her on the floor, he conjures a small, black blanket and wraps it around her shoulders. The chill he brings with him would make anyone shiver, and he wants her to relax in a moment like this.

A strange warmth settles in his chest. He tries to brush it away until he realizes it's on the inside. Without thinking, he rests his head in the crook of her neck. Before he can pull away, Clarisse leans her face against his. For a moment, they just sit and breathe. Her eyes close and her book starts to fall shut.

"I'm so scared, Death," she confesses.

A wrenching pain tears through his chest. *Of course she's frightened. How much more can she take before she breaks?*

The urge to bundle her up and carry her away to some far-off place only he knows grows in intensity. *I can keep her safe. Leyun won't find her if I take her.*

It's folly to believe this; he knows he can't outrun the inevitable. He can only hope to help her gain confidence in who she is so she doesn't feel the urge to give in when the time comes. The thought of losing her makes him angry—murderous, even. While no one has ever tried to murder the Neylka, he would make himself the first. *Consequences be damned.*

The wet sensation in his eyes is foreign to him. *Am I... crying?* She leans up to look at him before he can wipe the moisture away. Her wide eyes reveal that she's startled, but she says nothing. Instead, she reaches up and wipes them away for him.

Without thinking, he leans in and brushes his lips over hers, softer than a butterfly's wings. Pulling back, his cheeks grow warm as he realizes what he's done. He starts to stand, but she catches his shoulders and tugs him back down, crashing her lips against his.

Her kisses are a bit sloppy, but one would expect this from someone who's never been kissed. But Death doesn't care. He groans and kisses her back. He stops just before he brings his tongue into the mix. They pull away panting, clearly wanting more but holding back.

Clarisse's eyes look conflicted, but she leans into his embrace. He rests his chin on her head and neither of them speaks for a few moments. As much as he would like to continue whatever it is that just occurred between them, he knows they can't. *Not yet.* But his heart flutters. He curses himself.

Is this the bond?

With his conscience at war with itself, he reopens the book that lays forgotten on her lap, though he doesn't remove it or shuffle her out of the way. Together, they look at images of different gods and goddesses and Clarisse stops to ask a few questions here and there. Despite being an entity of ice, he's never felt so much fire in his bones.

"Do you think the bond means something else?" Her question echoes in his mind and his throat grows thick with worry.

"I'm beginning to believe so." He gently pushes her from his lap so he can stand. If Bast were here, she'd be laughing at him. Calling him names. Making sure he never forgot the fact that he slipped.

Except I want to slip again.

Turning, his eyes lock onto Clarisse's and they stare at each other for a few quiet moments. "Clarisse, I'm not sure what I feel or how to navigate this, but I do care for you, bond or not. So I can't tell you for sure if it's the bond or if I just..." He blushes.

"That's okay, Death, I care about you, too." Clarisse's cheeks are flushed and neither of them can figure out what to say. "We can take our time. I mean… don't we have eternity now?"

The sparkle in her eyes melts his resolve and he nods, allowing a small smile.

It's startling for Death to drop his act and allow others to see him take his mask off, real or otherwise.

Kreyuhl remains quiet, though his eyes are fixed on Death with daggers poised in them. The creature is jealous, Death is certain.

"I will protect her with my life, just as you would protect hers with yours," he vows.

This seems to please Kreyuhl, whose teeth are no longer poised to open and clamp shut on him for his insolence.

"I think taking time is the right answer," Death finally answers, almost having forgotten Clarisse's question entirely. "You need time to come into your own and I… well, I need time to sort through how I feel. I admit, I'm not very familiar with romance. It hasn't been my focus, you see."

To his surprise, Clarisse giggles. "What? You mean reaping the souls of the damned isn't the best place to land a girlfriend?"

A hearty laugh escapes him before he can stop it. "Not exactly a good setting for a date. Most aren't that appreciative of my attributes while I'm dragging them here for the rest of eternity."

They're both laughing now, and Death is grateful. That feeling in his chest, while still there, doesn't feel so intense and oppressive now. Had it stayed present any longer, he might've done something stupid like kiss her again.

Still, the dreaded bond tugs at him every time he looks at her. He won't ask Bast about it, though he's sure she'll figure it out when she returns. *Perhaps I'll summon Fal back and ask her. Maybe she can explain what's happening.*

He realizes they've both been sitting in silence again and chides himself. *I need to be more… open?*

"Yes, you do." Clarisse smiles knowingly. *"Heard that one."*

Deciding to ignore the heat in his face that never seems to truly disappear when he's around her, he clears his throat. "May I ask why you were so focused on Tryta and Siralto? How will learning about them help you figure out who you are?"

Clarisse shrugs. "They created everything, right? If I can get a sense of who they are, maybe it will help me understand the Neylka and why they would create a system where you can 'come back', even if only a little."

Death winks. "You're profiling the gods?"

"Profiling?"

Death feigns a gasp. "You mean to tell me that you've never seen a crime show?"

Shaking her head, Clarisse looks almost crestfallen. "I didn't get to watch much television. I heard about things or saw them in snippets when I went out in public and stuff, but I never really watched shows or anything."

Death shakes his head. "Don't be ashamed, Clarisse. We'll have to watch a show or two together to see if you like them. I think you might enjoy the dramatics. I confess, I've never understood why they scream so much when bodies are discovered… except for the gruesome finds. *Those* I can understand."

Clarisse's laugh this time sounds hollow, but he appreciates that she seems somewhat interested. The pull to spend more time with her increases with each passing day. It doesn't make sense why he's so drawn to her. Of course she's beautiful, but it's more than that. In the Afterlife, Clarisse is ethereal; a woman who no longer looks as if life might drain her of any spirit she has left. He has half a mind to go punish the Monroes on her behalf right now, but he knows better. Doing so would be reckless—foolish. It would be an idiot's task to harm the mortals while they still live, but when they die...

Almost chuckling at his own thoughts, he hums aloud. "Well, since we didn't turn up anything interesting, why don't we look at gods and goddesses who had the ability to wield stars?"

"Is that a unique power?" Clarisse looks down at her hands, effortlessly summoning one in her palm. "I mean… *you* do it."

"Sort of," Death admits. "They are tied to my power, but I don't conjure them. I have a fixed number within me that don't speak like yours do, whereas you create new ones."

Clarisse's face twists up with confusion. "I… I've never counted them."

The star in her hand makes a strange noise.

"What is it saying?" His curiosity gets the better of him.

"I think it's scolding me for not counting them," she says with a smirk. "You've gone and given them ideas."

Rolling his eyes, he finds himself wondering about the sentience of her stars.

"Hey, shouldn't my magic have the answers to who I am? That's how Kreyuhl knew to find me, right? So why not just ask my stars?" Her question hangs in the air. The answer sounds so simple, it's almost insulting.

"Do you think they could answer you with any level of coherence? I'm sure you could glean some things, but it's not like they can outright tell you. If that were the case, Kreyuhl would have already done so. Don't you think?" Death scratches his head and tries to understand. Like Clarisse, he's growing frustrated with the level of complexity that's arisen. "I'm sorry, Clarisse. I don't really know the answer, but I'm all for helping you figure it out."

Clarisse's sad smile threatens to break him. *Since when am I this emotional? Snap out of it, you dolt. You are the freaking Grim Reaper. Act like it!*

Putting on a stern face, he motions for her to stand. She seems confused by the sudden shift in his demeanor, and his mask almost slips. *Almost.* Sighing, he grabs her hand and motions for Kreyuhl to move away from the doorway. As they walk down the stairwell, he suggests, "Why don't we start working on using your powers? For starters, I'd like you to summon your stars so we can ask them some questions."

"We?"

He glances down at her. "Yes. Do you remember how Terrence amplified your powers?"

Raising an eyebrow, Clarisse nods. "It was bizarre. I didn't get as tired when I worked with him. At least not while I was conjuring. Afterward… well, I can't speak to that, or else I wouldn't be here right now, I guess. You were right about the impact of using too much magic."

Death ignores the admission, though it's not a moment where he's particularly proud of being right anyway. He'd much rather Clarisse have had the opportunity to live a normal life instead of being thrust into godhood so soon after dying.

"Well, I'm capable of supplying similar magic," he admits. "I can offer you some of mine so you can focus on using yours without overexerting yourself. Do you feel up to creating some stars? I don't think we could do too much, given what you exerted by finding your familiar…"

Kreyuhl hisses, but the sound doesn't appear as a threat. Death perceives it as his way of agreeing, though he's still wary of the creature.

"I'd like to try, but I'm not sure what to ask them or if they'll even answer." With slumping shoulders, her body seems to admit defeat before she even begins.

Death pats her shoulder reassuringly. "Clarisse, it's okay if it doesn't work. We can even wait until you feel more confident, if you'd like. I just want to arm you with as much as I can before Leyun shows up. I want you to be strong enough to stand against her. She won't attack in the traditional sense—she'll try and make you *want* to return and be recycled properly. And I don't want you to be susceptible to that narrative. If she wants to take you, she should expect a fight."

He's not sure if he's telling Clarisse for her benefit or for his own; their fates are inextricably tied together. With his fists clenched, he turns to face her on the staircase. "I want you to know that I'll do whatever it takes to ensure you have the best chance of survival. I know I couldn't intervene on Earth, but I can here. I don't have to worry about playing favorites here because you *are* my favorite. I'm not required to be impartial here. I'm also not going to sugarcoat the danger you're in."

A sigh leaves Clarisse, but her expression softens. "I know you're on my side, Death. I just don't know how I'm supposed to fight an unknown entity. I mean, what will she hit me with? It just… I don't know. It all very strange to me."

"I wish I had an answer for that one," Death acquiesces. He's been here his entire existence and it's difficult to fathom. He can't imagine how much harder this is for her to grasp.

I don't have to be in your thoughts to understand that this is a lot to absorb. But you're not alone.

Taking her hands in his again, he squeezes them. "Let's go try and conjure some stars. It's at least a starting point, and we can figure things out from there, okay?" Death tries to overlook the obvious hesitance in her gaze. He never tries to make anyone do anything they're uncomfortable with... *except die.* But this is urgent. If the Neylka weren't hunting her down and using Leyun, of all creatures to do it, he'd let Clarisse take all the time in eternity she needed.

As they walk through the ballroom doors, he's hit by a stark reminder of the time he found Ralun chasing her across the floor, then how he had to sit back and let Terrence be her savior. *Not this time.*

He claps his hands. "Okay, Clarisse. Let's start by me lending you one of my stars."

Pausing, Clarisse holds up a finger. "I thought you said the number of stars you had was fixed?"

Death waves off her concern. "I won't miss just one. Besides, you will keep it safe and it will continue to burn. If anything, it will make our bond stronger. It's a risk I'm willing to take." Her cheeks turn pink. *I might've said that wrong.* Swallowing, he conjures one of his stars. It isn't like hers—it doesn't move and talk on its own. It's a *piece* of him. Bright. Burning. Strong. And yet cold, somehow. He reaches out to her and places it in her waiting palms.

He watches her as she grasps it and studies intently. Her stars come out to greet it, circling the bright, cold light like hounds on the hunt. They buzz, squeak, and make a variety of strange noises.

A low musical hum erupts from his lost star. It starts to rise before joining its new friends, buzzing and chanting about, but at a lower octave.

"It seems that they're, uh, getting along well." Scratching the back of his neck, Death hopes he said the right thing. He's never communed with his stars before. Before now, he wasn't even aware they could talk. *Unless... she made them talk?* Shaking away that treacherous thought, he tries to think of what to do next. "I suppose you should bring more of your stars out now. Maybe start with trying to see if you can make more, or if yours are fixed like mine."

Clarisse bobs her head like she's attempting to nod through her fear. He can't help but notice the beads of sweat forming on her forehead. *The poor thing.* He must let her weather this, though. His constant nagging and interference won't help her find her way. In fact, he's certain they would make things far worse.

"I'm going to try something," she murmurs.

Clarisse splays out her hands and closes her eyes. Then, Kreyuhl creeps up behind her and does something odd. He places his muzzle in her hair, but he doesn't close his eyes. Instead, they start to glow. Death almost steps in—almost. But part of him knows that whatever is going on, it must transpire.

"I promise I'm just helping," Kreyuhl whispers.

Death exchanges a wary glance with the creature before motioning for him to continue. Only then does Kreyuhl close his eyes.

Clarisse doesn't speak, but Death feels an intense warmth travel through the ballroom floor and up into his chilled feet. By the time the heat reaches his nose, Clarisse is engulfed in a sea of her own stars. Every inch of the walls is covered in them. They sparkle, all humming and speaking, as hundreds more continue to pour out of Clarisse. Death can't tell if they all come from her hands or if they leak from her skin like blood from a gushing wound.

The stars are thunderously loud. He wants to cover his ears, but he knows he must listen. *If they have any clues about who she was, I need to hear it.* Shivering, he feels cold for once. It's a startling sensation that gives him only the slightest idea of how his friends or those he ferries might feel in his presence.

He watches as the stars spiral and wheel about the room. A few of them start to hover and swarm, much like bees do when they are startled from their hive. The humming, a distinct warning, gives Death just enough time to step back before they take a much more intricate shape.

A woman forms first, followed by a man. The stars then shift to make the figures move. The blinking drives Death mad, almost to the point of running from the room. He's never been a fan of flashing lights; he much prefers the subtle way Clarisse conjures her stars. Without her in charge, they don't take the same exquisite shapes and forms she gives them.

His eyes widen as he watches the woman start to run from the man. The man chases her before they disappear.

Is this… who she was? Confused, Death is still trying to make sense of it when the next figures start to take shape.

The woman is weeping, alone. She continues to weep, and a bundle of stars gather around her, a testament to the fact that Clarisse has *always* possessed this light.

She died sad. It's not surprising if she chose to be recycled.

Clarisse's eyes fly open. No longer are they a rich, brown shade, but bright gold. The light spilling from them is blinding. Death shields his own as best as he can. Stepping back, he waits for the inevitable explosion. Then, all at once, the stars disappear. Clarisse slumps to the floor, her lips trembling and her eyes back to normal.

"Did—did you learn anything?" he whispers, unable to contain his curiosity.

She looks up at him, her eyes stained with the gold light that no longer shines. "I was afraid when I died. Terrified. Sad. Broken. That's all I know. And I loved someone. But they betrayed me."

"Is that god still alive?" Death demands. He knows for certain if he gets ahold of them, they won't be for much longer. Clarisse doesn't need to know he's one of the few who can cast souls into the Neylka. *That's a secret I can keep for now.* It does make him uncomfortable, though, not being transparent with her. Part of him wants to pour out all his secrets to her, but he knows she can't handle them. Not yet, anyway.

"I… I don't know. I don't know what he looks like. All I could see were shadows."

Death huffs aloud. "Well, I'm sorry to have put you through that, Clarisse." She looks startled, as if he's hurt her feelings. "I don't mean it like that," he hurries, trying to gather up the pieces of the mess he just made. "I mean that I wish I could've helped you learn more from this session. I can tell it took a lot out of you." Her eyes flutter like she might lose consciousness. Rushing over, Death scoops her up in his arms. "Hey," he whispers. "You did great, Clarisse."

She smiles up at him, her eyes full of tears. "I wish I'd chosen you first, instead of whomever that was."

"I don't understand. What do you mean?"

But her eyes close and she's asleep in seconds. Kreyuhl growls a warning at him before motioning to the staircase just beyond the glass doors.

"I know. It's time for her to rest again. Bast is going to kill me."

Kreyuhl chirps in agreement. Death casts him a look but doesn't argue further. Hoisting Clarisse against his chest, he carries her back to her room.

Better luck next time, I guess.

RECKLESS

Terrence

he doors to the church screech in protest on unoiled hinges as Terrence swings them open. His eyes peer about in the darkness in the hopes of catching Simmons unaware.

But that would ruin the fun, he reminds himself. If Simmons reacts anything like the Monroes did, he is willing to wait so he doesn't spoil the entertainment.

Chuckling, he peers up to the balcony, deciding it will make a fine hiding spot. Even though the lights are out, he pinpoints the sound of someone's breathing. Somewhere, far back in the church, Simmons must be sitting in his office.

Resolving to wait until the man emerges, Terrence launches himself into the balcony, a comet of solid darkness and woe blinking through the air. His red eyes are the only giveaway that he's present as he settles deep into the seats high above. Remaining silent is an easy task for him, as is stalking. His specialty is hunting down the worst of humanity. Compared to that skill, Simmons should be a routine visit.

Except for the fact that I'm breaking every protocol in the book.

Terrence cocks his head to the side as the church doors swing open again, this time with a professional level of silence.

Who might this be?

He doesn't take the bait, opting instead to see if the creature who has come to visit will reveal itself.

"Hello?" a soft, familiar voice calls in the darkness.

Terrence notices the silver eyes too late. They lock on his with eerie precision and he tries to shrink away, but the panther lands on the balcony with him a second later. They remain silent as Father Simmons stumbles out of his office.

"Who's there?" he calls.

Terrence must use all his willpower not to fall out laughing. It's maddening how fun it is to watch this wretched human struggle.

Father Simmons pulls a flashlight from his pocket. The small light cuts through the darkness as he fumbles towards a light switch. *Why didn't the fool try to find one of those first?*

Bast glances at him, sensing the malevolence rising off his soul. She hisses at him, the sound barely a whisper. Father Simmons doesn't react, but it does little to ease the tension Terrence senses. Bast's eyes are alight with rage and... *curiosity?*

That particular emotion killed the cat... he jokes to himself.

Terrence can't dispel the grin that stretches across his face as the scent of Father Simmons' fear wafts to where he crouches in the balcony. He watches the priest fumble with the light switch before lights flick on and the priest turns about in all directions, trying to find the source of the noises that cause his heart to race. The steady *thump, thump, thump* makes Terrence delirious with excitement.

What a fun creature to stalk. He will make for fun prey. Licking his lips, he notices that Bast coils back from him in disgust. She's clued in on his intent, and it's clear she's not a fan of what he's up to.

As Father Simmons glances up at the balcony, Terrence conceals them both in shadow, closing his eyes and praying Bast does the same. All Father Simmons will see is shadows casting between the pews. The flimsy lights overhead don't illuminate the balcony all that well, relying on the sun to pour in through the windows as the dawn breaks.

But there is no dawn now, and the sun has long since retired for the night. Terrence holds back his sigh of relief as Father Simmons, with a shake of his head, returns to searching the pews below for signs of life. When he finally retreats from the auditorium, Terrence releases his shadow hold on Bast, who mouths a snarl at him, letting no noise escape her. He's grateful for the art of concealment, which she has long since mastered.

Her paw points to the door and she gestures for him to follow as she leaps from the balcony and prowls out into the night. Terrence almost decides not to follow her, but Bast is a formidable enemy. Truthfully, she's more terrifying than Death in some ways. Her agenda is murky, and her morals aren't tied to some false duty like Death's are. She's a free agent, whereas Death is bound by the laws of Fate.

The black wolf follows her, careful not to make a sound as he jumps from the balcony and scurries out the door. *I'll make good on my plans to torture this man later*, he promises himself.

Even after the door closes behind him, he's not ready to speak yet. The sound of the doors clicking will summon Father Simmons now that he's on high alert, and Terrence isn't ready to get caught yet. As much as he's ready to tear into the wayward priest's throat now, he wants to savor the moment. He and Bast reach the edge of the woods. Once they are well out of sight, Bast whirls on him, her eyes glimmering in righteous anger.

"What are you doing, you wretched fool?" Flames flicker in her eyes—enough to make his own fire sputter with trepidation.

"I'm exacting revenge," he purrs. He decides not to mince words or pretend he's on a noble errand. It's high time that the gods in the Afterlife learn there are other forces willing to exact justice, even if it falls to him alone.

"For whom?" Her voice is a sharp edge; a knife poised to slash through him and reduce him to smoking ribbons.

"Clarisse Monroe." Her name hangs in the air like a thick, poisonous fog. He's swallowed it enough times to know it's deadly. Betraying her may have cost her life, but it cost him eternity. *Not the bargain I was hoping for…*

It's strange how his grief ebbs and flows like the tides. He wonders if he might someday drown under the weight of all the wrongs he's committed. Illicit magic… plots to undo the entire system of Reapers, with Death at the head of his extermination… Terrence knows the last thing he'll see as he's pulled under the waves is Clarisse's face contorted in pain, as she was on that couch where he found her in the end.

Bast seems surprised. "You know her as well?"

Terrence perks up and a trickle of excitement bleeds through his veins. "You mean to tell me that you've met Clarisse Monroe?"

Bast nods.

"Was…was she damned?" He blurts the question before he can stop himself. If he had the capacity to sweat, he'd be drenched. Worry for her soul has consumed him since she departed her mortal body. He convinced her to engage in all sorts of magical exploits before she passed. *That's what got me into trouble… mostly.*

"No, Terrence." Bast seems confused by his question, and she draws out her response almost as a question. "How… how did you know her? Death mentioned you were involved near the end of her life, but not how."

At the mention of Death, Terrence bristles. Why is Clarisse with Death and Bast? What business do they have with Clarisse?

"I merely took her from her circumstances here on Earth," he replies cagily.

Bast pauses and stares at him for several long moments. "She showed me snippets of you in her memories."

Terrence is surprised, and maybe a little envious. "She showed you?"

When Bast dips her head in acknowledgement, Terrence's heart and stomach are set in an oven to broil. His heat rises, and the hiss that rips through his body is earth-shattering.

"Why are you prying into her mind and memories?" The grass beneath his paws is set alight and he doesn't bother to stomp it out.

"Terrence, she's safe… where she's at." The uncertainty in her voice douses the heat in Terrence's soul.

Does that mean she's not safe?

Bast isn't fooling him. She's never unsure of anything. She's a constant force of confidence and strength. If she can't say Clarisse is safe with certainty, then he doesn't believe her claim.

"You should really work on your lying skills," he sneers.

Groaning, Bast holds a paw over her face. "Listen, she's being looked after by Death and her familiar."

"Her familiar?" Terrence fails to hide the panic in his voice. "Why does she have a familiar?"

They stare at each other, neither willing to divulge secrets. Bast finally pipes up.

"Terrence, there's a lot about her that's… uncertain right now. She's more powerful than anyone could've guessed, and Death and I are working to help her navigate it all. I'm surprised you didn't call me when you knew she was suffering," she growls, baring her fangs for good measure.

Startled, Terrence steps back a bit to keep safe from harm. *Try to stay calm, Terrence. Don't let her get under your skin.* Safe from swiping distance of her paws, he stews. Then his skin crawls when he realizes what she said.

"What do you mean, she's *more* powerful?"

Glaring, Bast reveals her claws, only to sink them into the ground. "Terrence, you're not really in a position to be questioning me right now. I am the one who should be asking the questions! For starters, what the hell are you thinking? A shadow storm? And then I find you slinking about in the same church I glimpsed in Clarisse's memories?"

Terrence isn't fazed by her outburst. "I'm not buying it, Bast. Now that you've met her, wouldn't you do anything to protect her? She's a beautiful soul, and those evil people tarnished her. Abused her. Took advantage of her. And the powers-that-be allowed her abusers to go on like it was nothing!" He snarls, his body spasming from the anger coursing through his veins. His hackles are raised and even the earth is blackened from his fire.

Bast's eyes widen further. "Terrence, you don't mean to tell me that you're planning to seek revenge on your own, are you?"

Hissing, Terrence fails to find an answer to give her.

"Do you know what kind of trouble you'll be in when they find out?"

Glaring, Terrence snarls, "Why are you here, Bast? What are you trying to do? What are you looking to get out of this? You're not a Reaper."

Bast laughs. "Terrence, darling, I may not be a Reaper, but I know when there are distortions in timelines, and I can be called in when there are enough humans concerned with matters of Tyrladan. Why do you *think* I'm here? Fal asked me to check in. She knows you and I are… *close*… so I wanted to be the first to contact you." Bast looks embarrassed by her admission. "To warn you. You *have* to stop whatever it is you're trying. I know you care for the girl. I do, too. Believe me, I'm going to help her harness her magic. But you can't take matters into your own hands."

"Or what?" Terrence challenges. For a moment, he swears Bast flinches. He ignores the small pang in his heart when he sees her shrink from him. *She should never be afraid of me.*

Bast straightens. "You know the consequences for violating Tyrladan's laws. You've already been given a second chance… really a third, if you think about it. Don't you fear what Death could do to you? Or even Fal?"

"Yes, yes, the threat of being erased." Terrence waves away Bast's doomsday proclamations like he's unconcerned. While the thought weighs heavily on his mind, it's for a different reason. "Has it ever occurred to you that maybe, just possibly, I'm not afraid of being erased? I mean, look at me. You at least have your full form, but I'm stuck as a shadow for eternity!" Terrence's voice cracks a bit, but he doesn't care.

Bast steps closer to him, her paws unbothered by the smoke and flames curling up around them. She stands in front of him, nose to nose. Terrence's heart flutters. Even in this form, the regality and power that radiates off her is intoxicating. *Maybe in another life…*

He bottles that thought up and tosses it into the recesses of his mind. He has no business developing feelings for a goddess. He's a lowly Reaper, meant to drag out the souls of the damned. Even in his official capacity, he wasn't strong enough to keep his post.

Her silver eyes probe his searchingly and he swallows. "You deserve to have a chance at a second life, Terrence," she whispers. "Who's to say that this shadowy damnation will last forever? Try and hold onto hope for me." Her tone is soft and pleading.

Dipping his head, he tries to think of other things besides the ocean of pain stirring in his soul. He's lost so much. He failed Clarisse and now he's about to fail Bast.

"I'm sorry I didn't tell you about her, Bast. I was selfish – I realize that now. That's why I want to make it up to her… I want to bring her the justice she didn't get while she was alive." He thinks back to the news report he overheard that declared Father Simmons and the Monroes not guilty of all the crimes they'd committed against Clarisse. "I was so angry when I saw the news." Terrence clenches his teeth, baring them at the night sky and imagining her tormentors going free. "When will they pay for their sins?"

He gestures back to the church, suddenly bolstered by their closeness. "Bast, I can't keep going like this. I can't continue to pretend like this doesn't irk me. Death *left* her there with those monsters, knowing full well what would happen. I know magic is illicit when used improperly, but what we were doing wasn't. I never told her to do what I did, or to try and take over the world or anything ludicrous. I just wanted to give someone a chance." His voice breaks again as hot tears fill his eyes.

Bast's paw reaches up and gently pulls at his face so he can't turn away. "You have always been more than what meets the eye. You can't fool me, Terrence. You *did* try to help her, even if it didn't work out. It was her fate to meet her end early, regardless of what you tried, so stop blaming yourself. As for those villains... Well, I don't know what to tell you. You know how I feel, but there's not much I can do to change the outcome. I saw what she endured, and it's unspeakable. Why a goddess would choose to be born again into that kind of environment..."

Terrence perks up, almost brushing his nose against hers. "Goddess?"

Bast backs away, her eyes glistening. "Her light is unlike anything I've ever seen. I wish I could bring you back to Tyrladan to see."

Another reminder that I'm not truly forgiven, even if they're not actively hunting me. Huffing, he lowers his head and buries his nose in the embers where the grass once grew. The scent of charred earth renews him. A wave of energy crashes through him, ricocheting along his spine and down through his paws. He whips his head up and startles Bast, who cautiously backs away. This time, her hesitation doesn't bother him as the dull rage within him returns like the tide.

"I can't even see her. Why should I worry about losing anything? I am dead and cannot rest. I have never been allowed to rest or be made whole," he hisses. "Until Fal decides to reevaluate this decision, I will continue to do what I am meant to do. I am a Reaper who serves no master, which means I am free to do as I wish. You tell that overblown tree trunk to speak to me herself or expect the worst!"

Bast's eyes glaze with unshed tears, but she nods. "Don't say I didn't warn you, Terrence. I tried. If things were different, I would happily join you in this quest of yours."

"Why don't you? If enough of us take a stand against these foolish laws, we can make a real difference!" His voice is thick with emotion, and fresh tears trickle down his cheeks. He wishes she would hear him out.

She shakes her head sadly. "Terrence, I can't risk my position. I have a duty to uphold—"

"Why are you so obsessed with duty?" Terrence raises his voice, not caring that he's interrupting. "Why don't you care about what's right, too?"

"How dare you assume I don't have morals!" Bast sniffs.

But Terrence hears her voice break and knows he's getting to her.

"Why don't you bring Fal back to take me on? And don't bother trying to change my mind. I'll make that choice myself!" Terrence snaps.

Before she has a chance to respond, he turns on his heel and prowls back inside the church. To his great relief, she doesn't follow. She can't see the way his face crumples in defeat. Hopefully she can't sense the trepidation in his heart.

CONFESSIONS

Clarisse

*H*er head is pounding. The sheets, drenched in sweat, are proving to be more of a cocoon of suffocation than a fortress of reprieve. Taking that as a sign that it's time to get up, she opens her eyes, then immediately squints as the light from the three moons outside touch them. She's not sure how long she's been asleep. The memory of what happened in the ballroom is fuzzy. Swallowing, she realizes how thirsty she is. Looking down, she notices she's wearing flannel pajamas, for which she's grateful. The chill in the room is not as comforting as Death's.

Icy frost clings to the panes of a large, single window in her room. Pressing her fingers into the condensation, she draws a shaky smiley face. *A manifestation of what I want to feel…*

A low growl draws her attention. Kreyuhl, whose massive frame takes up most of the bedroom floor, is awake. He raises his head, his milky white eyes almost glowing in the moonbeams.

"How are you faring?" His sibilant voice washes over her like soft waves on a summer evening. Clarisse misses the warmth of that wonderful season.

She clutches the loose strands of her hair and ponders how to best answer his question. She stares through him more than at him and tries to process what she's learned. For starters, she learned she was married in her former life.

Swallowing, she slides down to the floor and finds solace in her familiar's embrace. The Aiyeliu gives a deep purr, similar to a cat. She savors such a normal interaction, choosing to ignore the fact that Kreyuhl is far from a cat and, in fact, is a strange nightmare creature from the Afterlife.

Pulling back, she stares up at him. "I'm coping as best as I can," she whispers honestly. "I don't know what to make of all this. Now that I know I was married, it brings up a host of other questions. Like… what does being married mean in the Afterlife? Does it mean my husband is still out there? Will he… remember me?" A pang of guilt tugs at her heart. "Would he be jealous of my bond with Death?"

The mere thought of the Grim Reaper brings warmth to her cheeks as she remembers her admission to him. That she wishes she found him first. Her heart aching, she reaches out to Death with her mind. She knows he can hear her, and he can even feel her emotions. Nothing is truly secret from him, even when she tries to focus on keeping her thoughts private.

Sure enough, his cold aura seeps through the doorway and she looks up to find him standing in the frame with a sad smile fixed on his face.

"Awake, finally?"

Clarisse rubs her bleary eyes and forces a smile. "Maybe. Give me a few minutes of quiet and I won't be."

Death chuckles and walks over to where she and Kreyuhl are still sitting on the floor. Kreyuhl doesn't budge, forcing Death to curl up in the beast's embrace to get close to her. His cold hands cradle her chin and his eyes, Clarisse swears, are wet with tears. He blinks before she can confirm what she thinks she saw.

Yawning, she leans into him. "What did you see in my stars?"

Taking a deep breath, Death clasps his hand on Clarisse's shoulder. "I saw the silhouette of you and your… husband… in the stars. You seemed unhappy in your past life."

His eyes drop the floor. As they sweep along, Clarisse wonders if he'll mention her confession, but it never comes.

"I want you to know that you don't have any obligation to him in this life," Death declares. "Your tie to him is null and void, or else this bond between us wouldn't exist. You'd be drawn to him instead."

Cocking her head, Clarisse nibbles her lip and picks at her cuticles, which is something she does when she's nervous. Death gently swats at her hands, forcing her to stop her act of minuscule self-destruction.

"Clarisse, I'm sorry you must endure this, especially after the trials you endured on Earth. The Afterlife is supposed to be a serene, relaxing place."

Anchored by his intense gaze, Clarisse wonders if it's possible to drown in the pools of gold that simmer in his eyes. She sighs. "It's okay. There's nothing I can do at this point except ride it out. I mean, what else am I supposed to do? Cry about it?" She clenches her fists. "No… no more crying. Or I'm at least going to get stuff done while I cry. I'm not worried about still being married, either. I'm more concerned about why I was afraid of him in the first place. I thought you said gods couldn't kill each other?"

Death studiously avoids her gaze and rubs the back of his neck awkwardly. "That's not *entirely* true. The Neylka can't force people to enter. It can deceive and deprive you of your will to want to escape, but you still must make the choice. However, there are some gods with the ability to kill each other."

Clarisse blinks. "Are you saying my husband might have murdered me? And that even here, there are ways I can be killed?"

Death laughs. "Everyone can be killed, Clarisse, even me. It's just that dying doesn't work the same here as it does on Earth. Here, energy cannot be created or destroyed. The Neylka exists to recycle us."

Her head pounding, Clarisse tries her best to follow his logic. "Why does the Neylka exist?"

Death shrugs. "It's part of the fabric of existence. It's where all energy originates, and, therefore, it's also where all energy 'ends' when it's time for it to be used in a different fashion."

"So what you're saying is that I've died twice and the person I used to be has no memories of my former life, which means I'm not at peace." Tears try to break free, but Clarisse won't let them. Kreyuhl nestles his muzzle in the crook of her neck as he emits various humming noises that send soothing vibrations down her spine.

Death glares openly at the beast. Clarisse fights the urge to laugh at how jealous they both act over her, but she can't stop her eye roll. She sighs and wonders about the life she lived before.

"What do we do now? How am I supposed to figure out who I am —who I was?"

Death shrugs. "We keep trying things with your magic, I suppose. We haven't gathered enough information yet, and we don't know what else to try. But now we know your stars hold the key. I have a feeling they'll help you figure things out, whether you like it or not. Maybe Kreyuhl will start to remember the history of your magic as well."

The beast nods his gangly head. *"I will continue to search, Clarisse. So far, I am not as helpful as your stars, but I will try."* Kreyuhl lowers his head, his eyes closed and his expression pensive.

Clarisse runs her fingers between his ears. "You don't need to beat yourself up over that, Kreyuhl. You're very helpful. You keep me company and give me the reassurance I need to keep going."

Kreyuhl's eyes open, but he doesn't lose the look of intense focus on his face.

"This is a mystery that will take time to solve, Clarisse. But in the meantime, I think we should get up and help you learn to use your magic in general." Death extends his hand and Clarisse takes it. He gracefully ushers them both to their feet and Kreyuhl follows suit.

"How do you do that?" Clarisse can't hide her tone of jealousy.

"Do what?" Death glances back at her with a surprised look on his face.

"Make everything look easy."

Laughing, Death leans down and kisses her cheek. He pulls away, still chuckling. "I have plagued the existence of the living since the first being died. I have had eons to perfect things. You'll get there, too."

Clarisse's cheek burns from where he kissed her, but she doesn't let on how much it affects her. She knows he can tell anyway since he's in her mind.

Before he can say anything, she jogs down the stairs, not caring that she's still in her pajamas. Now is not the time to care about such things when she has a mystery to solve. Stopping at the base of the stairs, she waits for Death and Kreyuhl to catch up. "Come on, guys, you're too slow!"

In answer, Kreyuhl leaps from the top stair. He's hardly more than a pale streak in the air before he lands quietly at her side.

Death rolls his eyes. "Sorry, but I'm not coming down with that kind of flair." Instead, he steps gracefully down the stairs, his black robe swishing around his feet.

"Hey, Death?"

"Yes?"

"Why do we all wear robes here? I mean, I know you found me some pajamas to wear, but what does Tyrladan have against modern fashion?"

Death stares down at his chosen ensemble. "Don't you think it's on brand for Death to be wearing a black robe?"

Clarisse snorts. "You're not a skeleton, though."

"Are you saying I don't look the part?"

The cruel taunt in his eyes glitters and Clarisse gulps as she takes a measured step back. "Not at all." She holds up her hands. "I'm just saying it… I don't know. I just think you'd look good in jeans and a t-shirt. They might be more comfortable, too."

Groaning, Death shakes his head. "Only *you* would focus on something like that at a time like this." Hovering over her, he grins. "Maybe I'll go around as a skeleton for a while. Shake things up a little."

"No, that's okay," Clarisse protests. "I was just curious. I wanted to know why I was given robes, too. I mean, I know that's what we arrive in, but why don't we have… You know what? Forget I asked." Her cheeks burn and she almost smacks herself for thinking about underwear in the presence of Death.

Chuckling, Death runs his fingers through her hair, tousling it. He walks off before she can sputter a response and starts to rifle through the kitchen, opening cabinet doors before settling in front of the pantry. With the door flung open, he scans the shelves.

"Isn't it a little late to be eating?" Clarisse jokes.

Death raises an eyebrow, but he doesn't answer at first. After a few moments of staring at his options, he speaks. "I'm using this as an opportunity to teach you magic," he calls, his voice muffled through the walls of the pantry.

"What does food have to do with teaching her magic?" Kreyuhl's frustration is evident in every syllable.

Emerging from the pantry, Death carries a single sack of flour. Clarisse bites her lip, wondering why it took him so long to find something so simple. *Didn't I stock the pantry before I died?*

Death's face twists up. "Are you seriously wondering if you bought flour before you died?" He shakes his head and sets the bag on the kitchen table. "We're not going to bake, but you are going to use this as an ingredient for creating something."

Nodding, Clarisse realizes this is the first request he's made that makes sense. Smiling, she rolls her shoulders and holds out her hands.

Death reaches out and lightly grasps her wrists. "Not so fast. We're not ready to start just yet. So far, we've discovered that your power only has two amplitudes—small and large. We need to figure out how to get your power to settle somewhere in the middle so that you are in control of how intensely it works or doesn't." He beckons her with his free hand. The chair nearest her slides out without being touched and she settles into it. "I'm going to put this in front of you, and I want you to imagine something as simple as moving flour into a bowl."

Clarisse looks around. "What bowl?"

Death holds out his hand and one comes flying out of a kitchen cabinet to land in his outstretched palm. He places it on the table by the bag of flour and grins, adding a wink for good measure. "Forgot that part."

His quiet confidence makes Clarisse's cheeks flush. It's hard to imagine what it might be like to be so comfortable in your own skin.

"Okay. See if you can get this flour into the bowl." He stops. "Without using your hands," he smirks.

Clarisse snaps her fingers. "Darn!" she says, her voice coated with sarcasm. "I was just about to do that. Thanks for foiling my plans."

When he doesn't answer, she turns her attention back to the bowl. Staring at the flour, she pulls on the images in her mind. *It was so easy when I built the house, so a little bit of flour should be no problem, right?*

The smell of smoke curls up to her nose. When she opens her eyes, the bag of flour has caught fire. Panic sets in her lungs and she waves her hands, desperate to put it out. As she imagines the fire being extinguished, a giant stream of water comes rocketing from the sky, dousing everything in the kitchen. Now soaked, Clarisse refuses to glance up at Death.

The Grim Reaper roars with laughter, unable to hide his amusement. "Well, Clarisse, I would say bravo, except we weren't looking for grand acts and miracles. Just a simple act of getting the flour into the bowl. What are you nervous about?"

She crosses her arms with a pout. "How do you know I'm nervous?"

Death gestures to the soaked table and the spot where the bag of flour once was. His eyes still full of mirth, he snaps his fingers. At once, the kitchen is dry again and a pristine bag of flour is back on the table, along with the bowl. The smell of melting plastic still lingers in the air, the pungent stench assaulting her nose.

Now, she's afraid of what will happen. She's worried she'll set the bag of flour on fire again. Her emotions bounce around faster than she can catch them. Closing her eyes, she tries her best to focus. She imagines her emotions wheeling about like her stars, blinking various colors like Death's do. His own, lingering star that he gifted her emerges to the front of her mind to lead the others. It changes its hue on command, trying to lure the others closer, but they don't follow suit.

When she opens her eyes, she's no longer in the kitchen. She's surrounded by a bland, white expanse. No light or dark seems to penetrate the space, and Death is nowhere to be found. There is only nothing.

The Neylka! She breathes in deeply, terror dousing her veins in ice water. She doesn't have to be told where she is. Sweat pooling on her forehead, she tries to convince herself that she's imagining things.

Then, in the distance, she sees her. Blazing silver eyes drill into her own as Leyun steps out from the void, her golden mane dull without the sun or moon dancing through its gilded strands.

"*Clarisse,*" she calls out.

Clarisse's hair stands on end and her limbs are frozen in terror. She tries to find the strength to move, but can't. If her heart beats any faster, she fears it will explode. Her eyes dart everywhere, looking for

Death or Kreyuhl, but her friends aren't with her. Clenching her fists, she prepares for the worst. Her skin tingles where the fiend bit her last time and she slams her eyes shut as she waits for the inevitable.

She wishes her feet didn't feel like lead bricks. She wishes she could laugh in the face of danger and fight, or at the very least, run away.

Where is the Clarisse who fought Ralun? she thinks miserably.

"She's still there," Leyun whispers.

When Clarisse opens her eyes, she finds Leyun standing so close, the beast's horn almost grazes her forehead.

Up close, the unicorn creature is even more marvelous than Clarisse could have ever imagined as a little girl. *And far more terrifying.* Her razor-sharp teeth are hidden, but Clarisse knows that within her maw sit knives sharp enough to cut through mortal souls. Swallowing, Clarisse tries to lean away, but Leyun doesn't budge. She's trapped.

"What do you want from me?" she calls aloud, hoping and praying her friends can hear her.

"Friends?" Leyun tilts her head, her ears twitching forward like two roving satellites, lost in the stars and praying for a signal.

Clarisse's fear begins to subside. A strange sense of safety curls around her like a heavy blanket. Before she can second-guess her intuition, she yields to the desire to reach out and touch Leyun.

With trembling fingers, Clarisse touches her soft, white muzzle. To her surprise, Leyun doesn't pull away. Her leonine tail flicks, the golden tip waving in a breeze that neither of them can see or feel.

"What do you want from me?" Clarisse whispers.

"To understand," Leyun answers.

When the unicorn straightens her neck, Clarisse loses her grip on Leyun's muzzle. "To understand what?"

"How you escaped unscathed. How did you leave the Neylka in one piece? How can I do the same?" Leyun's eyes water, and silver tears pour in rivulets down her face.

The sadness that wafts from Leyun breaks Clarisse's heart. When she reaches back up to pet her again, Leyun remains still. "You're the only other person like me, and yet we're so different," Clarisse murmurs. "But at least you remember who you are."

With an indignant hiss, Leyun rears back. *"I don't know who I am, stupid girl. I do not remember, just as you do not. I am more like you than you know!"*

Before Clarisse can sputter an apology, Leyun rears up, her cloven hooves nearly bashing in Clarisse's head. She stumbles to avoid being mauled and falls onto her rump. With a loud whinny, Leyun gallops away. Clarisse blinks, and the unicorn is gone. Seconds later, the blank void fades.

When she opens her eyes, she's back in the kitchen again. Tears trickle down her cheeks and Death and Kreyuhl both descend upon her.

"What was that?" Death demands. "Where were you?"

Sobbing, Clarisse clutches him fiercely. Kreyuhl's muzzle roves over her frantically as he tries to scent out where she'd disappeared.

"I was nowhere," Clarisse chokes. "There was no light or dark. There just *was*."

Death pulls back in surprise but continues to run his thin fingers through her hair, as though desperate to confirm she's real. "You were in the Neylka?"

Shuddering, Clarisse starts to cough as the weight of her sadness chokes her. She wonders if she'll ever breathe comfortably again.

"She was," Kreyuhl confirms, his soft voice echoing through both their minds. *"Leyun was there. She saw something interesting. Leyun's tactics are stronger than ever."*

"Stronger than ever?" Death demands. "Are you saying you remember her from another time?"

"No, but I sense her magic has shifted. You can taste it in the air. Something is wrong," Kreyuhl answers, unbothered by Death's veiled accusations. *"Clarisse must be on guard. Using magic will be dangerous moving forward. Leyun is too similar to her. Her magic will draw her in."*

"But I need to learn how to control it!" Clarisse whines. "How will I ever learn who I am if I can't tap into my magic?" Her voice cracks, but she doesn't care. *I'm constantly being told I can't use magic. Even though I'm dead, it's still not safe to wield it? What gives?!*

Kreyuhl's voice is calm, which Clarisse finds unsettling. *"No, Clarisse, what I'm saying is that by using such a strong spell, you made yourself more vulnerable. You must practice this more with Death to learn control. In the meantime, we must figure out how to handle Leyun. She will keep coming back. You will make mistakes. We must plan on them."*

Clarisse tries to tamp down her rising agitation. *If you don't remember our past lives, then how can you be certain that I should practice my magic? How can I possibly prepare to be manipulated like this?*

"You must be free of want when she arrives. You must prepare yourself before wielding magic to rid yourself of desires. If you go in with obvious weaknesses, she will use them against you. What do you think she was trying to get at with this?" Kreyuhl looks at her with a pointed stare.

Death, though irritated, shrugs his shoulders. He watches them both with dogged fascination. Clarisse wonders if he might whip out a pen and paper at some point and start taking notes.

"Don't be silly, Clarisse," Death mumbles. "I would use a pencil. Easier to erase mistakes."

Clarisse opens her mouth to say something, but the pull of Kreyuhl's voice interrupts her retort.

"You saw Leyun, and she spoke to you about how you are the same. How neither of you can remember who you were in your former lives. She will try and utilize this fact to draw you out. You may not even realize you're agreeing to being erased. Gods are much like tricksters and fae. They easily twist words and use them against you. You may think you're going away to help her, but in reality, you'll be signing your death warrant."

Kreyuhl's face never changes and his eyes don't reveal any emotions, but the magic Clarisse shares with him betrays a certain apprehension, followed by shock.

"Is it true that you touched her?"

Before Clarisse can answer, Kreyuhl reaches forward and pulls her hand to him, though he's careful not to break the skin with his mouth. Her palm opens at his unspoken command. In the center sits the etching of a sun, freshly cut, with dried golden blood around it.

Death hisses. Goosebumps erupt along Clarisse's spine and she stumbles back in her chair, nearly tipping it over. He walks over and grabs her hand. "How dare she mark you!" His voice is dark and full of thunder.

Clarisse winces as though she's afraid he will strike her. Noticing this, Death puts his face close to hers. She hears his breaths, heavy and full of rage. His nostrils flare.

"Don't you *ever* be frightened of me."

His hushed voice sends butterflies careening through her stomach. With a shaky nod, she allows him to inspect the wound. When Kreyuhl leans in with him, they look like the most mismatched pair of surgeons to ever operate. Clarisse cringes and fights the urge to pull away when Kreyuhl sticks out his long, slimy black tongue and licks the mark.

"She can't track you with this, but she left it as a subtle reminder that you two are linked. She's playing tricks with your mind even when she's not here." Kreyuhl's conclusion makes Clarisse shiver.

Death's eyes drill into Clarisse with a hundred unasked questions. Squirming, she tries to pull away, but he doesn't release her hand.

"Clarisse, why would you touch her?" he demands. "Why?"

"I... I was drawn to her." Clarisse voice hitches. "I don't know why, and I didn't plan to go with her, even though the pull was there. I want to survive this, but something overcame me. I was so sad for her, and I wanted so badly to help her. She's broken like me."

She begins to sob before she can stop herself. In truth, she knows what the mark is—it's a symbol of the unspeakable pain of having to live again in the shadow of who you once were. *And Leyun is stuck serving the Neylka, which means she'll never learn who she is.*

Her chest crashes in on itself and Death scoops her up. Kreyuhl follows them, his strange paws silent on the staircase as Death ascends the steps. They hurtle through the door to her library and Death holds her as he stoops to the floor. For a few moments he simply rocks her back and forth, like the gentle swaying of the sea. His cool skin sends sparks of electricity up her arms as he peppers her forehead and hair with featherlight kisses. He whispers to her, shushing her.

Eventually, the little bunker that hides them from Tyrladan darkens as the moon disappears behind gathering thunderclouds. A distant boom pulls a squeak from Clarisse, and she huddles deeper into his embrace.

She looks up at him. "Why did you bring me in here?"

"This library is sealed off from detection, remember? I think, moving forward, we will practice magic in here. When you are overwhelmed, we will come here. Moments like these when you are most vulnerable, Leyun will strike." He sighs. "I must think practically. This library was created so you could hide from

Terrence. You can choose the people to let in. Leyun can't enter this space because you won't issue an invitation. Manipulation doesn't count—I specifically designed it against malevolent intent such as that."

Clarisse's heart is full as she basks in his comforting gaze. His dark hair falls into shadow as the room darkens. The only light to penetrate the gloom arrives in the form of a handful of stars she's conjured without realizing it. They hover around the library, casting their glow into his golden eyes.

Her breath is labored, but she's certain it's due more to the handsome being holding her than any lingering health issues. "Why can't I breathe when I'm around you?" Why bother hiding her questions when he can hear them?

"I could ask you the same," he drawls, his eyes glittering.

He leans in, and his lips crash onto hers. She fervently returns his kiss, this time parting her lips so his tongue can explore. She greets it with her own, groaning as he pulls her against him. His hands trace circles along her back and she threads her arms around him, gripping his back and sagging against him.

He finally breaks away, their panting the only sound in the dark library. "Clarisse," he groans.

His lips return to hers, and this time his hands start to roam. Clarisse's skin seems to catch fire as he elicits tingles down her back and over her spine, his fingers rubbing circles along her skin. Suddenly, a scream breaks the stillness.

Jerking apart, they look up to see Bast standing in the doorway clutching a lantern.

"I leave for a few days, and *this* is what I come back to?" she shrieks.

Kreyuhl looks positively homicidal as he snarls at her from behind the doorway. *"I tried to stop her, Clarisse,"* he hisses. Bast casts an angry glare back in his direction, but Kreyuhl is unmoved.

Death looks back at Clarisse hungrily, but the frown on his face tells her that whatever just happened will have to wait. Clarisse mutters and swears in her head, her heart still tied up in his long-gone embrace.

"So *this* is what the bond is?" Bast taps her foot.

"Bast, I thought you were going to find resources to help her learn magic," Death growls.

"Yes, and *I* thought you were supposed to be helping her manage her magic in the meantime! Not doing whatever *this* is!" Bast sneers just as hotly.

Her dismissive tone sparks outrage in Clarisse's chest. "I was on board with whatever 'this' is, thank you very much," she huffs. "I know it's the bond, but he's not manipulating me, if that's what you're implying." If it were brighter, Clarisse is certain she would see the fierce feline goddess blushing.

"I-I wasn't implying anything of the sort," Bast stutters.

"Don't bother, Bast," Death interrupts. "I'm not going to explain what's happening between us, and I don't think you're looking for an explanation anyway."

"Way to make it sound worse than it is," Kreyuhl complains.

Death's glare is concealed by shadows, but Clarisse feels its icy burn from where she's standing. She giggles.

"Listen, Death, we have a problem." Bast's voice breaks. "Terrence… he's breaking laws. He's… he's seeking revenge for what happened to Clarisse."

The blurted revelation hangs in the air, and no one speaks. Clarisse hears Death's breathing in the darkness.

"I beg your pardon?" he finally asks.

"He lost control," Bast continues. "He became a shadow storm that everyone could see. The mortals are investigating. Fal is angry. Death, he's haunting the Monroes and Father Simmons. I tried to get him to see reason, but he's so stubborn," Bast chokes as tears spill from her beautiful silver eyes. "He usually listens to me."

Seeing Bast tremble doesn't sit right with Clarisse. She pulls the goddess into her arms. "Bast, whatever is happening with Terrence, it's not your fault," Clarisse whispers. She pulls back to look at Bast and wipes away her tears.

Bast's eyes widen at the softness of this exchange. "You must have been a motherly deity," Bast remarks as she dabs at the few remaining tears that try to escape.

"Tell me more about this shadow storm," Death demands. "And what do you mean by haunting?"

Clarisse could throttle him for overlooking Bast's pain, but she sends him a pointed look instead. *We'll talk later.* He raises an eyebrow in response, but says nothing to betray their conversation.

Bast sinks to the floor and curls up with her legs crossed. She throws up her hands. "He's lost his way! He's completely insane. I don't even know where to start."

As Clarisse joins her on the floor, her heart sinks. Bast starts to explain what she learned, describing the way Terrence became a shadow storm, engulfed in grief and rage. Death sidles up right behind her and she leans back into him. He's silent, giving Bast the space to speak, and he curls his arms around Clarisse to steady her.

I'm afraid for him, Death. Why won't he just move on? You forgave him because I asked… Tears threaten to break her resolve and her lip quivers.

"Be strong, Clarisse," Death answers. *"You gave Terrence a chance. He was your friend. It's okay to be upset. But you can't blame yourself or question anything that's going on. This is his fate."*

Clarisse closes her eyes for a few moments and tries not to focus on the images of a shadow storm that Bast describes. "Why is he so angry?"

Bast shoots her a grim smile. "I believe your torturers were acquitted when they went to trial. He's enraged."

Clarisse's heart shatters. Behind her, Death stiffens and the library grows colder.

"So you mean to tell me that's why he's exacting revenge? Because the human court system didn't reach the conclusion that the Monroes and Father Simmons are cold-blooded murderers?"

The knife in Death's voice grazes past Clarisse, but it still makes her shudder. She leans back to look up at him and finds that his eyes are a monsoon of rage. "Hey," she whispers. He looks down at her. "They'll pay, even if it's not through Terrence. I'm dead. They can't get me here. And people will eventually learn something is off about them. That's all we can hope for, right?"

Death settles his chin into her hair. "You're incredibly mature. And kind. They did not deserve you."

"I can see why Terrence wants so badly to make them pay," Bast interjects. A sad smile is all the goddess seems capable of mustering.

"So, how long have you been in love with Terrence?" Clarisse guesses.

Another silence envelops the room.

"In love?" Death inquires. His focus lands on Bast and Clarisse wishes he would stop making things more intense than they need be.

Bast straightens her spine. "Yes, Death, I love Terrence. I don't know if he feels the same, but we grew close working on a few rough cases together when he was still a Reaper. I… I don't know what else to tell you." Then Bast slumps, the relief of her confession evident.

Clarisse smiles. "You two would make a lovely couple. I'm sorry he's not listening to you. Would you like me to go down there and talk to him? Maybe I could let him know I'm okay and he shouldn't try to take revenge on my behalf."

Bast shakes her head. "It's deeper than that, Clarisse. He and I have witnessed… terrible things. Especially with children. We've witnessed first-hand the worst depravity that humanity can offer. He may have stopped doing his Reaper duties after the failed insurrection, but he definitely hasn't stopped seeing the worst in people. He was always tired of the lack of inherent justice in the universe. It ate him alive then, and I doubt it's stopped now. I think you were simply the final straw." Wringing her hands, Bast pulls in a shuddering breath. "I can't say I blame him."

"You and Terrence did always bond over your hatred for the vilest of humans," Death remarks. Rather than being angry, Death looks… thoughtful.

What's on your mind now? she asks through their bond.

"The reality of how the universe does not exact justice as it should. Free will comes at a steep price." Death's stony mask may be locked firmly in place, but Clarisse feels it cracking. *"I'm so angry that they aren't paying for what they did to you. I confess, I would almost root for Terrence if he did go after them. Were it not for my duties, I would be down there in an instant helping him. But I must retain some level of neutrality, as I always do."*

Clarisse's chest swells. *Don't get yourself in trouble for me.*

At this, Death laughs aloud. Bast pulls back from them with her face twisted in confusion. "Are you two having a conversation without me?"

"Always," Death taunts. "I'm in her head and she's in mine, even with me doing my best to keep things secret."

"You two are disgusting," Bast retorts. "I can't believe it took you as long as it did to realize your bond is a representation of romantic feelings for each other."

Death pauses. "It's… only been a few days."

"Yes, but you know how powerful these bonds are. You've seen them before. You've watched them and laughed at how naive people were about them, yet here you are." Bast's sharp-toothed grin grows wider as she watches Death struggle to find a response.

"Fine, perhaps you're right. Clarisse and I are inexplicably intertwined, but that's how it is sometimes, I suppose," Death sniffs. "We're merely navigating our feelings at this juncture. No need to panic."

Bast rolls her eyes. "Right. Okay, well, let me know when the wedding is."

Clarisse almost chokes. *Wedding?*

"I believe that was a joke, Clarisse," Death teases.

She almost reaches up to swat him. Almost.

"So, how has everything been here?" Bast asks with a knowing glint in her eyes. "Since you two are clearly talking, I'll just insert myself into your conversation."

With a last eye roll aimed at Death, she turns to Bast. "Um, well, Death's been helping me learn to use my magic. We learned I was married in my former life, and apparently, I didn't like my husband much. Oh, and I can't use too much magic without being in a warded room like this one, because otherwise it summons Leyun." Clarisse holds out her palm to show Bast the golden sun etched into her hand. "She marked me with this because I touched her in the Neylka."

Bast is on her feet in a flash. "You *what*?"

Kreyuhl lifts his head, but Death answers for him. "She was drawn in. Kreyuhl explained to her the dangers of how gods deceive. The trickery they utilize to secure contracts and agreements is unparalleled, even by the most nefarious of Tyrladanian species."

Bast blinks. "Since when did he become so well-versed in Tyrladanian law and customs?"

Death nods. "Apparently, he can remember certain aspects of the Afterlife, even if he doesn't understand why."

"Fair enough," Bast mutters.

The panther goddess' eyes reflect her distrust of Kreyuhl, but Clarisse doesn't doubt her familiar. If he's anything like her stars, he remembers her past, even if it's buried somewhere deep down.

"Clarisse," Bast warns, "you must be more careful moving forward. You cannot continue to put yourself at risk. It is improper—reckless, even. You must put your emotions aside. I take it you've been unable to master your magic yet?"

Before Clarisse can protest, Death steps in. "She's been doing marvelously. She's aware of what she needs to work on, and she's been practicing. She knows her magic is comprised of two extremes and she needs to work on shifting somewhere in the middle. I hardly think Leyun showing up was a result of her 'lack of trying.'" He narrows his eyes at Bast. "Clarisse has only been dead for one week, to be fair. Barely even that. A few days isn't enough to master something we've had millennia to perfect."

Bast clicks her tongue, but her response is lost beneath Kreyuhl's growl. The beast attempts to squeeze further into the library, coiling himself around Clarisse as much as he can.

"Clarisse has more power than most. To ask her to learn to wield it so swiftly is a fool's errand!" Death defends. "It would take far too much for her to learn that fast without great sacrifice. I would rather her learn in safe environments such as this."

Kreyuhl tips his head and gestures to the library and Death snorts.

"If you continue to patronize her, I will have Kreyuhl remove you from the room and allow her to continue, despite your protests."

Kreyuhl bares his teeth and lets out a low growl, confirming Death's threats.

Bast's fist clench. "I beg your pardon?" Her silver eyes glow and flames curl within them.

If Kreyuhl doesn't move, Clarisse fears the burns he'll undoubtedly suffer. Stepping between them, Clarisse clears her throat. "While I appreciate everyone here trying to protect me, I don't think it's anyone's job to determine how fast or slow I should move. My magic will tell me. Kreyuhl and Death have helped me a lot, but this will take some time." Holding out her hand, she pulls in the direction of the kitchen. An instant later, a white puff of flour lands in her palm. "Not exactly what I was going for," she mutters, "but at least I didn't set it on fire this time."

"Were you trying to retrieve the bag of flour?" Death's eyes are wide.

"Yes. I only got a little, but that's better than the last time I tried it, right?" Her tone is uneven, betraying her uncertainty.

Death smiles. "I think that's great progress!"

Bast rolls her eyes. "What? You think teleporting a sack of flour from a different room will prepare you for what you're about to face?"

"N-no," Clarisse stammers. "But don't you think it's a start?"

Shaking her head, Bast storms from the room. Clarisse steps forward to chase after her when Death grabs her elbow. "No, let her have some space. She is fond of Terrence and facing the prospect of losing him. She's going to lash out while she comes to terms with it. Until Terrence reins himself in, it won't be pretty."

"Is he going to be erased?" Clarisse's voice shatters, her heart along with it. "Is that the punishment for violating Fal's laws?" Death's silence confirms her worst fear. Her mind burns with memories of the shadow wolf: how he found her in the barn, convinced her to leave her parents, and taught her magic. Yes, he pushed her too hard, but was it intentional? Did he mean for her to die? Her soul remembers how he stood and wept over her body, his body shaking with the rage of his failures. Now, her body shakes with his.

I couldn't save him. He's going to end up the same way.

"Not true, Clarisse. He still has a chance," Death argues. *"At the end of the day, his foolish choices will lead him to his end. As much as I sympathize with him and what he's trying to do... you can't alter the fabric of existence and twist laws to your desires. People must choose for themselves, even if it's wrong."*

It's not the answer Clarisse wants to hear. She'd like to have a word with Siralto if she ever gets the chance. *Why would she design life to operate like this?*

"Tryta played his part, too. Siralto allowed mortals to have the power to choose, but they both used me as a threat."

Would you exist if Earth had not been created? The thought feels dangerous to even acknowledge.

"*I'm not sure. I was created in relation to Earth, but there were discussions of me prior as an agent to usher errant gods to their erasure, if need be. It's why that power was entrusted to me.*"

Are you the only one with that power?

"*No, Clarisse. As I've said before, there are others. But unlike the others, endings are my specialty.*"

Clarisse looks up at him, mesmerized by how calm and sure of himself he is. His hair glistens in the light of the moon, betraying dark mahogany strands within the rows of black waves. His eyes are lost somewhere in the distance. Clarisse would like to follow him to where they go. *Don't leave me here by myself.*

Looking down at her, Death smiles. "I'd never leave you. You're my most favorite star, after all." He tousles her hair again before walking to the door. Kreyuhl steps aside for him as he did for Bast earlier, though the movement is not as abrupt.

They're getting comfortable with each other, she muses.

Death and Kreyuhl exchange a wary glance. "Don't be too sure of that, Clarisse," Death sneers.

Kreyuhl makes a strange growling noise in response—like a howling wind being chopped up in a blender. It makes Clarisse's hair stand on end, but she overcomes the fear and puts it away for later. *I'm glad you're not my enemy.*

The light dancing in Kreyuhl's pale eyes grows brighter. "*Me too. You wouldn't be very tasty.*"

Tasty? Clarisse's question goes unanswered as Kreyuhl gets up and seems to glide from the room on his stilted legs.

Clarisse hopes Bast will be okay. Seeing the goddess in such a state of distress saddens her. Summoning Death's star, she strokes it like a little bird as its light turns blue. Startled, she wonders if Death is sad.

"*Of course I am, Clarisse. Bast is like my sister and Terrence like my brother.*" Death peers through the door to the library. "*Even so, I'm powerless to the laws. Violating them has consequences none of us can understand. The last thing we want is the Selyento stepping in.*"

The tree?

"*Yes, she's the last living agent of Siralto. The world would crumble within the strangulation of her roots if we were to disrupt her strings by that much. Don't you know? Fate strings come from her roots."*

Death speaks of this as though it should be common knowledge, but Clarisse's jaw drops. "Are—are you serious?" Death nods. "So we're being governed by a tree?"

Laughing, Death motions for her to follow. With Kreyuhl out of the way, she follows Death with her familiar hot on her heels.

"Sort of," Death answers as she steps out of the library. "Siralto cut off a piece of her soul to lay within the tree, so the Selyento possesses a part of her consciousness. She did it so she could keep an eye on her creation at all times, since Earth was already an experiment that never should have happened… according to how Tryta viewed things, anyhow."

"Do you think there's a way to convince her to pardon Terrence?"

Death glances at her, but his face reveals nothing. "I wouldn't go down that route. Many of us have tried petitioning her throughout the centuries but failed. Don't waste your time. I'm sure you'll try anyway, but we can discuss that later."

"But Death, Terrence is running out of time!" Clarisse protests. "We have to save him *now*."

Sighing, Death smiles. "You're a merciful little thing. I love that about you. Perhaps we can schedule some time for you to speak to her, but be warned that we've tried it all before. I don't want your hopes crushed."

Seeing Bast standing at the bottom of the stairs with tears staining her cheeks, Clarisse's concern for time wasted is dissolved. "I'm going to try and help, anyway. I want Bast to know I tried."

"Tried what?" Bast calls.

"I'm going to try to convince the Selyento to pardon Terrence. I have an idea about something I might be able to use as leverage."

Bast laughs, disbelief evident in the way her smile falls and her sobs return. Clarisse rushes to her, leaving Death behind. She crushes Bast in a hug, which the panther goddess eagerly returns.

"I love him, too, you know," Clarisse whispers. "I don't want him to die. And I promise I'm trying to learn my magic. It's hard, but I'll keep trying. And I won't stop trying to convince the powers that be that our mutual friend deserves mercy. You deserve to have him in your life, Bast. This is how I'm going to pay back my debt to you... *and him.*"

"You owe him nothing!" Death snarls, descending the stairs in a flurry of black robes.

Clarisse holds up a finger. "He got me out of there, Death, and helped me grow comfortable with magic. It may have killed me in the end, but imagine if I'd died and learned about this all at once?"

Sputtering, Death can't find the words to respond. Bast grins down at her. "I suppose I'll allow that to be part of your payment to me."

"Agree to nothing, Clarisse," Death orders.

Her spine runs rigid. *What are you doing?*

"Using the bond to keep you safe, now hush."

"I will oversee this exchange. We should make haste in getting to the Selyento, if this arrangement is agreeable. However, *I* will be the one to settle the terms," Death commands.

For once, Bast doesn't push him. The eagerness in her eyes at even a sliver of a chance at saving Terrence is enough to spur Clarisse onward. She rushes to the door, ready to step out.

"Where do you think you're going?" Death demands.

Clarisse turns to face him with a quizzical expression. "To see the Selyento." Believing two can play at this game, she wordlessly pleads with him, hoping he can see her resolve.

"Fine," Death acquiesces. "I'll allow this. But Bast and I will accompany you and you will stay close to Kreyuhl at all times. Understand?"

With a grin, Clarisse nods and opens the front door. "So which way do I go?" She realizes that her memory of where the Selyento is, while altered, exists across multiple timelines. *I'm remembering!* "Never mind. I think I know."

Before Bast or Death can say anything, Kreyuhl dips his head so Clarisse can climb aboard his back. Smiling, she shimmies up and settles into place, wishing she had something to hold onto. In a blink, a stretchy rope fashions around his neck. The rubber is flexible so it doesn't tug at his throat, but it's enough for her to feel more in control. To her surprise, when Kreyuhl takes off at a trot, the movement feels familiar. She bounces around a bit, but her balance doesn't betray her.

"Wait up!" Death calls.

"Then hurry up!" Clarisse turns to see Death and Bast stumbling after her through the doorway and smiles.

For once, she feels like she's the one with power. Despite the dread pooling in her gut, she draws on the power of the moon as it casts its cool light over her. Her stars curl up at her fists and she grins.

"I can do this," she whispers.

As Death and Bast catch up, she nudges her heels lightly against Kreyuhl's sides. He urges forward in the direction she feels in her soul.

Time to petition a tree.

GUILT AND VENGEANCE

Terrence

When his eyes flutter open, he has no idea how long he's been asleep. Terrence doesn't remember the last time he dozed off, which is something he tries not to do because it renders him helpless to the world around him. *And of all the places to fall asleep…*

Still up in the balcony, Terrence has resigned himself to damnation for his actions. *Someone must do something to change the system. Someone must start caring when people do horrendous things. Those who torture children should not get a pass. Those who use people for their own means should not get a pass.*

He winces at this last thought, because he's fairly certain he used Clarisse.

With a shake, he stretches his limbs, letting every vertebra in his spine pop itself into place. He hopes the loud cracks and pops won't alert Father Simmons to his presence. Hiding as a shadow is one thing —it's easy when you're silent. But if you make noise… humans tend to fear shadows with a voice rather than shadows who don't speak.

A dangerous mix up. Grinning, he peers over the edge and tries to get a read on where Simmons might be sitting. Tilting his head, he listens. No breathing or heartbeat is discernible.

He hops down from the balcony and curls around the corners of the church, searching for signs of him. Prowling down the hallway, he comes just short of the door to Father Simmons' office. The door is open, but no one sits inside. Listening, Terrence wonders if he might be in the other room or using the restroom.

It would suck for him if he died in the bathroom. Terrence swallows a chuckle, turning over several different ways to humiliate Father Simmons in his last moments.

"Who's there?" a voice calls.

So Simmons is here….

With no time to think, Terrence dives into Father Simmons' office. He curls up in the corner and closes his eyes so he won't stand out from the dark shadows casting from the room itself. *I will hide in plain sight.*

When Simmons steps within the room, he shivers. *That's odd. Most people burn.*

The priest holds a briefcase. He sets it on his desk and disappears from the room. Deciding to test the waters, Terrence decides to laugh, the sound just above a whisper. In a flash, Father Simmons is back in the room. His pale eyes dart back and forth, searching for whatever might be lurking.

I am your worst nightmare, cretin.

Still, Simmons doesn't discern the shadows for what they are. Eyeing the briefcase, he puts his withered hands upon it, deciding not to leave it in case the owner of the offensive noise seeks to take it.

"Who's there?" The priest's voice trembles.

Terrence knows the man can sense him. Father Simmons, whether he knows it or not, has magical aptitude. It's the only explanation that logically determines how he was able to deceive people so well and for so long. *Some people are simply gifted at screwing others over. The man is a master manipulator. A trickster.*

When Simmons leaves the room once more, Terrence hatches a plot. Sliding out from his dark corner, he sweeps his tail across Father Simmons' desk. Pens and papers scatter everywhere, and the disruption doesn't go unnoticed. Terrence hears Father Simmons' hurried footsteps, but he slinks into the hallway before he is noticed.

The sound of Simmons' shuddering scream stamps a grin on his face. He can't help the giddy feeling sliding through him, even if there is a twinge of residual guilt.

I shouldn't be doing this.

Stomping that thought out is growing more difficult. *Why do I feel guilty?* A pair of feline eyes stare at him, piercing deep within his soul. *Because I should know better.* Still, he wants to see Simmons writhe and scream. To see him pay is Terrence's greatest wish.

Other than being able to apologize to Clarisse. And... to spend more time with Bast.

Seeing the goddess did little to help him stay firm with his wishes. He knows that beneath her feline guise stands a powerful goddess. Her sweeping dark hair that she does up in the most intricate patterns. The hair cuffs she chooses are always engraved with curious symbols he's always wanted to know more about. And her eyes... they captivate him most.

A strong, vexing being. He takes a breath and wills himself to stop thinking of her. He's certain Bast doesn't think of him that way... not really. He's stuck like a shadow, anyway. No one will solve his problems. No one will heal him. No one will set him free of his chains. The most he can ever be is a shadow.

The price for freedom is high. Deep down, he knows his attempts at securing power are to blame for his damnation. Some greater plan is at play, too, but hearing those things is harder than stomaching them. Even with the number of centuries that have passed, he's not ready.

What does one have to do to earn freedom from a damnation such as this?

His mind won't quiet as he stalks out of the church on silent paws. Part of him regrets burning down Clarisse's home. He wishes he could go home. *Home.* Deciding to clear his mind, he angles back to where the structure once stood.

Haunting people, as it turns out, is an exhausting practice, and he's only gotten started. He wonders how ghouls and demons have the stamina.

Charging through a copse of trees, he stops to ponder the way the sun has chosen to rise today, cast within pale clouds that amplify the few beams that manage to break through. The warmth of their rays bathes his face and brings him solace.

"I wish I could see what you're thinking, Clarisse. I wish you could know what you've left behind. And Bast, I wish you knew how hard it is to deny your wishes." His confessions, though heard by no one, leave him with a wave of relief as they are spoken aloud.

Stepping over leaves and twigs, he loses himself in the sounds of them snapping beneath his paws. The harsh winter has left them brittle and broken. He's doing them a favor, squashing them out and helping them along the path to becoming compost.

His mind is a fervor of strange, fleeting thoughts when he stumbles back to the clearing where her house once stood. *Their* house.

Settling down on his haunches, he tries to think of what to do next. His soul tugs him in so many conflicting directions it's hard to tell which way is up. He slumps down and rests his head on his paws. He doesn't care if anyone stumbles into the Grim incarnate as he lies out in the open. His grief tumbles over him and everything inside him hurts. As a shadow creature, the light becomes painful to bear. His eyes squint every time he looks up.

"Clarisse, I wish I'd left your house alone. I wish I'd thought things through a little better before I went and gathered everyone's attention. But who will make these monsters pay for their crimes if I don't?" The exasperation in his voice carries through the echoes that boomerang back to him, which snaps him out of his woe.

"What am I doing? Why am I taking so long to come to terms with this?"

Having to hold still for so long is beginning to take its toll. He's not being chased anymore. He holds no post, and his duties have been abandoned. He doesn't know what his purpose is. What is he supposed to do if it's not to seek out vengeance?

From above, Terrence catches a gleam of light that tumbles from the sky and rockets down to Earth like a meteor. When it crashes into the place where the house once stood, he rushes over to investigate. He almost tumbles over his paws as his eagerness overflows. *It's like being a child on Christmas!* That's an experience he's always wished he could've had. *I almost had that with Clarisse.* The idea stops him in his tracks, and he curses as yet another pang of guilt washes over him.

"I need to stop that," he mutters. "That's not helping anything."

He slows his pace as he pads gently toward a small, glittering object. As he draws near, his eyes widen. In the dirt sits a tiny crystal seed. *An... acorn?* Glancing around, Terrence waits for someone to come bursting from the tree line. Maybe a Reaper hoping to tease a former target. Or maybe an errant Selben here to mock him for being incomplete.

Nothing comes. No one comes. Terrence is alone with this tiny acorn, its glittering shell almost blinding in the light. Irritated, Terrence snatches it up. *Consequences be damned.*

Holding it in his heavy paw, he holds it closer to his nose and takes a sniff. The powerful stench of magic makes his eyes water and he drops it. Stepping back, he examines his paw for signs of marks, symbols, or anything that would indicate being affected by the strange magic radiating from the acorn.

"*It's a gift,*" a voice calls.

Whirling around, Terrence snarls, preparing for a fight. But once again, he finds nothing nearby. Hackles raised, he lowers into a defensive position. Should anyone or anything come after him, he's ready to launch and attack. His teeth are coated in saliva, which is a characteristic he normally hates about being a wolf. But it's a terrifying sight to potential prey and, for once, he's grateful for the visual deterrent.

Mess with me, I dare you.

"*I'm not messing with you. Consider this an aid to you in your journey.*"

Terrence counts to ten in his mind. It's always jarring when something from the Afterlife chooses to engage with the mortal world. The creature Ralun stuck out like a sore thumb, terror radiating from his strange body, while this being—although unseen—has a power unlike anything Terrence has ever encountered.

In a thin strip of sunlight, he catches its presence.

A... unicorn?

Stepping forward, the creature approaches Terrence. It looks serene, like something from an innocent fairytale. But Terrence knows better. He's heard of this creature before.

"Leyun," he hisses. "Why are you here?"

The unicorn tips its head back, its golden mane fluttering in a cool, chilling wind that blusters the closer she gets.

"I came here to give you a weapon, which you can use in honor of Clarisse."

The unicorn licks its lips, a silver tongue washing over its muzzle. It's creepy enough to make even Terrence shudder.

"Why are you helping me?"

"Committing a crime against a goddess demands vengeance, regardless if the laws of Fal and the Selyento state otherwise. You were in the process of exacting revenge, were you not?"

Shivering, Terrence tries to come up with an answer that doesn't implicate him in any nefarious plots. It's not easy being caught red handed, even if he has decided to walk away. *Or… have I?*

"You don't want them to get away with desecrating a Selbeno like Clarisse, do you? It's bad enough that she had to be reborn the way she was… The poor dear doesn't even remember who she is! But then to be forced to endure some of the most horrible abuses imaginable…" The unicorn lowers its head and pins its ears in a mixture of rage and sorrow. *"I'd do it myself, but I can't work alone. I can't bring souls into Kohlu… but you can."*

The unicorn's eyes glimmer with hate, kicking up strong feelings within Terrence's soul. "Why should I trust you? Why should I work with you? Bast told me you're hunting Clarisse."

The unicorn whinnies, but the sound is more like a cruel laugh. *"I'm afraid you don't have much of a choice."*

With a flick of its horn, Leyun produces an image in the air of Clarisse walking alongside Death and Bast. Seeing his favorite goddesses near each other sets his heart ablaze. Part of him – a tiny part – is even happy to see Death. As his eyes adjust to the vision, his heart seizes when he watches them step into the boundaries of Kreyuhl. The Aiyeliu with them, though calm, gives him cause for even more concern.

"Why are they in Kreyuhl? And why is that Aiyeliu with them?" His eyes lock on Leyun with a sinking feeling in his gut.

"Clarisse plans to tell them of the crimes that were committed against her. To try and petition the tree…"

"For justice?" Terrence guesses.

"Yes."

Terrence's heart sinks. The image dissipates. A nagging voice in the back of his head tells him not to trust the unicorn. She could have warped the image. She could have made him see what she wanted him to see to further her own selfish agenda.

But why else would she go to the tree?

The shadow wolf narrows his eyes suspiciously. "Why aren't you there hunting her?"

The unicorn doesn't even flinch at this question. Her ears are pitched forward and her eyes are bright. *"She and I are quite alike. I'm rather fond of her, and truthfully, I don't want to harm her. I want her to be whole again, just as you do. I want her to remember."*

Terrence doesn't detect any deceit in the words, but something still feels off. The unicorn, sensing his hesitation, leans into him. Seconds later, a strange calmness washes over him. By the time he realizes she's casting a spell, it's too late to fight it off. He blinks, his limbs sluggish and tired. His eyes adjust and they focus on the beautiful, angelic creature standing before him. "What's your name?" he slurs.

"Leyun," the unicorn chirps. *"I heard you need some help!"*

Turning, Terrence glances around. "Help with what?" He glances down at the acorn that sits between them, covered in winter mud and a few leaves, and reaches down and picks it up between his teeth. Then he buries it in his shadows for safekeeping, instinctually knowing it's his.

"That's for you to use to capture Father Simmons. Don't you remember? You were hunting him down because you were ordered to exact justice on him for killing a goddess."

Terrence frowns. He remembers Simmons abusing Clarisse, and in a flash, his plans to haunt him come swirling back to him. With renewed vigor, he growls. "You're right!" His head, in a fog, seems to have forgotten its true purpose. "Why are you here, again?"

"I came to show you that Clarisse went to petition the Selyento for justice, remember? She wants justice, Terrence."

His mind flickers for a moment. The memory of Clarisse, Bast, and Death striding through Kreyuhl is fuzzy, but it's there. "Why can't I remember?"

"Father Simmons is a trickster, remember? He cast some sort of spell. But I heard your cries for help."

On an ordinary day, Terrence would question this. No deity, no matter how beautiful, is ever this kind. Not for free, anyway. The only truly neutral party in Tyrladan is Death, and that didn't turn out well for Terrence, even with Death's unbiased nature.

Smiling, Terrence is overwhelmed with gratitude. "Thanks, friend. What's your name?"

The creature smiles. *"I don't have a name. I'm an agent of Siralto."*

The goddess' name perks Terrence's ears. "She's been dead since the beginning of Earth! How can you possibly be her agent?"

"The Selyento is part of her, remember? How do you think the Selyento gets information to Earth for people like yourself? Now go get justice, Terrence!"

Before Terrence can ask any further questions, the beam of light disappears and the unicorn fizzles out with it. Were it not for the crystal acorn tucked securely in his shadows, he would think it was all a dream.

I must go back. But who do I kill first? And how do I do it with only one acorn? Shuddering, he tries to shake off the feeling that something is wrong. *Why was I even back here?*

Nausea curdles his stomach, giving him pause. *Something is wrong.* Shaking himself, he tries to remember what he was doing before. *I'm grieving. That's the gist of things. There's no other explanation. I came here and got lost. And Simmons cast a spell…* A low growl rumbles from within his chest.

"I'll show him what magic looks like," Terrence vows aloud. He wonders how long it will be before he is punished. But then he recalls how Leyun made it sound like the Selyento wanted this. Could it be? Could Terrence be the harbinger of Tyrladanian-sanctioned punishment? He licks his lips as glee courses through him, pleased that he can finally do what he was meant for with reckless abandon.

He breaks out into a skip rather than a prowl. Prancing to the Monroe's house was the last way he planned on making an entrance, but it's even funnier to imagine what might cross their minds at the sight of him. *A happy shadow, here to reap our souls.*

A maniacal laugh tears through the trees. At first, he doesn't even register that it belongs to him. His skipping picks up and he breaks out of the trees, gliding through the dying, tall grass that surrounds the Monroe house.

He slows before reaching the door, and hunches down to a low prowl. *It's not the right time to be seen.* Slinking about, he decides to invade the home. He melds through the walls, embracing the darkness rising within him, and journeys to *her* room without thinking. When he looks around, he is mortified.

Her room is filled with *their* belongings. Even her bed sags under the weight of boxes filled with pictures, clothing, and other forgotten items.

All remnants of Clarisse have been buried and piled up, dust collecting in every corner of the room. It makes him sick. *How are they able to move on so easily?*

From beyond the door, he hears arguing.

"What are we going to do?"

He picks up on Deborah's voice first. Her tone is urgent. "He's demanding that we pay him for the inconvenience, and he's threatening to sue us if we come forward!"

Terrence's blood runs cold. It doesn't take a genius to realize who they're talking about. It takes great effort not to take off for the church. *Why should I care about them? They deserve whatever evil deeds he brings into their lives. Clarisse would still be here if they hadn't listened to him in the first place.*

"Deb, I highly doubt it will escalate that far. The man values his reputation."

Terrence spots Arthur, his thinning hair wispier than the last time he saw it. *He should really get rid of that awful comb-over. He'd look better bald. No matter… it won't look any better where he's going.*

"How can you know that, Arthur?" Deborah snaps, wringing her hands anxiously. Her once sable hair is completely gray, and her eyes seem haunted by the weight of her many sins.

Arthur sighs, seemingly unaffected by her tone. "Deb, he thrives on extorting people for cash, but he has to maintain a low profile. If he sues us, then we'll countersue and subpoena his records. Using a child as a performance act? He's not going to risk his wallet. We may have been acquitted, but there's a lot of risk going civil for this. For one, we'd be testifying against him together and not keeping our mouths shut."

Overwhelmed with rage, Terrence swings the door back and forth, creating a loud screeching noise from the hinges. He hears both of them jump and Deborah shrieks as he hurtles toward the closet and slips through the door. He watches them through the keyhole, glee passing through him again and a bit of solace at seeing their palpable fear.

That's how it should be. You should feel what she felt. Afraid.

Grumbling to himself, but quiet enough beneath their commotion to remain undetected, Terrence observes their behavior keenly. They're jumpy—even more than one would expect the average haunted family to be. He notes how Deborah twists at her wedding band every time Arthur speaks.

"There must be a draft in here." Arthur swipes at the air, his annoyance a sharp blade that cuts through Deborah.

She steps back. "You're right," she mumbles. She twists the ring tighter, her finger turning white as the circulation is cut off.

She's terrified.

Arthur storms from the room, but Deborah lingers. Her hand passes over one of the boxes, her fingers trembling at the flaps. She heaves a whispered sigh but leaves the box alone, denying herself whatever nostalgia may lie within it.

As soon as she disappears from the room, Terrence rushes over to see what's hiding within the box. Tearing into it, he doesn't care about leaving evidence. *What's a good haunting without making a mess?*

When he peels back a flap, he has to steady himself. Old scrapbooks fill the box to the brim. His eyes water and he steps away to gather his resolve. When he's certain he won't start sobbing, he delves back into the box, sniffling at the dust. These boxes reek of memory—he can smell them. Memories pouring all the way back to the date of Clarisse's birth. Her magic betrays the age of the contents inside, her essence written all over it. It smells of happiness—of her stars. All of which have been trapped within this carton.

He wonders why Deborah has these mementos. Up until now, he was convinced that Deborah hated her daughter and the memory of her just as much as Arthur and Father Simmons. But now? He's not so sure.

Indecision clouds his heart. On one hand, Clarisse was abused mercilessly at the hands of her parents. On the other, it appears that maybe Deborah wasn't always a willing participant, if at all.

Humans confuse Terrence more often than not, even if he was once one. Existing as a Reaper for as long as he has, he's learned that many of the things he once considered problematic are largely trivial.

Why does this man have such a hold on her? Why not leave? Why not take your child and leave?

It occurs to Terrence that Deborah probably didn't have many readily available alternatives. For starters, where would she have gone? And how would she have gotten there?

Arthur has resources—a strong accounting firm and rich elbows to rub. He would've been able to stop her… but why did she turn to the church? Everything he knows of the parents, he learned through Clarisse's memories. Deciding he needs more intel, he slinks back into the walls of the house. It takes a lot of energy to be a shadow, but he feels compelled to understand things better.

Creeping into the living room, he stays hidden between the insulation and listens. Terrence can no longer sense Arthur's spirit. After a few seconds, he realizes Clarisse's father has left the house. Stifling a snort, he focuses in on Deborah. *You're the one I'm interested in, anyway.*

Her muffled sobs reach him first, the sound distant. Pinpointing the sound to her bedroom, he slips within the bedroom walls, promising to get some serious rest later. *Today will not be the day I strike.*

His eyes gleam with satisfaction as he watches the woman writhe with guilt. *You're the one who called in Father Simmons—you used Clarisse to fulfill your own sick requirements for peace.* Still, his heart softens. It's not within him to be cruel. Even at his angriest, he knows this woman has suffered, too. Part of him wants to make himself known now and demand answers to questions such as why she allowed Clarisse to suffer so long, or how a mother could bear a child only to use them for their own nefarious purposes.

A growl almost slips through his lips and he curses himself for being so reckless. If he wants justice to be served, he can't mess this up.

He notices something in Deborah's hands and realizes she must've taken a photograph from the box of Clarisse's things. Climbing up into the ceiling, as fatigued as he's become, he manages to focus on the picture. In it stands Deborah and a very young Clarisse—before the incident with the stars that Clarisse feared and hated so much.

Deborah's tears have smudged the photograph; Terrence fears it's damaged beyond repair. In a sudden fit of rage, she shreds it. The scream Terrence swallows would chill even the most damned souls to the bone.

Why would you do that?

His heart races, his mind focused on the remaining keepsakes in Clarisse's old room. *What if she destroys those next?*

"What have I done?" Deborah whispers aloud. "I've... I've killed my only child." Her head collapses into her hands and she begins to sob.

Terrence blinks. He doesn't do well in moments like these. The duality of mortals never ceases to amaze him.

As much as he wants to sympathize with a mother mourning her only child, he holds his cards close to his chest. Rushing to comfort Clarisse's mother goes against every stretch of loyalty he has left to give to his friend. Even though she's dead, he refuses to betray her like that.

Without warning, Deborah vaults to her feet and storms from the room, leaving the torn photograph lying on the mattress. Tilting his head, he waits a few moments. When Deborah doesn't return, he collapses through the ceiling with a sigh of relief, the extent of his shadow powers tapped for now. He worries he might end up sleeping for decades after such an exertion. *Now I know why Death keeps his emotions out of things. It makes things so much more difficult.*

Swallowing, he strides to the mattress to collect the photo pieces. Then, he rifles through Deborah's dresser to see if there is more evidence of her regret in the form of journals, photos, or letters. Each drawer comes up empty.

"There must be something in here that will help me figure this cretin out," he mutters. No longer sensing Deborah's presence, he's emboldened to look in less obvious places. It occurs to him that he could've hidden in the closet instead of seeping into the ceiling. Maybe if he had, his mind wouldn't be so clouded with exhaustion.

This is why we don't let our feelings get the better of us.

He cringes as he remembers Death's constant reminders. In this moment, he misses his former boss. Death is an expert sleuth and would know exactly where to look. With a snort, Terrence wonders why he ever thought he could overthrow him.

Rooting through shirts, pants, and coats, Terrence hopes to find something substantive. When he comes up empty, he wonders if the evidence might be in Clarisse's room, tucked away for future disposal.

Before he can move in that direction, he hears footsteps again. In his exhaustion, he missed Deborah's return. She races down the hallway and he almost doesn't make it into the closet before Deborah rushes in, her eyes wide and a knife clutched in her right hand. Glaring at the closet door that just slammed, she hoists the knife high, ready to stab whatever intruder is hiding in the closet.

Terrence knows he's out of luck. He has no choice but to jump out and scare her. He'll survive a stab wound, but he won't have the upper hand he so desperately needs.

Just as she grips the doorknob with a trembling hand, he leaps out, a snarl ripping through his chest. The booming sound makes her stumble back, and the jarring reverberation mixes with the woman's terrified screams. Tears spring from her eyes as she falls to the floor, the knife clattering beside her, forgotten. She drags herself backward, trying with all her might to scramble to her feet. Terrence watches her hair bleed from gray to white, the short strands falling from her head in feathery tufts.

Her pupils go wide; Terrence feels it before he sees it. Her soul departs her body.

I scared her to death!

A Reaper has yet to arrive, but Terrence knows his time here is limited. The house will be under strict investigations from Tyrladan. A haunting like this will be unmistakably tied to him. His malevolent handiwork is known by all who once worked with him.

He grits his teeth and chastises himself. "How could you trip up like this, Terrence?"

Before anyone arrives, he takes off running. His long strides eat the distance faster than a blink, his heart racing as he surges to put distance between him and the scene of the accidental scaring-to-death.

While a small part of him regrets his actions, peace washes over him the farther he retreats from the house. Partial justice has been served. One down, only two more to go.

By the time he stops running, a wide smile splits his face. *Not half bad for an ex-Reaper*, he thinks. His eyes climb to the top of the church, the empty balcony awaiting him. Within him, the acorn glints like the stained glass in the windows.

I know what to do with this now.

FATE

Death

He senses it before the Reapers even send him a message. Calling forth one of his stars, he awaits the news. Terrence will need forgiveness now more than ever.

Sure enough, the star turns red in his hand to announce the blood of Deborah Monroe that's freshly spilled. Cause of death: cardiac arrest.

Terrence's power and presence, he knows, are the ultimate reason. It won't be long until this conclusion is made by the other Reapers, assuming it hasn't already been figured out. Fal will be informed. There will be a hearing, but it's always an open and shut process. Falme are never to be disturbed under any circumstances by supernatural forces.

Frowning, Death pulls up a summary of Deborah's timeline. He's doing his best to retain an expression of neutrality, but his worry is not missed by Clarisse, who turns to look at him. He swears he sees a glimpse of silver in those lovely brown eyes of hers, but he dismisses this thought as foolish and returns to his task.

When the timeline becomes clear, he breaks into a cold sweat.

Deborah… was on time? He goes over the record a few more times, reviewing the potential outcomes that were supposed to be the result. In the end, the facts are clear. Her timeline wasn't altered.

Growling, Death pockets his star and tries to figure out how Debora's death could possibly be correct. On one hand, it means Terrence isn't in trouble. He's acting within the bounds of the Falme, whether he knows it or not. Then again, if they learn the cause of the cardiac arrest… he may not be out of the woods yet.

Death looks up just as he tumbles into Clarisse. He throws his hands out to try and catch himself; instead, they topple to the ground, his body squishing hers.

"Death, what in the world are you doing?" Bast demands.

Looking down, he's mortified to see the blush spreading on Clarisse's cheeks. He places his hands on either side of her and pushes his body away from hers, careful not to hurt her in the process. "Are you okay?" His eyes rove over her as he offers a hand to help her to her feet.

"Yes, but what about you? What's wrong?" As she stands, she dusts the dirt from her chiffon dress.

He finds it funny that she spends so much time curating outfits when she hardly cared about the clothes she wore on Earth.

Clarisse snaps her fingers. "Death, focus! What's going on?"

Sighing, Death does his best to curate a response, knowing how frustrated and confused she is already. "I don't think Terrence is going to be in trouble. I think Fal is wrong," he starts. "I have the evidence to prove it."

Bast blinks. "What do you mean?"

Death takes a breath and looks at Clarisse, unsure how she'll respond. "Your mother… just passed. Terrence frightened her to death. On accident, it appears. But apparently, she was due to die today anyway. It means he didn't alter her fate at all. In fact, he just sealed it."

Clarisse doesn't speak for a few moments. The turmoil brewing in her eyes will sweep Death away if she doesn't say something soon.

"Is it bad that I feel relieved?" Clarisse's shoulders slump beneath the weight of her confession.

Death feels the guilt writhing within her and isn't sure what to do. *Do I hug her? Do I leave her be?*

Clarisse answers by stepping forward and wrapping her arms around him. He feels the wetness from her eyes stain his cloak, confirming his fears. Unsure what to do next, Death looks to Bast.

"Clarisse," he starts, "I don't think it's bad at all. You were abused. Severely. Your mother used you. There is no shame in being relieved that a monster is gone."

Pulling back from him, Clarisse's puffy red eyes make him uncomfortable. "Is she going to come here? Do I have to talk to her?"

Shaking his head, Death leans in closer, uncaring that Bast's face twists into an obvious cringe. "No, you do not. I doubt she will come to Kreyuhl. Remember, your scenario was unique. Most decisions about where a soul will end up are decided long before someone arrives in Tyrladan. And someone like Deborah is slotted for Kohlu, I'm sure of it."

"My mom is in Hell?" Clarisse gasps. "I… I don't know that I… Is that really how…"

Clarisse's stammering fades to silence. Death is touched by the mercy she wants to extend, even for the worst people in her life. Nestling her closer, he's overcome by the urge to whisk her away someplace where she won't be bothered by those who would wish her ill.

"Clarisse, there's nothing you could've done to save her. Her actions had consequences. Does a child abuser deserve reprieve in the end? Does someone like your mother really deserve mercy?" Death growls. "Justice must play out. If it's not allowed on Earth, where else will it be served?"

The flicker in her eyes doesn't convince him that she buys his explanation, but a dark piece inside him revels at the thought that her oppressors are now going to face proper punishments for their evil deeds. Just thinking of all the things Clarisse endured in her short life makes his stomach churn, accompanied by the guilt of leaving her, even if he didn't have a choice. Rage festers in his soul, which is new for him. It's rare that he ever feels an emotion as intense as *rage*.

"Bast, would the Selyento know about the bond Clarisse and I share?" For once, he doesn't care about sharing his concerns. Their bond is growing treacherous by the minute. *Since when do I have the hormonal control of a teenage boy? What is it about her that's so intoxicating I can't walk away?*

He hopes Clarisse can't sense his thoughts, but the hurt in her eyes confirms she does.

"Clarisse, don't start. You know full well that I care for you, but even you must admit we have a strange connection. Doesn't it concern you in the slightest how attached to you I've grown? How attached to *me* you've grown?"

She pouts, but her thoughts cloud and he hears the turmoil in her soul. She deserves a reprieve. But what does that look like?

"Death, the Selyento will only tell you what you already know, deep down. It's best not to fight it, as disgusting as that is for those of us in your company," Bast adds snidely. "Denying your feelings for each other will only make things escalate. As a matter of fact… it might make her an easier target, the longer you avoid the truth."

Groaning, Death claps his face into his hands, letting Clarisse slide from his grasp. He knows what he's doomed to hear, but he doesn't dare think it aloud.

"Back to the point at hand," Bast interjects. "Are you telling me there's hope for Terrence? That the Selyento called out for justice, rather than condemnation?"

Death can't stand to see the naked hope in Bast's eyes. He knows hope leads to devastation in moments like these. Time and time again, calls for justice have gone unanswered, despite his own discomfort with things. The last thing he wants is for Bast to get her hopes crushed.

"I won't confirm or deny anything. The only facts I have are the ones I can see, and those facts point out that Deborah Monroe was scheduled to die today. Where the circumstances and timing of Clarisse's death were vague, Deborah's was concrete. Deborah was due to have her soul reaped from the Earth, and now she will face the fires of Kohlu. Whether Terrence is responsible or not… Well, I don't know what kind of implications his involvements hold for him."

If things continue like this, Death will have his first migraine in decades. The last migraine was when Terrence decided to try and overthrow him. Looking down at Clarisse, he ponders again why he chose to let this mortal female sway his opinion on Terrence's punishment. Her brown eyes are soft, and her mind doesn't seem to be as plagued with concerns as it was a handful of minutes ago. He wonders why she's calmed down.

A glance at Kreyuhl answers his question. The Aiyeliu, like a proper familiar, has sensed her distress and began the process of unraveling it. He'll store her thoughts for safe keeping, giving her time to process things one at a time. Death knows he should explain this to Clarisse, but it will have to wait as they handle more pressing matters.

Kreyuhl casts him a glare, which is outrageous given that the creature's eyes match his pale skin. Death has words he would like to exchange with Kreyuhl, but he contains himself to save Clarisse the heartache of watching them bicker. Part of him would trust Kreyuhl with Clarisse's life; the other part of him can't stand the beast. He knows the Aiyeliu has more information than he's chosen to reveal, but he also knows it's likely that the Aiyeliu doesn't remember it all, just as Clarisse's stars struggle to recall what her life was like before.

His mind returns to the fact that Clarisse was *married* to some deity who took her for granted, and more rage stirs in his chest. *I wonder if Asclepius would take a look at me. Something is wrong!* When Clarisse looks up at him with concern, he stuffs away those troubles for later.

"I hope you're right," Bast finally says. She's irritated at the silence, knowing that Death and Clarisse have retreated to their thoughts again, though this time Death can at least defend himself and say they weren't conversing without her.

"I do, too," Death concedes. For once, he's in Terrence's corner. Clarisse didn't deserve to be treated that way, and he's glad one of those monsters has paid the price.

It's high time *someone* does something to change the way that Earth's natural justice operates, even if he doesn't agree with how rash Terrence can be. If someone asked Death a few months ago of his thoughts, he'd be appalled to know how much he's changed in such a short period of time.

What's becoming of me? He worries that, if his actions continue like this, he might become unworthy of his post. It's something people have murmured about for eons. Now, here he stands... in Kreyuhl, helping a soul that's long since passed on and could, theoretically, be left in Bast's care or someone else equally as capable.

I can't abandon her. It's out of the question. Death can't stomach the idea of Clarisse being alone in Yehta, navigating the treacherous reality of being on the Neylka's hit list. His Reapers are functioning fine without him and, eventually, he's certain he can return to his tasks. *Perhaps Clarisse can accompany me.*

He's not certain she's cut out for a title like Reaper, but he's sure he has something she could do. With her sensitive spirit, perhaps she could be the calm force that helps bring errant souls to their senses. She could capture them with her sweet voice and sing them into compliance.

The heat growing within him makes him blush. Bast stares at him, but wisely remains quiet. The sparkle in her eyes tells him she'll be bugging him about this later, whether he likes it or not.

"Come on, team. We're getting off task. The quickest way to find out if Terrence is in trouble is to ask the source of our woes directly," Death grumbles. He takes off in a flurry of black robes, ignoring the startled stares from Bast and Clarisse. *It's time we finish this so I can help Clarisse train and figure out what to do with her.*

They're not far from the Selyento. Death scans the tall grass and the leaves of impossibly tall trees, their neon greens, blues and purples almost blinding in the moonlight. The dawn will be upon them soon, and he doesn't want to be caught stumbling around in broad daylight. He has a plan—he always has a plan, even if it isn't apparent right away. He's hardwired for logic and sound decisions.

How did I end up on a quest like this?

It occurs to him that he could probably step out for a few moments while Clarisse petitions the tree to sort out any hard decisions that have piled up with the Reapers. Unclear deadlines, hard to catch souls, and a few situations that border on necromancy have come through his team's communications, and his stars are in a daze at the prospect of going much longer without dealing with the unrest.

I must get a handle on things. His mind is aflutter with possibilities of how he might get things sorted as they inch closer to the Selyento. It takes him a few moments to register that he's arrived. He almost goes tumbling into the tree's trunk.

"Death, are you going to pay attention to where you're going, or are you trying to get us all killed?" Bast calls after him, standing several hundred meters from the tree. Most Selben are hesitant to approach the last remaining piece of Siralto. The Selyento can be cruel and conniving—a tie-in to Fal, her rules are rigid and unforgiving.

Why have we come to bow for a tree?

Clarisse fixes him with a stare that's unfamiliar to him. Her eyes almost glow in the low light of dawn, now that the three suns are creeping above the horizon. In the morning light, her brown hair turns cinnamon and he's breathless at the sight of her. Where most would crumble in the face of danger, her face is fixed with a firm, brave mask. Wherever the Clarisse from Earth has gone, she left behind a phoenix within her ashes. Her whole being is on fire with power and grace.

Death wonders how this part of her stayed hidden for so long. Even in the mortal realm, her magic broke free, but it's difficult to imagine the magnificent power that radiates from her now being trapped.

He reaches out to her, helping her find her footing as he grasps her hands and keeps her from setting something else on fire or drowning them all. *Somehow, I'd be okay with that, too.*

"Selyento, I have a proposition to make," Clarisse calls past him.

Death looks up at the tree, half expecting it to say something aloud. *It never does.* "My darling, Fal has to be here to translate," he says smoothly, surprised he used such a term of endearment.

"Why does she have to be here to translate?" Clarisse's question doesn't sound suspicious, but Death senses an uneasiness within her. *How do we know she isn't lying to us?* she adds in her mind.

Shocked, Death stares at her a few moments. He tries to think of a suitable answer, but the notion of Fal deceiving everyone for millennia? *Seems a little preposterous, my love. The tree always gives a sign of its assent, and then the magic flows a certain way to carry out the curses. I'm certain that Terrence's current form is not a product of Fal's magic.*

Still, Death wonders how Clarisse came to that conclusion so quickly.

"I just find it hard to believe that a tree is your government. Seems a little weird," Clarisse confesses. Death agrees in the quiet of their minds, but refuses to speak this aloud. While the Selyento doesn't govern the

undead, he knows it wields power, and Fal wouldn't like that power to be questioned.

The last thing I need is another deity gunning for you, my love.

He doesn't realize what he's said until it's too late. Clarisse leans into him, though she chooses not to ask aloud what he shared in their minds. The bond burns him now; he doesn't want to cut it out, though. He wants to be charred by its flames.

"If Fal isn't here, there must be another way to commune with the tree," Clarisse says aloud.

Snorting, Bast rolls her eyes. "Good luck with that. Fal will be here any minute. Just hold on and wait, okay? Let's not get hasty."

But Clarisse isn't listening, and Death doesn't expect her to. She rushes up to the tree and eyes it as though she's a child seeking the right branch to climb up.

"Clarisse, please be careful." Death sidles up to her and tries to think of ways to get her to calm down and wait, but the curiosity shared between their bond overwhelms him. He nearly caves to it himself. He knows it's a moot point to try and argue with her now.

Clarisse glares and sticks her tongue out at him.

"Clarisse, I hardly think that's a mature response." Death crosses his arms, desperate for any shred of sanity he has left to come rising to the surface to save them. His emotions have never been this unstable. *All it took was one woman?* Gazing at Clarisse in her element, he shakes his head. *One goddess, I should say. She's definitely not human.*

He hears Kreyuhl lumbering up behind him, then the beast rests beside Clarisse where she stands just in front of the Selyento. He settles his muzzle in her hair and Death clenches his fists. Just then, a startling thought dawns on him. *Am I jealous of Kreyuhl?*

"Took you long enough to figure that one out, bonehead." Kreyuhl's eyes laugh for him, though his mouth doesn't move.

Death swallows several angry comebacks and decides to store them for later. Right now, Kreyuhl seems much more focused on whatever energy Clarisse has started to draw from the tree.

What is she doing? For once, Death is the one breaking out into a nervous sweat. He's not sure if he should interrupt or not, for fear of making things worse if her magic becomes too volatile.

Her breathing slows. Death almost doesn't step back in time when

146

her hand connects with the tree and her magic courses through it. Her eyes, when he looks again, are definitely silver. The brown has been eaten alive by whatever molten magic resides within her. The power radiating from her frightens him, which is a feeling he's never felt before.

Even so, he's unwilling to budge from his place beside her. He's aware Bast is calling out to him, but he can't hear her words over the deafening song of Clarisse's energy coursing through him. Bearing witness to it, even through a bond, makes him weak. *Whomever Clarisse was… she was everything.*

The last resistant pieces of him that want to run from her give in. He is truly and wholly captivated by her, every inch of him yearning to help her any way he can. He fears for her. He wants to protect her.

From within their bond, he hears someone else talking.

"Terrence is pardoned. The justice he demands must be sought out. The Monroes shall end how they shall end. His purpose is greater than what Fal would have for him."

Clarisse speaks these words aloud, her voice christened by the sound of the Selyento's whistling chimes, her body a strong vessel.

Death's stomach churns. Before he can decipher anything else, Clarisse is overtaken by exhaustion and her power fades as the tree loosens its grip on her. One moment she's standing, the next, she's slumping down the tree.

Rushing to her, tears well in his eyes. Pulling her to him, he pats her face gently to try and wake her. Deep in her sleep, he senses her contentment. Her proposition, though unnecessary, worked.

"She can speak to the Selyento," Bast whispers, her voice laced with awe. The goddess, spurred by watching Clarisse, no longer shakes as she approaches. Leaning over them, she studies Clarisse with astonishment. "Thank you, little Selbeno." She grabs Clarisse's free hand and plants a reverent kiss on it. "You have saved my Terrence." Bast snaps to look at Death. "I still want to learn magic from her, and I expect to have that wish honored, whether you broker the deal or not." She points a finger at him. "And if you hurt her, I'll erase you. I don't care if you're the one with that power and I'm not; I'll figure out how to wield it."

I know, Death thinks to himself. He's glad that Bast can't probe his thoughts. They've been rebellious lately, planting all sorts of foolish notions in his mind.

Clarisse's eyes flutter open. He brushes a loose strand of her hair away from her forehead and smiles. "You okay there?"

Nodding, Clarisse clutches his hands. "I'm alright," she whispers. "Just took me by surprise, that's all."

Laughing, Death is amazed by how well she's handling such a significant amount of raw magic that's just coursed through her.

"I don't know who I am anymore, Death," Clarisse says, her eyes welling with tears. "I don't feel the same. I still don't know who I am, but I feel… old. Powerful. I'm not so afraid anymore. And as much as many things here don't make sense, somehow they do. I don't know if it's me, Kreyuhl, my magic, or a mixture of everything." Her voice shudders and her breath gets choppy.

"Listen, don't panic," he says, his voice soft. Death holds her face rigid so she can't look away. "You are going through something I've never seen, and you're shouldering it like a true goddess. No one can truly explain everything to you or help you navigate your path, but Bast and I are damn well going to try. I wish I could tell you why the Selyento is able to speak to you. I wish I could tell you exactly what it means to be chased by the Neylka. I've seen things like this, although never to this degree. But you're hanging on, and that's all that matters."

His heart swells with pride as he realizes just how much Clarisse is doing to try and understand this new world, especially after learning that she doesn't know who she really is.

"I know our bond makes things more intense, but I am genuinely proud to know you and bear witness to who you're becoming. And your past self be damned. Who you are now is just as important. *You* define who you are. Never forget that." Death winks.

Clarisse is grinning so wide, he fears his heart might take flight and soar off into the morning suns somewhere.

"What's happening here?"

Death turns to see Fal approaching them, her six eyes contemplative and her faces carefully blank. He clutches Clarisse closer to his chest, ready to take on Fate incarnate if it means protecting Clarisse.

Holding up her hands, Fal laughs. "I'm not here to take your Lafura from you, Death. Nor am I angry. I'm merely curious… Did she manage to speak to my Selyento?"

Death looks down at Clarisse, unsure how to advise her. *Should I have her answer Fal truthfully or not? Granted, the Selyento will tell her if we lie…*

"Yes, she told me that Terrence was pardoned," Clarisse blurts. Death can tell in the urgency of her voice that she doesn't trust Fal. He's beginning to think she might be onto something, though he's not sure why her hunch makes sense.

Just then, Death's internal alarm bells start ringing. *My LAFURA?*

"If someone could explain to me what a Lafura is, I would appreciate it." It haunts Death how mature Clarisse is starting to sound. The age of her magic has a clear effect on her personality.

And for some reason I'm drawn to that.

If he could beat himself with a shovel, he would. *Now is not the time to focus on our feelings.*

Fal chuckles as she draws closer to the tree. Death's hair stands on end. He braces himself for a fight, even though he knows he's being delusional. Fal's eyes meet his and she grants him three knowing smiles.

"It's normal to feel this way when the bond first solidifies. Everything that's not about you two starts to feel foreign and like a potential threat. I felt the same way about my Aynda. She and I were very closed off from the world when we first acknowledged our bond."

At the mention of Aynda, his heart sinks. *No one has seen her in centuries.* Not daring to broach that subject, he casts Clarisse a look and hopes she knows not to push.

"*I won't,*" she promises.

Death lets out a breath and takes a moment to rest in what little relief that offers.

Fal explains, "A Lafura, Clarisse, is a mate. A soulmate, specifically. When a Selben meets their Lafura, it usually starts slow, but becomes an undeniable force between the two of them. You may have only been with Death a few days, but your souls have known each other forever. They were destined to be together."

Clarisse's face is one of blank shock. Death wishes he could be wholly inside her thoughts to understand how she feels. Everything continues to plummet into her Afterlife at such a rapid pace, he fears she'll go insane.

Clarisse glances over at him, her gaze shy—embarrassed, even, and it breaks him.

"Clarisse, you take all the time you need to process this, okay?" Death manages to say, though he himself is spiraling. "This—being close to people… I think it's new for both of us."

Clarisse nods, her hands trembling. "I don't know who I am, Death. How can my soul know it loves you when it doesn't even know itself? I'm just some girl who was abused for cash by a false preacher. I make stars. That's it."

Her eyes are wide, and her heart races so fast that he begins to worry that she could have a heart attack in Tyrladan. She's drifted from his arms, but he reels her back in. She rests her head against his chest and takes a deep breath.

"I see she's been using her magic."

This time, Fal's interruption is welcome. He needs something else to focus on. If Death keeps his focus on Clarisse's pain much longer, he's going to fall apart himself.

"She's been learning to regulate her emotions and understand how they tie to her magic. She must be careful though, as using too much magic draws Leyun to her," Death explains. At this, he realizes how vulnerable they are after Clarisse used so much of her magic to speak to the Selyento. Kreyuhl stands close by, but he hasn't started growling like he did back in the kitchen right as Leyun arrived to take Clarisse to the Neylka.

Nodding, Fal hums and sits next to them both, which prompts Bast to sit across from them. Until now, she's remained silent in the presence of one of Tyrladan's most feared beings. Goddess or not, when Fal is in her element, she's positively terrifying.

"I've been looking around for signs of her Falme, and I can't find it. Her fate is woven somewhere that even I can't see," Fal sighs. "It doesn't surprise me that she's so closely tied to Leyun, though. Has she forged a bond with her?"

Clarisse holds up her hand, quietly revealing the sun mark on her palm. Fal clicks her tongue. "You touched her, I see? Brave. Not exactly the kind of brave we need you to be, though. That won't gain the answers you seek; that will just get you killed. And now your death won't only hurt you… it will hurt Death, too. Why do you think he's been unable to return to his job?"

Death hates how the reality of Fal's words crash down on him. *I've found my soulmate. Of course she comes first! She's my everything.*

His soul aches at the very thought of losing her to Leyun. Everything about the Neylka's hunt for Clarisse has been personal from the moment she landed in Tyrladan. The guilt of leaving his soulmate in the evil clutches of the Church of Light is sure to eat him alive. Granted, he didn't know she was his mate until she died. *She must be a Tyrladanian I know… only Selben mate with Selben.*

Gripping her tighter, he wants now more than ever to carry her away someplace safe. *We can rule the crossing to the Afterlife together. She can be the Mrs. Grim Reaper I never thought I'd have.*

Across from them, Bast sits and stews. For the moment, Death doesn't care that she's upset. Right now, he's only interested in learning how to help Clarisse.

"Death, I don't know that I trust Fal," Kreyuhl calls. *"My magic is unsure of her."*

I appreciate the intel, friend. It's hard poison to swallow, calling the Aiyeliu friend, but he can't deny that the being has been quite an ally. *I appreciate you looking after Clarisse.*

"What about my husband?" Clarisse asks, picking at her cuticles. Death wants to stop her but refrains from smacking her hands apart. *I'll have to help her channel her nervous energy elsewhere.*

"Your husband?" Fal looks confused now.

Death holds out a hand in a feeble attempt to wave away the cloud of questions headed for her. "She was married when she was alive last, and she's worried that she still bears some connection to him. I've assured her this isn't the case with her new soul, or else it wouldn't be bound to me."

Fal nods, her eyes no longer clouded. Death breathes a silent sigh of relief. Accusations of infidelity are not what Clarisse needs. She's not capable of being so disloyal, anyway. He swats away any jealousy that tries to root itself within him. Their bond is enough for him. *I'm just happy to have her at all.*

Bast shuffles from where she sits. "Doesn't it bother you that she can speak with the Selyento? And… why is she able to wield such powerful magic? It wears her out, so I know she's not done… developing it yet… but I mean, have you seen what she's capable of?"

Hiding his urge to throttle the panther goddess is difficult. Death wants to clap a hand over Bast's mouth and insist she ask her questions later. *I don't want Clarisse on anyone's radar, for Siralto's sake!*

"That's a good question, Bast," Fal comments.

The sparkle in her eyes gives Death reason for pause. His own radar is going off—something about Fal isn't right, and he's not about to leave Clarisse in her clutches. "Fal, as much as I'm sure Clarisse would love to speak on this further, I think she needs to return to her abode and rest." Death scoops Clarisse up in his arms and motions for Kreyuhl to follow him.

Clarisse's eyes are wide, but she clutches him without a word.

"Oh, are you eager to take your Lafura home?" Fal wags her eyebrows and Death swears he must be the darkest shade of red fathomable.

"I'm sure he is," Clarisse teases, choking on her own comment before bursting into laughter.

Death almost drops her, mortified at the implications. Behind him, he hears Bast snickering and thinks of several things he'd like to say to her later. *I have a whole list of insults ready to go.*

Clarisse is laughing so hard her eyes are watering. *"Let it go, Death,"* she manages to think. Her own cheeks are bright pink when she buries her face in his cloak.

As much as he wants to argue, he's somehow grateful for the excuse, even if he has no intent of bedding Clarisse. Besides, they haven't known each other long enough. Death fancies himself a traditionalist in many ways. He's budged enough on his ethics and responsibilities; he's not about to throw away his morals when it comes to her.

"I would like to take my Lafura home," Death manages to respond, ignoring how hot his face is, or how hard it's become to breathe.

I am a being of ice, not fire. That's Terrence's job! he grumbles.

"I suppose we could table our conversations for later." Fal winks. "But I expect you all to keep in touch. I want to talk to Clarisse some more about her newfound powers. It's not every day I get to meet someone with the same uncanny abilities I possess. Speaking to the Selyento is no small feat. As for Terrence... he is to be left alone. He will be allowed to create havoc in whichever ways he deems best when dealing with the Monroes and Father Simmons. We'll re-evaluate his situation and actions later if they persist past these specific individuals."

Death takes a breath, relief overwhelming him now that he knows Terrence won't be erased. *He was my friend once.*

Bast begins to weep, her joy no longer containable. "Can I go see him? Would that be considered interference?"

Fal shakes her head. "As long as you are not impeding his path, you are fine to go see him. You may go to him now, if you wish."

Bast casts a look at Death before sprinting off. Death doubts that it will be more than a few minutes before she's back on Earth with Terrence. He knows it's been hard for her to be separated from him for so long. He can think of a few choice taunts he could make at her about having a Lafura, but he'll have to save those for when she returns.

He looks at Fal. "Thank you. I will let you know when we're ... uhm... less occupied." He whips around, ignoring the chuckling that echoes behind him. He clutches Clarisse to his chest, doing his best to drown out the sound of her heart beating.

Clarisse blinks, then speaks through their bond. *"I don't trust her, Death. Something seems off. The Selyento was trying to tell me something else, but it got cut off by a burst of magic. It didn't seem like very friendly magic, either. It was something about Fal, though."*

Death clicks his tongue, but he doesn't respond right away. He tries to think of any reason why Fal would be acting malevolent. Fate has always had strange inclinations about how things should work; he assumes it has something to do with her rigid, peculiar beliefs. *But if the Selyento was trying to warn her...*

He decides to return to this thought another day. For now, he focuses on getting Clarisse home. Now that Terrence has been saved, they need to refocus on their quest to learn about Clarisse's past. Their time is ticking by.

We must figure out who you were, Clarisse. Who you are now depends on it. We need to kick things up a notch.

Nodding, Clarisse nestles into his chest before dozing off, her body spent. As far as he's concerned, deadline or not, she can sleep there as long as she likes.

PARTNERS IN CRIME

Terrence

He opens his eyes, unsure how long he's been asleep in the balcony. Once again, he's let his guard down. He's grateful it hasn't come to bite him in the ass... *yet.*

With a jaw-popping yawn, he stretches his tired muscles. It takes him a few moments to figure out what time of day it is. The sun is high, which means he's been out cold for at least a day. The previous days seem to run together. He half wonders if he was dreaming about his foray to the Monroe house, but Deborah's bloodcurdling screams tear through his memories, dissipating any doubts. *I killed her.* Wincing, he remembers being convinced that it was best to murder them, but he can't remember *who* or *what* convinced him. All he remembers is a bright light and a crystal acorn, which he checks to find still firmly tucked within his shadows.

He hopes he isn't murmuring aloud, but when no one comes rushing out, he gives a relieved sigh. Terrence strains his ears and hears Father Simmons busy clicking away at his computer inside his office. He feels a small wave of relief and turns his attention to the rest of his plans.

I know what the acorn is for... but what do I do about Arthur? The

Monroes, he figures, aren't the intended target for his Tyrladanian weapon. Father Simmons is a trickster; this seed from the Selyento, which he remembers mimics that of a pin oak, is meant for a soul that's harder to catch. Father Simmons has, in some ways, a divine heritage. *He must never know this.*

Grumbling, he sees, once again, his dear Bast entering the church. This time, the door doesn't squeak and her pace is more targeted, therefore, less likely to disrupt Father Simmons from his work-induced stupor.

Her eyes lock on his and she jerks her head to the side, motioning for him to follow. He feels a sense of deja vu overwhelm him as he creeps down from the balcony a second time to greet her. They stay quiet as they creep out of the church and head back to the tree line. He braces himself and waits for her to berate him for killing Deborah. *Why do I even trust that she won't turn me in to Death?*

He knows deep down it doesn't matter anyway—he'd forgive her. She's one of the few for whom he'd overlook such a transgression. Her and Clarisse.

When they're out of earshot, Bast faces him. "I'd like to help you, Terrence."

Of all the things he expected her to say, this isn't it. His jaw drops and she rolls her eyes. The glimmer of mischief doesn't dampen, though.

"Listen, the Selyento has condoned your actions, stating you are not to be disturbed in your process of seeking justice. I must say, I'm impressed you managed to kill Deborah with nothing more than fear." She chuckles, her grin ferocious. When she licks her lips, Terrence knows just how much she envies him. Bast wishes she could sink her teeth into the flesh of a child abuser.

Maybe I should let her have Arthur… He chews on the thought.

"Hello? Earth to Terrence? Did you malfunction, or do you need me to repeat what I just said?"

Terrence chortles, the sound a little too merry given the nature of their conversation, but he doesn't care. "I know, Bast. I don't know how I knew, but I remember seeing a bright light, and then I was given a divine weapon." He produces the acorn from his shadows and places it on the ground between them. "Father Simmons is a trickster. His specialty is manipulation, so I was given this tool to make reaping his soul a bit easier." Terrence gives a sinister grin. "It won't be so hard to capture him now."

He can't quite swallow the smug smile that wins out, staining his face with cruel satisfaction. He's nearly delirious with the thought of what it will be like to see Father Simmons writhing—screaming—as this weapon does its job. *I can picture it now.*

"Terrence, who gave this to you?" Bast tilts her head, though she doesn't dare touch the acorn herself.

The energy emanating from it is toxic. Terrence isn't sure how he's managed to stomach it, but he knows it's not meant for him. He blinks, realizing how jumbled his memory is. In ordinary circumstances, he'd panic, but he's never felt so sure of anything in his life. "I'm not sure, but whomever it was, they wanted justice for Clarisse as badly as I do."

Bast's smile drops and her eyes cloud with concern. "Don't you remember who gave it to you?" She inches away from it, her instincts overriding her curiosity and her fur standing on end. Her eyes dart from side to side as though she expects someone to come popping out of Tyrladan, ready to swallow them whole.

"I think they wiped my memory," Terrence confesses. "I do think it's a bit odd, especially since the Selyento already approved these actions I'm taking."

Frowning, Bast takes a step toward the acorn and sniffs the air around it before batting it with her paw.

"Be careful," Terrence warns. "I know it's set to trap Father Simmons, but I don't want there to be a chance of it going off on you. If you're going to help me, I need you in one piece."

Bast perks up. "You mean you'll let me come along? I was wondering if you would." She laughs, though it's shaky. Her eyes never fully leave the acorn between them.

She knows something I don't.

Terrence narrows his eyes. "What? Do you think I've missed something important?"

Bast shakes her head. "I mean, you have, but you haven't. Someone altered your memories and delivered something *vile* to you to kill Father Simmons. We know the Selyento has approved these actions, but this just... it feels iffy, Terrence. I'm not worried for you, but I'm concerned about what it means that the Afterlife is conspiring to bring justice to the universe for Clarisse. I mean, who would...?" Bast's question drops off, but her face remains contemplative.

Terrence has always made fun of her for cutting off mid-sentence, as she tends to get lost in her thoughts and forget that she's supposed to keep speaking. Now doesn't seem like the right time to tease her, though, so he decides to table that opportunity for later.

"Terrence, if you don't mind, while I'm with you... could I hold onto this? I want to see if I can get any clues about its signature to figure out where it came from and who gave it to you."

Terrence dips his head. "I don't mind if you carry it, just please, be careful. Besides, I need your help... I know this is for Father Simmons, but I don't know the best course of action for Arthur. I don't want his death to be easy, but I can't draw attention from the mortals more than I already have. And something doesn't seem right. I know I'm supposed to take him, but the time doesn't feel right yet."

Bast giggles as she scoops up the acorn and makes it vanish, undoubtedly into some interdimensional pocket. *She's always been good at hiding things in places that don't exist...* Terrence stuffs away his envy, trying his best to not let it eat at him.

"I guess you never stopped being a Reaper. There's an order to things and, whether you like it or not, you do try to follow it to some degree. You're not haphazard—you never have been. Not really. Though you do tend to be a little more... creative... than the average Reaper." Bast winks.

Terrence slaps a furry paw to his chest. "Are you saying I'm messy?"

Pointing her nose in the air, Bast stalks away from him. "Some might use those words, but you're the one who said it."

Terrence bites his tongue, choosing instead to catch up to his friend. "So, should we take on Arthur or Simmons first?" He changes the subject, hoping to get closer to his goal now that he has Bast with him. *Maybe she's the reason I haven't felt ready to go through with it yet.*

Bast doesn't answer until they've traversed deep into the woods. He wonders if she even knows where she's going. *Shouldn't I be leading this front?*

She finally stops and turns to look at him. "I think Father Simmons should be the finale, don't you? Besides, I'll need some time to get used to this thing's magic before we take him down. Let's chart out a plan of action for how we want Arthur to go. How do we want to kill him?"

Terrence blinks. "I didn't think about that, to be honest. Deborah was more of an accident than a purposeful murder. She seemed… remorseful in her final moments. There are boxes everywhere full of Clarisse's things in her room, and she was weeping over photographs of her. She was afraid of him, too."

"Who, Deborah? Are you saying she was afraid of Arthur?"

"Yes." Terrence nods. "I was hoping to gather more intel on that to figure out where things went wrong and get an idea how far the abuse went, but now Deborah is gone and it's hard to say what's been going on. I searched everywhere in her room for journals, photos, anything that would clue me in. I'm embarrassed to admit, but I was almost at the point of granting her mercy if I could find anything to save her case. She just had to go looking through her stupid closet."

Bast chortles. "You were hiding in the closet?"

"I wore myself out hiding in the walls!" he blusters. "I was in the ceiling before my magic started to falter, so I slipped into the closet. Most people can't distinguish shadows, you know. But I suppose it really was her time. Jumping out at her probably didn't help, though, come to think of it."

Bast's laughing escalates to the point where she has to sit down and collect her breath. "What were you *thinking*? You stuffed yourself in the walls and then jumped out at her from the closet? I can't buy that it was an accident."

Tears stream down Bast's leonine face and Terrence finds himself joining in. "I was desperate!" But his chuckling defense is lost to more amusement.

"Oh sure, I can tell."

When they catch their breath, Bast gets lost in thought again.

"I was thinking…" she starts, "that perhaps we should go back to haunting him as you were before. We could make a real spectacle within the house. Torment him. Ruin him. Whatever hair he has left will dissipate." Bast's eyes glimmer in malicious glee.

Terrence stops. "How do you know his hair is thinning?"

Bast waves a paw at him and scoffs. "As if I wouldn't scope the place out first. It's like you don't even know me!"

Terrence is reminded why he fears Bast. *And love her for it. But she can't know that.*

She exchanges a knowing glance with him before starting to walk again.

"Bast? I take it you know the way to Arthur's house from here?"

"Of course I do," Bast calls over her shoulder. "Now come on. We need to get there and put our plans into action. We can alter the killing part as we see fit."

Terrence smiles.

UNCOVERING THE PAST

Clarisse

Opening her eyes, Clarisse relishes the feeling of being ensconced in her blankets. She tugs the soft covers up around her shoulders to trap in the warmth, dreading the bite of coldness that waits for her should she peel them back.

On the floor, Kreyuhl sleeps soundly. It takes her a moment to remember where she was before she woke. Then she remembers. *In Death's arms...*

A blush floods her cheeks as she recalls why she was being carried. The moonbeams outside tell her it's night again. She curses herself for sleeping so much.

I have to work on staying awake more. No one else needs sleep like me.

"True," Death whispers.

She bolts upright, realizing he's standing in the doorway, staring at her. His eyes sparkle, causing shivers to rocket down her spine.

"I trust you slept well?" He raises an eyebrow, which sends fluttering butterflies sweeping through her midsection. Stammering, it takes her a minute to think of how to answer. "What does it mean by soulmate?" She finally manages to utter the question to him, even though it comes out weird. "I mean… what did Fal mean by soulmate? Am I allowed to have a soulmate bond with you even though I was married before? And, like, how does that change things? And is Terrence really pardoned?"

As her rambling turns desperate, Kreyuhl wakes from his peaceful slumber. He turns his head to glare at Death, undoubtedly blaming him for the disruption.

Death doesn't answer for a few moments, his gaze lost in the moonlight that pours through the window. Clarisse fears he might drown in it before he ever answers.

"It means our souls are inextricably intertwined. I am doomed to fall in love with you, and you are doomed to fall in love with me. For whatever reason, we are matched. Siralto and Tryta were soulmates. I don't doubt that Terrence is Bast's Lafura. You were married before, but you can be married to someone who is not your Lafura, though as you can see, it didn't end well. The gods don't typically marry unless they're mated. Things get messy if they do… Although that's not to say you're to blame, either. Millennia of loneliness are not easy to bear."

He looks more pensive than ever, but the way he speaks of falling in love as though it's as mundane as picking up a loaf of bread at the grocery store concerns her.

"How… how can you be so calm about things?" Clarisse can barely ask the question, and tears start to form. "What if it's wrong again and you don't love me? What if… what if you end up hating me? What if my husband comes back and tries to hurt me?"

The worry about her former husband coming back has become an ever more persistent feeling in the back of her mind. Whatever her magic remembers of him, it's not good news. "And… what if he hurts you? Death, I can tell he was… dangerous."

At this, Death throws his head back. "You really think your *ex-husband* has any power over me? That's funny, Clarisse. He can try to rip you from my cold, erased hands, but he will fail. You are *mine*." He growls so loudly that Clarisse whimpers in fear. He's at her side at an instant, his eyes almost in flames. "Don't you *ever* be afraid of me," he hisses. "I will *not* harm you."

His lips collide with hers, but they leave her so quickly she questions whether it was a dream. She fears she'll freeze or melt under his gaze, so she looks down at her hands.

"I just worry," she admits. "I worry about you. About us. About doing the wrong thing. This is all so new, and now you're telling me I'm bound to you? Won't I get in the way of your work? You eventually have to return to reaping souls." She bites her lip.

"Yes, and you will come with me."

Clarisse is envious of the confidence in Death's voice.

I wish I could make plans in a snap like that.

Chuckling, Death grabs her hands and pats them between his. "You'll get the hang of it. I've been around a lot longer than you." He looks proud of himself for his last statement.

Clarisse rolls her eyes. "Yes, oh, wise one. Thank you for that. And what am I supposed to do when I'm with you?"

Grinning, he winks at her. "We can figure that out when we get there. I think your skills will come in most handy for helping me and my Reapers. Plus, being together may help you discover your own path. I don't think it's a coincidence that you and I contain stars and galaxies within us, don't you agree?"

It sounds like a wonderful plan, even if Clarisse finds her stars more confusing than anything else if she thinks about them too much. She loves them, but they chatter like the humming of bees unless she listens. But listening is hard.

Maybe that's the key. Maybe I'm not listening enough.

"*Listening to what?*" Death's eyebrows are furrowed as he waits patiently for her to answer, his fingers still running over hers.

"I think maybe I don't understand my stars well enough because I don't listen. Most of the time, all I hear is a low hum of barely-there music, but maybe the answer is that I'm not ready to listen to them. Or haven't been to this point, I mean. I think I'd like to try again. Kreyuhl, can you help steady me if I try that?"

Kreyuhl is on his feet and padding over to her as soon as she mentions his name. "*I think that is a wise idea,*" he hisses. "*You shouldn't try something like this alone. I don't think it will be accomplished right away, either. I suspect you'll be wiped out each time you try. I hope you like your bed.*"

Clarisse groans, but Death laughs.

"I think it's only fair that you get to rest in your Afterlife, Clarisse, since you weren't able to in life," he adds gently. "I'll stay by your side to keep you safe from Leyun, and I have a few ideas on how to prevent her from reaching you when you sleep. How do you feel about sleeping in the library?"

Her face scrunches up in mock horror. "Oh, no! I'll be surrounded by books while I sleep? In a cozy little nook in the wall? How terrible!"

"Alright, I'll put something together. For now, I want us to hold down the fort in there. No major magic unless it's within those walls."

"I will also see about erecting barriers around you," Kreyuhl adds. *"I think I know of special magic I can weave as your familiar. At the very least, if you are abducted, I will go with you. Your bond with Death will make it easier for him to find us. Two pieces of you gone will leave a trace. I'll just have to tie myself to him more permanently, but we can work that out."*

Death frowns. "You mean I'll be stuck with you forever, too?"

"Death, it's high time you accept me as part of your family. I know you want to, anyway, so stop denying yourself. I'm your Lafura's familiar. Is that not enough?"

"It's enough," Death grumbles.

"You don't have to be jealous of Kreyuhl, Death," Clarisse whispers. She leans in and kisses him on the nose. His eyes widen. *"He's* not my Lafura. *You* are. But he's an important part of my life."

Death takes a minute to wrap his head around the idea of being around Kreyuhl for the rest of his existence. Silence creeps up all around them, but it's not uncomfortable. Their lack of words doesn't seem awkward anymore.

Smiling, she reaches up to him. "I trust your judgment, Death." She leans in and wraps him in a hug. He molds his body into her embrace and she feels safer than she has in years. Then she remembers something from earlier. "Did you say you thought Bast and Terrence were soulmates?"

When she leans back to look at him, he smirks. "Yes, and they've been playing a game of denial longer than we have. Granted, she was banned from speaking to him for several decades…"

Clarisse gasps. "You banned them from seeing each other?"

Death shrugs. "He was exiled! What was I supposed to do? I didn't want her getting damned alongside him. But now, your act of mercy and the Selyento's decision to let him carry on have removed those barriers. I don't want either of them to be erased."

Clarisse pouts. "Ugh. You and the rules. Listen, I followed them, too, and look where that got me."

"Yes, and breaking them got you killed," Death blurts.

They both stare at each other for a beat, then Clarisse surprises them both when she laughs. "Yes, but then I found my way to you that much faster. So, yes, I died, but then I found out I wasn't meant for that world, anyway. Did I learn my lesson, or did I just learn that sometimes Fate has other plans?"

Death leans into her so that their foreheads touch. "What am I going to do with you? You must promise me not to be so reckless."

Clarisse giggles. "I promise nothing."

He tackles her, guessing correctly where to tickle her. "You will not put yourself in danger."

Clarisse squeals and tries her best to escape his grasp. "Let me go, you beast!"

But Death doesn't let up. After a few minutes, tears run down her cheeks from laughing and Death finally releases her. "There's more where *that* came from if you get yourself into any major shenanigans!" he warns with a grin.

Clarisse sticks her tongue out, but she's too wary of him attacking her again to offer a retort.

It's not like him to loosen up like this.

"No, it's not, you wretched thing. This is all your fault," he pouts.

"You're both weirdos," Kreyuhl interrupts.

Clarisse reaches out to pat her familiar on the muzzle. "Sorry for leaving you out, Kreyuhl. We'll tickle you next time," Clarisse promises.

"I should think not. You two are getting distracted from your duties. Do you want to know who you are or not?"

Clarisse nods. "Could we get some cookies first? And maybe some other snacks? I get hungry when I do magic."

Death doesn't seem surprised by her confession. "That's not uncommon," he confirms. "Magic, especially when you're new to it, can tax you significantly. I'll make sure we have ample fuel for you. You'll need it if you're going to try and petition your stars."

"Perfect!" Clarisse chirps.

*D*eath enters the library with a plate of warm cookies. Clarisse has stuffed her arms with chips, a large bottle of juice, two bottles of water—*since someone insisted*—and a box of cereal. *Only the sugary stuff will do.* She laughs as she remembers Terrence's insistence that milk would ruin the experience.

"That moron didn't want milk with his cereal?" Death looks incredulous.

Her eyes widen in surprise. "Don't tell me *you* like cereal?"

Death takes the box from her. "Of course I do. Did you bring milk?"

Clarisse looks down, realizing she forgot it. "Oops."

With a wave of his hand, a gallon of milk appears, along with two bowls and two spoons.

"I guess I forgot that, too," Clarisse admits sheepishly.

He pours them both some, then hands her the bigger bowl. "You need more energy than I do. You're about to engage in some serious magic." He winks as he takes a large scoop of cereal in his mouth. He chews on it with so much grace, she's almost disgusted.

"You'll eat cereal, yet you wouldn't drink coffee when I offered to make it."

Death grins over a spoonful. "Hotel coffee is gross, and you were nervous. I wasn't going to impose on you like that. Now eat." He points at her bowl to indicate there will be no further discussion until she gives in.

"Oh, I didn't know it was gross," Clarisse mumbles. "What kind of coffee do you like?"

Death pauses in the middle of another spoonful. "I suppose I prefer dark roasts."

"And let me guess – you prefer your coffee black, with nothing added." Clarisse laughs. "So it matches your soul?"

Death winks. "Right you are. Why aren't you eating your cereal?"

With a groan, Clarisse begins to eat, appeasing his wishes. She polishes it off in no time and moves on to the snacks. She doesn't remember being this hungry in a long time. Shoveling a handful of chips into her mouth, she freezes when she realizes Death is staring at her, only halfway through his cereal.

"I suppose this has all been very taxing on you?" He raises an eyebrow. She knows he's teasing, but she self-consciously slides the bag of chips away and clears her throat. "I'll wait for you to finish your bowl before we start. In the meantime, could you hand me a cookie?"

The sugary smell is intoxicating, and she wants at least one bite before descending into the tragedy of her past again. *Why suffer without cookies? That would just be suffering twice.*

Death snorts and passes her the plate of chocolate chip cookies. By the time he finishes his cereal, she's blown through her third cookie. Her stomach gurgles, signaling it's time to stop. She rubs her belly.

"I… may have overindulged just a bit."

"You think? Well, let's hope this doesn't impede your abilities to summon your stars."

Hesitation builds in her gut. *I don't think that's the cookies. I think that's nerves.*

Sighing, Death reaches out and clasps her hands gently in his. "We're going to try a new approach, okay? The last few times, I haven't given you much direction for how to look for your stars. You're a natural, which I'm afraid I've taken advantage of. In order to better understand them, I'm going to tell you the way I understand my own powers. My stars are more like maps or blueprints than living beings, but it's a start, so don't expect this to go perfectly, okay?"

Frowning, Clarisse drinks a glass of fizzy soda—a brand she was never allowed on Earth—before setting her mind to work.

"Okay, Clarisse, I want you to ease into it. What I want you to do is envision yourself descending within your magic. Whatever you feel most strongly, I want you to focus on that. Close your eyes, take a deep breath, and descend. You'll know the feeling when it starts—that part will take over, given your natural inclinations. Pull on myself or Kreyuhl for help. Do not overtax yourself," Death commands.

Kreyuhl grumbles behind her, assenting with Death.

You two will be the end of me, I swear.

Rubbing her hands together, she begins to focus, setting aside her irritation for later inspection. But focusing proves difficult. She envisions the pain in her stomach as a twisting vine; grabbing hold of it, she lowers her consciousness deep into her soul. With her eyes closed, bright lights shimmer in the distance. Wherever she's headed, her stars are already there.

"Where are you now?" Death calls.

I don't know the name for this place. Clarisse feels her connection falter.

"Never mind, ignore me. It's alright. Just keep focusing."

Clarisse's eyes fly open, and her breath comes in panicked gasps. "I can't, Death. I can't do it! It's dark. I don't know where I am!"

He scoots closer and pulls her into his lap. Tilting her chin, he forces her to look up at him. "You are in this room, safe with me and Kreyuhl looking after you. Anything that dares to try and come in here to mess with you is a fool. Now, I want you to close your eyes again and feel where your power is. You'll know what to do. I can't explain it any better than that, except to say you'll know it when you sense it. Magic is a unique experience to each user. Use my words as a guide, not the law."

Clarisse nudges her head free of his grasp and nestles against his chest. The sound of his breathing calms her.

"Just try again," Death whispers.

Closing her eyes, Clarisse expands her senses to feel for the threads of her pain again. It settles against her, wrapping around and pulling her under, deep into the shallows of whatever ocean hides beneath her skin. Somewhere in her soul, she feels her stars crying out to her.

Swimming to them, she kicks her legs and pulls against the currents, desperate to stay afloat. *Is it possible to drown inside yourself?*

Her nostrils flare when she pulls in deep breaths of air that propel her forward as she descends deeper into the murky depths. Her stars are closer now, their humming and singing calling out to her.

She finds Death's star first, because its hue is more subdued than the others. It whispers to her and beckons her to come closer. Her curiosity drowns out the warning that threatens to dispel the allure, the inhibition she once held slipping away with every floating step towards it.

Somewhere, she hears Death's voice echo. Nearing his star, she reaches out to touch it, her mind alight with a buzzing song that intoxicates her. When her fingers grab it, a jolt of power courses through her. The other stars rush at her from all directions, drowning her in glittering light.

All at once, she comes crashing down. Her eyes fly open.

Everywhere is gray.

REFLECTIONS

Clarisse

"**D**eath?" she calls. Her voice echoes in the cavernous chamber, but nothing answers. Shivering, she tries to ignore the chill that settles over a grand expanse of nothing. Straining, she tries to listen for him. She knows he must be nearby. *I can't be taken from the room,* she tries to convince herself, but her conviction is feeble.

Clearly I've been taken anyway, … but how?

Swallowing, she braces herself as reality crashes down. This place is familiar. She knows she's submerged within the Neylka. The ebb and flow of nothingness crawls up and down her shoulders, threatening to swallow her whole and spit her back out again.

"I know you're here, Leyun," Clarisse says aloud, her voice cracking on the unicorn's name. Over her shoulder, she notices the flickering light of Death's single star. It's blue, pulsing in the gray and shedding color in its wake, a defiant rebellion. "Why are you sad?" she asks the star.

Perplexed, Clarisse reaches out to the star, setting aside her feelings of trepidation in favor of making sure the celestial being is soothed. It needs reassurance just as much as she does.

It settles into her palms, and the cold fire almost passes through her skin. Stars are strange beings, nothing like their sisterly bodies in the sky. Rather than flaming gases, these stars are encased in fiery magic—but this star doesn't burn her. It freezes her skin, leaving small crystalline snowflakes creeping up and along wherever it touches. A testament to its owner.

This inspires her. From within, she pulls one of her own stars, wondering if their actions are a clue to who she was.

Death's star hums, its eagerness apparent in the way it shakes and dances around her. Giggling, she peers at her star. It's a lighter blue, betraying her fear. She knows she's being watched, but she won't give Leyun the satisfaction of a larger reaction. *She's just another goddess. I'm powerful like she is.*

She reels her star in closer. Warm to the touch, it's less transparent than Death's and appears more like a shimmering gem than a ball of fire, though it still laps at her skin like a flame.

It looks like the ocean and fire had a baby... The star glimmers a bit brighter at this thought. It shoots up, hovering close to her face before turning a happy shade of bright yellow.

She gasps. "Are you guys color coded to my emotions? Like Death's stars are to him?"

Death's star, though still blue, sidles closer to her yellow one before they both start to dance around. Mesmerized, Clarisse forgets her mission for a moment and watches them with building fascination.

"Comfortable?"

Clarisse jumps at the voice, but she doesn't turn around right away. Leyun's breath washes down her spine, sending shivers ricocheting down it. Clasping her hands together, Clarisse turns carefully. "I am, thank you," she answers smugly. "Death loaned me a star and it's getting comfortable with mine."

Facing the unicorn in person is no easier than it was in her dream or the last time she was snatched up into the Neylka, but she does her best to be brave.

"Why do you show up every time I do magic?" Clarisse inclines her head. "How did you manage to break into *my* sacred room?"

The unicorn's nostrils flare, and its bright, silver eyes alight with mischief. *"Bold words from one who shares more with me than she thinks.*

Not to mention, I saved your friend, Terrence." Stomping her hoof, Leyun allows herself a wide, toothy yawn.

Clarisse is surprised by the unicorn's claim. *"You saved Terrence? How so?"*

"He's about to engage in battle with a trickster who came to Earth. The Selyento agreed it was time for that trickster to be subdued, along with your parents for harming you. It's high treason to harm a goddess of your standing."

Blinking, Clarisse chews on this answer. "Why is it not high treason to harm any child? Why is it only considered treason if the soul belongs to a goddess?"

Leyun laughs, a breathy sound, almost like a hiss in the wind. It reminds Clarisse of Kreyuhl.

"You forget, I am a type of Aiyeliu, just as Kreyuhl is," the unicorn answers her unspoken thought. *"As such, we should sound the same. Your thoughts are not sacred from me. And yes, I did save Terrence. I petitioned the Selyento and received permission to sanction Terrence's violence against the Monroes and Father Simmons. I delivered him a weapon that will kill John Simmons, as he cannot be slain by traditional mortal weapons. He is a minor god, though I doubt he knows it."*

The thought of Father Simmons being more than human sends nausea curling into Clarisse's stomach. "Why... would you help him?"

"Why wouldn't I?" Leyun purrs. She brings her muzzle within an inch of Clarisse's face, her hot breath almost burning her skin.

Clarisse recoils from the heat. *Do you have a built-in furnace?*

"Maybe. It does burn to be stuck like this for so long."

As much as Clarisse would like to laugh at Leyun's play on words, the unicorn's sharp teeth keep her mind far from humor. Sweat breaks out along her forehead, but she doesn't yield to the creature's closeness. Emboldened by the magic swirling in her veins, she stands straighter and forces herself to look Leyun in the eye.

"I still don't know what you mean. Why would you help Terrence? He's my friend, but don't you want me to be erased?"

"Do I? You all assume so..." The unicorn's crafty gaze shifts. *"Tell Death I said hello. Maybe you'll figure out my motives, and maybe you won't. But time is running out sooner than you realize. Soon, he will know."* Leyun

makes an abrupt turn, flicking her tail so the very tip of it brushes Clarisse's chin as she trots away.

"What do you mean? Who's *he*?"

Peering behind her, Leyun stretches her lips, revealing sharp, angled teeth. *"Your husband."*

---

*C*larisse gasps. Her chest heaves, desperate for breath as Death holds her in his lap. His grip is so strong she fears he might crush her in his arms. Weeping, Clarisse loses any strength she has left. She buries her face against his chest and grips him for dear life.

"I thought," she begins to blubber, "you said she couldn't get me here!"

"Clarisse, you never left the room," Death whispers back. "You weren't in the Neylka this time."

Her body shakes, and her shoulders almost collapse under the weight of her fears. She still feels Leyun's presence—her breath washing down her spine and over her face—and she wants to disappear into the walls of her library. Instead, she curls closer into Death's solid embrace. His fingers weave into her hair and he runs them through, almost desperate in the way they grasp onto her blond strands.

Her stomach howls for food and her exhausted body aches. She pulls away to check for any remaining snacks and munches on everything in sight. Even after no cookie or chip remains, she's still not sated.

"Clarisse." Death grips her shoulders and shakes her out of her mindless binge-eating. "You need to stop and take a breath. What happened? You zoned out and started talking to Leyun, but she was never here. You didn't disappear. How were you in the Neylka?"

Clarisse chooses to ignore the obvious panic in his voice for now. If she focuses on that too much, she'll join him and hurtle off the cliff of insanity not long after.

Maybe fading away wouldn't be all that bad. Nothing makes sense. I'm lost. I don't know who I am. My magic won't tell me anything. I...

Death crushes her in his embrace before she can continue to spiral.

Her thoughts are darker than they've ever been. She wonders if she'll ever see light again.

"You will go nowhere," Death whispers. "I don't care if you never remember who you were. You belong back and alive. You deserve to exist, no matter how broken you may feel."

Closing her eyes, Clarisse ignores the humming that kicks up in her veins, her power desperate to escape.

"What happened, Clarisse? You must tell me."

She pulls away just enough so that her words won't be muffled. "She found me, Death. Leyun told me she was the one who saved Terrence, and then she claimed she doesn't want me to be erased. Then she warned that I need to figure out who I am before *he* finds out." Clarisse could feel her thin grasp on sanity start to unravel. The path before her seemed insurmountable. "My *husband* is going to find out, Death. That means he's alive somewhere and he's going to be a problem. I don't want to disappear again. I don't want to be with him. I—"

Death gently presses a finger to her lips to halt her downward spiral. "Let's start with the first part. Are you sure you actually talked to Leyun and it wasn't some strange memory resurfacing? You left to tinker with your powers and found Leyun, even though you never actually left this place. You weren't in the Neylka, though I suppose the bright white I kept seeing in your mind was some rendition of it from the first time, yes?"

Clarisse's lip wobbles but she manages to nod. Just the thought of that blank expanse of nothingness makes her want to vomit. *On second thought, I don't know that I want to go back to being nonexistent… not like that.*

"*And you won't,*" Kreyuhl hisses. Though still in the doorway, her familiar looks ready to pounce, his teeth eager to sink into any man, beast, or goddess who would dare to drag her to such an end.

I love and appreciate you both.

Kreyuhl hums, but says nothing. Clarisse can sense through their bond that he's irritated, though she's not sure why. *Maybe it has something to do with being "gone" where he couldn't reach me?*

"*That's about the sum of it,*" Kreyuhl answers before returning to stony silence.

The nausea from messing with her magic is fast returning. Leaning forward, she tries to put her head between her knees in the hopes that her innards won't end up spilled all over the library carpet. She would hate to stain the pristine cream fibers.

Death gently traces his hand up and down her back in comforting circles. In a few minutes, she feels strong enough to ask her next question. She appreciates that he has the curtains pulled, as she's almost certain it's daytime. Since joining the Afterlife, she loses track of the days and nights with stunning regularity.

"So, you're saying you think what I just experienced is a memory of Leyun from my past life?" Her question sounds more choked than she would've liked, but she knows Death doesn't mind.

"I think you are. She must be central to your memories in some way."

Her vision blurring from brimming tears, Clarisse slides off his lap and slumps to the floor. "Death, this is too much for me to handle right now. I feel like I'm going insane! You're telling me I didn't actually see Leyun? Then why the message about Terrence?"

Death's face twists up in confusion, which unsettles her. She's not used to seeing him perplexed by something. *You're supposed to know everything.*

Chuckling, Death shakes his head. "I'm afraid not, love. That's not how this works. I'm not omniscient, though I'm flattered you think so. What else happened, Clarisse?"

Closing her eyes, Clarisse ignores the humming that kicks up in her veins, her power still desperate to escape. When her knees buckle as she tries to stand, Death hoists her up by her armpits and steadies her. Hobbling to the window, she throws open the curtains and nearly shrieks as the brilliant light from the three suns almost blinds her. Squinting, she puts a hand in front of her face and seems to assess the world around her for the first time. Panic crashes around her in waves. Every other second is another battle to rein in her emotions. She wonders if she'll ever capture them or if they'll run away with her into some distant realm.

Not unlike how I ended up being swept away into the Afterlife at the tender age of eighteen. I don't even feel like the same person anymore.

Her voice is hushed. "I really am dead, aren't I? This isn't a dream…"

Death rubs her shoulders. "I'm afraid so. And besides that, you're the center of a mystery of mythological proportions, and have had more information chucked at you than anyone could ever ask. Your shadow friend is on the hunt for your murderers, and you're wrestling with a goddess who claims she doesn't want you erased from existence as you know it, but is known to operate on those orders. And you may or may not have an enemy with Fate herself. Any questions so far?" His eyes twinkle, but there's a darkness in Death's voice that gives Clarisse pause.

"I really am screwed, aren't I?"

Resting his chin on her head, Death sighs. "No. You're not alone, and it's okay to be overwhelmed. But you need to let me help you unpack what happened. Your magic is trying to tell you something if it's creating images of Leyun. Did Leyun ask for Terrence to be pardoned, or did you? Is that version of Leyun some version of yourself, and that's how your magic is helping you cope?"

A weight settles in Clarisse's stomach. "Why would my magic use her to tell me these things?"

"Why do you think? Try to grab that memory, Clarisse. Grab it and don't let go. What is your magic trying to help you piece together? You haven't told me everything. Help me help you."

Clarisse notices for the first time the garden that sprawls out behind her house. Relief washes through her when she doesn't see any roses. Her eyes settle on a little purple bird with black tinging the end of its feathers. She chooses to focus on it, relaxing as it sits and preens on a fountain carved in the shape of… *a unicorn.*

"I think she's part of my past. She says she doesn't want me erased, and maybe that's true. Maybe I knew her in my past life as a friend and not an enemy." She turns to face Death. "How old is Leyun?"

Death clicks his tongue. "She's several thousands of years old, Clarisse. She's been a broken soul for a long time."

Her heart thuds. "I think I knew her a long time ago, but I'm not ready to think I might be *that* old, either. I'm also going to set aside my question about how old you are again, because something tells me I'll be horrified to find out."

Out the window, the bird chirps and hops from branch to branch across various bushes that dot the winding flowerbeds, fluorescent flowers swaying under its delicate weight as though touched by a breeze and not a living being.

"How does the memory of magic work? If it's part of me, how does it know so much and I know so little?"

Death releases her shoulders and joins her where she stares out the window. "That's a lovely bird. Not sure I've seen one of those, or else I'd tell you its species."

She turns to him with a raised brow. "Don't you know everything that lives here?"

Chuckling, Death shakes his head. "No, love, I primarily work on Earth. I must say, it's nice to stop and enjoy Tyrladan properly, rather than popping in and out with various souls to return to its keeping."

Grumbling, Clarisse tries to hide her irritation that he's ignoring her question.

He casts her a side eye, a grin tugging at his lips. "Listen," he begins, "magic is personal. For us, it's tied to emotions. So, for you to understand your magic, you have to grapple with them. And as for why? Magic is a living being, much like that bird out there." He points a finger at it with a gentleness that softens Clarisse's resolve.

Something about the way Death moves is calming. She tries not to consider why that might be the case. "But how does my magic remember who I am and I don't?"

Shrugging, Death leans in so that their noses almost touch. "Magic is the only thing that neither lives nor dies—much like me. It just *is*. It is the fabric upon which life and death are balanced. It is the thing that runs in all our veins and keeps us moving, some more than others. What makes you a goddess is that you are not simply *filled* with magic, but *made* of it. You were not born the same way that others were. When you shed your mortal shell, you were set free. You returned to a state of magic to which your mortal memories have not yet caught up. Your magic will always know you because that's all it's ever been—*you*. The more time you spend with it, the more you will understand."

Heat floods Clarisse's cheeks as he plants a soft kiss on the tip of her nose. She slumps into his arms. "I don't feel like I'm full of magic," she mumbles, her voice muffled in his cloak. "I feel strangely detached from life. I don't fit. And Leyun has me worried... What did she mean? Aren't I bound to you? My ex-husband can't take me, can he?"

Death hugs her tighter. "No. Our bond is not severable, but the bond you shared with him was. However, there is one thing I've been hesitant to acknowledge. I have neither lived nor died, and I operate in such a way that I have the power to use the Neylka."

His confession sinks deep into her and she gasps. "So you could shove me there?"

"Yes," he whispers. "But I would know how to put you back together if I did. I would know where the pieces were."

Tears burn Clarisse's eyes. She knows he's not responsible for her current predicament, but she sorely wishes he could fix her now. If he could just grab hold of her soul and glue the pieces together...

"Would you be able to pull on my memories?"

Death buries his face in her hair. "No, love. They're uniquely yours. And they're not dead or dying. They're just... asleep. And you must be the one to wake them. If I could, I would gladly awaken them for you. I can help by lending you power, but yours is a unique situation."

His voice hovers like orchestral thunder when he whispers. Clarisse is almost lulled into sleep—almost. Blinking, she pulls away to look at him. His golden eyes are misty, but she doesn't dare point that out to him.

"You swear Leyun wasn't here? She can't get me as long as I stay here in the library?"

Death chuckles. "I'd like to see her try. That star I gave you is twofold... it's also a tracker." His cheeks redden and he rubs the back of his neck.

"It's a what?"

"The magic takes a bit to take effect, but if anything were to happen to you, I would be able to find you in an instant. It alerts me when you're in pain or when you're afraid, and since it is a part of me, I'm tied to it."

For some reason, Clarisse finds this comforting. Knowing that Death can find her no matter what happens gives her peace of mind. *They won't take me without a fight and without someone knowing, at least. How come I can't do that to you?*

Death stares at her a moment, deep in thought. "You actually can, I believe."

"Do I just give you a star like you did for me?"

Nodding, Death holds out his hands. "Give me one and you'll see what I'm talking about. While we continue to explore this path for you, it will reassure you knowing you can find me like I can find you."

"So… how do I give you a star? Like… how does it know to stay with you?"

Shrugging, Death grabs her palms. "You'll have to work with your magic to find out how. There are general theories but, on the whole, you and I are different. Everything will operate in a way that coincides with how you feel. And your magic… it's truly *alive*." Winking, Death smirks. "You're a natural, Clarisse. Don't overthink it. Just *do* it. You built an entire house, for Siralto's sake. Terrence may have amplified you, but you were stuck in mortal form at the time. Giving me a star should be a breeze."

Huffing, Clarisse closes her eyes and tries to think of her stars. *Treat it just like when you built the house. Just feel it.* Part of her would like to smack Death for having such blind trust in her abilities, but she knows that won't solve anything.

"Glad to know you aren't resorting to violence because of logic, not because of any feelings you harbor for me."

Clarisse opens her eyes to glare at him and finds him struggling to hold in laughter. She almost laughs, too, but she's too focused to let herself get lost in the mirth. *Maybe once I've accomplished something.*

Death opens his mouth to say something, but she's already back to focusing on reaching her stars. She thinks of the one that danced with his and wonders if it might make the best candidate. With little effort, she manages to produce it. It hums and bounces about; Death's star emerges to dance with it.

She feels something odd—sadness. She wonders if they don't want to be separated. The two of them seem happy together. Clarisse wants to cry at the thought of severing their bond, so she searches for another willing star—one that might want to join his. A volunteer surfaces, although it's much more sluggish than her other stars. Upon seeing Death, it brightens some, its light spilling farther out than when she first retrieved it.

"Are they... capable of individual emotions?" Death's eyes are locked on it, his bewilderment apparent in his dropped jaw, which he quickly snaps shut.

"I think so," Clarisse answers. "They're still tied to me, but they are very much... independent. I think this star is in love with yours." She giggles at the thought of two stars in love. It's both beautiful and endearing.

Death brings his hands out to grasp the star that has taken a liking to him. When it settles into his palms, Clarisse feels something click and knows, somehow, that it's tied to him. *I think I can find you now.*

The star hums from within his palms, pleased with its choice in a new master, then it winks out and disappears inside his chest. Death stares down at his torso in silence for a few minutes while Clarisse busies herself staring at their remaining two stars, which are still dancing about the room.

The stars settle onto a shelf and hover over a cluster of books. Her curiosity piqued, Clarisse wanders over to them, noting the strange names that line the very top one: BarulatyeNaSelben.

Death joins her at the bookcase, and his eyes widen at the sight of the title. "Clarisse... I didn't put that book here."

Her hands hover over the tome, almost afraid to slide it from its spot nestled safely between other books that don't feel quite as sinister. "What does 'na' mean in Mansalo?"

"Dead... or death. Not 'Death' as in me, but the idea of being dead or experiencing death."

"So... this is a book about dead gods?"

Death nods, then holds out his hand to stop her from touching it. "I've never seen this title. I have no idea who's penned it and *I* am Death. Surely this is a prank—some form of mockery that Bast left behind."

Shaking her head, Clarisse looks up at him. "Your star and mine led me here. I think I'm supposed to open this. I think it's a legitimate source."

With a groan, Death looks at her, desperate to see any signs of hesitation. The creeping dread in her gut, though almost unbearable, isn't enough to stop her from taking a closer look.

"Let me hold it," he offers. "You're weakened from your latest magical dealings. I can withstand a blow if something is wrong. You cannot."

"What? It's not like I can die again," Clarisse teases. "Only someone like *you* can kill me."

"And I never would," Death vows solemnly. "I would never purposefully harm a hair on your head. But there are things worse than me, and I don't want you to bear something so terrible. So, step back so I can grab this, okay?"

The finality of his tone annoys Clarisse. She hates feeling fragile, even now, after being dead.

"When will I be able to stand on my own? When will I not need help anymore?"

Even as she asks the question, she finds that her eyes are bleary and, unfortunately, she yawns.

"When you stop needing to sleep every time you use magic. It will get better, I promise. You didn't even pass out this time!" Death gives her a thumbs up and she's certain she might scream at him for doing so, but he's already ignoring her and pulling the tome from the shelf.

It's covered in dust, giving the illusion that it's been housed there forever. But she knows better. Death would remember a book like this, let alone placing it in *her* library.

"I think I ought to read through this before letting you touch it. It's magical, but so far, I'm not experiencing any adverse effects. Why don't we get some more things in here to make you comfortable? Some blankets and such? I think I'd prefer if you slept in here. Even if Leyun's appearance was an illusion, as I believe, the fact that she failed to remove you from the room in a physical manner means it's best to stay in here while we continue to investigate your magic."

Clarisse is giddy at the thought of sleeping in the library. She looks at Kreyuhl, who scampers from the room before returning with more pillows and blankets to line the floor. After tucking pillows beneath the window on the wall, Kreyuhl, who looks just as exhausted as Clarisse, curls against the furthest pillow and drifts off to sleep.

"I think I've drained my familiar."

Death smirks. "I believe he's finally out of magic to lend you for now. He'll have to recharge just as you do."

In his sleep, Kreyuhl hisses. Clarisse envies his ability to drift away so quickly. Settling in next to him, she runs her fingers along his head. His eyes almost drift open at the touch, but he keeps snoring. Smiling, Clarisse gazes up at Death, inviting him to join them under the blankets.

He hesitates. Clarisse wonders if he feels awkward about joining her. *Does he even sleep? I feel like I should know this.*

"Not often," he answers in her head. *"I can, though. Sometimes it is enjoyable to recharge. But I don't have to do it often."*

When will I reach that point?

"Soon. You're already awake much longer than normal. I just suggested we gather blankets so we can be more comfortable."

Clarisse has noticed she's not as drained as she used to feel. She wonders if the exhaustion was transferred to Kreyuhl, who is now drooling all over the floor. Laughing, she does her best to stay quiet and not disturb him. She's grateful to him for staying by her, even if the idea of having a familiar is still strange and concerning. Being tied to Kreyuhl for eternity isn't something she ever thought she'd have to consider.

"And yet you're not concerned about being bound to me?"

Turning to face him, Clarisse smiles at Death. "No. You just seem to fit. Now read me this dumb book."

"I hardly think it's dumb. It may carry bad omens, but it is not dumb. You should be careful of the things you say regarding magical items. Magic has a mind of its own."

Clarisse groans and motions for him to open the book. He rolls his golden eyes, but his smirk is playful as he lets it fall open in his lap. Leaning over his shoulder, Clarisse tries not to breathe too much and make things uncomfortable.

"You aren't going to make me uncomfortable, Clarisse, though you could always sit next to me so we can hold it in both of our laps."

Shrugging, Clarisse puts the left side of the book's pages on her knee, so it sits propped up for them to peruse.

The pages are full of colorful images of Selben. Clarisse tries to decipher a few of the words, but it looks like gibberish to her. She looks at Death, hoping he'll stop and read things to her. He mutters under his breath, but lost in his own thoughts, he fails to say anything aloud.

Rather than pester him, she decides to try some more magic. She feels inspired, knowing that she's not too tired to stay awake for once. *Maybe I have a chance of being powerful… of not being needy. I'd like to be able to stand on my own and perform spells without draining myself.* Guilt twinges at her as she glances back at Kreyuhl, who slumbers soundly. His strange paws twitch in his sleep, not unlike a dog who dreams of chasing bunnies.

Turning back to the book, she sees that Death is still inadvertently ignoring her. Snapping her fingers, she summons her stars. This grabs his attention, but she doesn't care to stop. She whispers to them and hears them whisper back, just as they did on Earth.

"Help me read," she orders.

Her stars zoom to the pages and shrink down to the size of the font. Dancing about, they form the ridges and curves of various letters, all too eager to help her decipher the BarulatyeNaSelben's secrets. Grinning, she looks up at Death, who crosses his arms and glares at her.

"You could have just *asked* me to translate," he scolds her. "You didn't have to use your magic for something that mundane."

"Yes, but I did, and I wanted to. Now we can both read!"

Before he can protest further, she starts thumbing back through the pages he's already scanned. As she flips the pages, an image makes her heart stop.

She lets the pages fall. On one gilded page, a half-man, half-spider stares up at her with haunted eyes. She can still hear his cruel laughter from when he chased her through the ballroom as she hurled stars at him, unsure of herself or her powers. *It's a miracle I escaped him.*

"Why… why is he… why is he in the book? I thought you said 'Na' meant dead or death?"

Death nods. "He committed a grave crime against you. You may have sent him back to Tyrladan, but I disposed of the bastard."

Swallowing, Clarisse feels her blood run cold. "You killed Ralun?"

"Technically I had him erased, but yes. His energy will now serve greater and better things. Terrence may have told you he was simply back in the Afterlife, but I take such transgressions of hunting mortals very seriously. Trying to kidnap you and harm you was uncalled for."

"Okay, so this book… it's really full of dead gods?"

"It appears so. Look here – you have Thoth, who went mad with too much knowledge a while back and chose to let the Neylka consume him."

Clarisse's heart is crushed as he flips to a page with the image of a man with a bird's head. "Would Siralto be in here?" Looking up at Death, she feels a bundle of nerves go up in flames in her core.

He flicks through the book and countless gods and goddesses shuffle by on pages lined with gold script. Clarisse wonders how many died because they wanted to have their energy taken up and how many were killed. *And how many by Death?*

"How many gods are capable of killing other gods like you do?"

"Not many. But most of the ones who can are bloodthirsty. Like Ares, for instance. He's always had a penchant for murder. Or Horus. Those two hate each other. So many lives lost."

There's an actual god of war?

"Both Ares and Horus are gods of war, as you mortals decided to give them those titles. You can imagine how much bloodshed there was for them to earn such names. They've since been reprimanded and had their powers stripped from full capacity. That doesn't stop mortals, though. They're still the most violent of species."

Frowning, Clarisse is mesmerized by the various depictions of gods and goddesses from long ago. *How many were killed in war? How many chose to leave the immortal plane? And how many are back in the form of something else? Do they remember their past lives? Are Leyun and I the only ones partly whole?*

At this thought, her stars begin to hum a strange melody. They rumble, swatting at Death's hands every time he tries to turn a page.

"What the heck are your stars doing? Are you messing with me?"

Clarisse shakes her head. "I think they want to show me something." She looks at her stars and whispers to them. "Show me what you know."

Zipping into action, they flip the pages, wind kicking up with their urgency. Clarisse can't decipher any of the photos as the pages flip by faster and faster. *How many hundreds of gods have died? Or are the entries all just super long?* Clarisse wants the stars to stop, but they keep pressing forward before finally settling onto one page.

"Death?" Clarisse's lip trembles.

Silver and gold ink threads across the page, making it impossible to

overlook the shining image of the creature from her nightmares…
Leyun.

"Why is she in the book?" Her voice is a whisper.

Death's hand grasps hers. His eyes are wide, betraying his fear. "Clarisse… this means Leyun is dead. Erased. There should be nothing left of her."

She feels panic clawing up her throat. "Then how has she been able to reach me?"

"Whoever is chasing you is *not* Leyun."

INTO THE SHADOWS

Terrence

Darkness settles in Ashville. A crisp Winter wind ruffles Terrence's shadows and he almost shivers. *Almost.* The cold always reminds him of Death's unrelenting powers; the way his gaze could very well turn a soul to stone if they defied him.

Bast stands beside him as they take in the Monroe house. He knows she's angry—she's frothing at the mouth at the prospect of seeking justice for Clarisse, even though she doesn't know Clarisse that well.

Bast has always taken victims of abuse to heart, especially when it came to kids. It's a tender subject that Terrence doesn't broach. He can't fathom where such a personal rage stems from.

Her claws are out. She sharpens them against the ground, digging and scratching eagerly. He fears he might not be able to get his revenge at all. Bast looks ready to beat him to the chase.

They spoke at length about how they might approach this one. Deborah was granted a modicum of mercy by not having to experience true punishment before she died. Her soul passed over to Fal before Terrence really got to seek out something that would work best for her and the pain she caused Clarisse, but he won't make the same mistake twice.

"Where should we enter?" he whispers. He's not sure why they're taking their sweet time about entering the house. His mouth drools at the prospect. *We will have so much fun toying with him.*

"I was thinking through the back door," Bast purrs. "We can slip in through the kitchen or their bedroom. I believe I hear his heart pounding somewhere in the living room. I hear the clinking of beer bottles, too, so this should prove quite fun... if not a bit too easy. It's a shame, really."

She examines her claws as if appreciating a new coat of nail polish instead of razor blades built to slice and tear. Terrence can't think of a time when she's looked more beautiful.

Grinning, he follows her as she slinks towards the house, her inky black fur shining in the moonlight. From the front windows, he makes out the faint light of a television screen. *Funny... I don't think they had one while Clarisse lived there, and now Arthur can't get enough. Does he even miss Deborah or his daughter? Doesn't he wonder how things could have been?*

Sighing, he decides it's best not to ponder those thoughts for long. Terrence finds it odd that he's never gone through the back door before. It's much less pristine than the front. The stairs are worn and the door is rickety. He's certain he could rip it from the hinges with ease, and it has nothing to do with his Reaper strength. A child could damage this door.

Bast growls, "They have a lot of faith that no one would come after them for what they did. What about the police? The tailor she worked for?"

"I suppose they hope justice will eventually prevail. I believe that's why we're here." He winks. "Here, their laws are stacked against the ones who have been wronged. Victims suffer, especially the ones punished for taking justice into their own hands. I don't hold this against them. Though... now that I think about it, it would be wise to check in on Mr. Harris..."

Bast doesn't wait for Terrence. She slips through the back door without making a single sound to betray her. He wonders how anyone could ever be so elegant.

He tries to follow her as soundlessly, but the wooden stairs leading up to the door creak beneath his weight. He wishes he'd thought to float in or embrace being a shadow more. His magic almost always seems to serve him in his efforts, but not when Bast is around.

Everything falls short near her.

Terrence finds her waiting for him in the hall. Annoyance flickers in her eyes, but it dissipates when she sees he's not far behind. Smiling, he motions for her to follow him. He knows this house like the back of his paw.

He wants to spend more time going through the boxes of Clarisse's things to find clues on what will work best to haunt Arthur. But when they step inside her room, Terrence's wishes are cut short, along with whatever fuse he has left.

Clarisse's room lies empty, save two boxes gathering dust on the floor.

Terrence's feelings of rage, uncertainty, and terror bubble to the surface. He seethes as he tries to fit all the puzzle pieces together. Before he knows it, he's spilling everything for Bast to see.

"He's gotten rid of *everything*!" he hisses. "There's not a fraction of her left. There's no piece of her—not a shred of her memory. He's in there drinking away his pain and forgetting everything. His wife *just* died, and what's he doing? Drinking. Watching television. Destroying evidence, while Father Simmons plans his escape so he can earn his next fat check. Speaking of, don't you find it odd that Father Simmons is still around? Why not skip town? What does Arthur have against him that makes him want to stay? What would a trickster even want with a man like him?"

Terrence doesn't care that he's rambling. His voice is soft like thunder, so as not to wake the mortal man. He's almost certain he's speaking in Mansalo, but his thoughts are too fast for him to register this.

His throat is thick with tears that run so hot they burn, but fortunately, his flames are not enough to match or engulf them. He buries his head in the first box, trying to catch any scent of what might be left of evidence—of any testaments to what Christine went through.

What will I use against them? What will I talk to him about? What will I taunt Father Simmons with?

Terrence continues his angry spiral. Arthur might as well have poured kerosene over his daughter's corpse. The shadow wolf's breath is ragged and smoke curls from his body.

Bast places a comforting paw on his shoulder. "Terrence, stop for a moment. We can sort through all that when we finally nab Simmons. Then we'll learn what his motivations are by drawing out his memories."

Terrence sours when he realizes just how badly Bast plans to torture Father Simmons. Taking memories by force is dark magic. *Does she realize what she's asking?*

Bast doesn't flinch and Terrence doesn't push her on the subject. Right now, he's hedging his bets on a crystal acorn. If he can avoid utilizing such dark magics, he will.

"Fine. But how will we torture Arthur? If we're taking one man's memories, we'd best not do it to both," he finally offers.

Bast rolls her eyes. "We don't really need to go that route with Arthur. This man's motivations are simple. Control. Money. That's it. Men like him have little else to live for. The same can be said for Father Simmons, except there's some reason he's staying here or else he would have fled. Now, do you want to do this or not? We shouldn't stretch this out any longer. We can grab those boxes on the way out, but right now, we need to seek vengeance for the little girl who was lost here."

Her cold reasoning, though solid, concerns him. *Does she think that of every man? Does she think that of me? Is she right? Is that all that would motivate someone like me?*

Bast is unconcerned by his inner monologue as she directs her focus toward the living room. Her ears perk as she crouches into a predatory prowl. Terrence watches with rapt fascination as she stalks toward Arthur, unseen and silent.

But he's tired of the theatrics. Something deep inside him clicks. He hears Death's wisdom, even if he can't see the Reaper. His time serving as Death's right-hand man reminds him of something important.

There's no point in delaying the inevitable.

"Arthur," he growls.

Bast whips around and hisses at him for blowing their cover. But Terrence doesn't care. The images of those boxes in Clarisse's room are burned into his mind, but she's no longer in pain. It's time to let Kohlu do its job.

Puffing out his chest, Terrence makes himself larger, his shadows swallowing the room in inky darkness. When Arthur stumbles to his feet, Terrence feels a gust of power ripple through him. He surges forward, unafraid. "Your soul has been sanctioned for punishment by the laws of Tyrladan!" he calls in a booming voice. "How do you plead?"

"How do I plead?" Arthur slurs.

Terrence is bored in this man's presence. All he wants to do is tear him limb from limb, but defeating a drunk, selfish human won't give him the satisfaction he desires. Killing Arthur won't teach him anything.

"What are you talking about, foul demon?" Arthur jabs a finger at Terrence, his eyes glassy, full to the brim with drink.

"Arthur, you have degraded and tortured a goddess from Tyrladan. How do you plead?"

Arthur blinks before slumping to the floor, dead from a massive heart attack.

Bast shrieks. "What are you *doing*? We could have tortured him and had a blast! What happened? Your resolve just *shattered* and you decided to play by the book?" She angrily swipes a paw at him; he almost doesn't duck in time. The wind from the tips of her claws passes so close to his nose, it stings.

"Bast, I... I don't know. I just feel like Death and I have spoken about this a million times before. Look at him!" Terrence motions to Arthur's body, lying still on the floor. "I've been ordered to exact revenge, but that man wouldn't understand what that means right now. This is a fool's errand! We struck at the wrong time and, even if we chose the right time, this man holds *nothing* sacred. He has power and money and he's *still* trying to drink away his sorrows, wasting away in front of a TV screen. He should have left, but he's still here. Has it ever dawned on you why?"

Bast sucks in a breath, ready to yell at him, but he doesn't give her the chance.

"It's not worth it. We should just collect his soul and toss it in Kohlu, then let it do what it does best. It creates terrors unimaginable, tailored the right way for the right people. The only thing that would terrify this man is the image of the past he can't have back. He's destroyed everything that would tie him to Clarisse or Deborah. You can't get through to someone like this. He won't repent or beg forgiveness. He's not even in the right state of mind to comprehend what he's done."

Terrence's chest feels heavy. Time and time again, Death tried to tell him. Tried to explain why justice is so finicky in the mortal world. Mortals are feeble. They are bound by time in ways that gods and goddesses are not. Gods must choose an ending or keep soldiering on. Mortals have no choice—they must always have an ending. Their souls carry on, but that's a journey for a different time and state of mind.

Siralto gave them free will and a life on Earth... and Tryta gave them consequences. But those consequences were never placed upon Arthur during his life.

Terrence can think of a million reasons how he would have made things different, but it's not his place.

"I think it's time to let Tryta's design play out the way it should. Who better to give him punishment than Tryta's own torture chamber? It's built for mortal souls who have transgressed to this point. You and I might not understand it, but I don't understand being mortal, either. I think I used to, but now I can't fathom it. To be so focused on the short term and the here and now seems unthinkable to me now. How can we truly get Arthur to understand what he's done if *we* don't understand *him* anymore?"

Terrence's heart lodges in his throat. *Death... Death was right.*

He swears he hears that orchestral laugh and almost spits on the floor.

"By Siralto, Terrence... Does this mean you finally understand your position? Is *this* what it took for you to get it through your thick skull? We get all the way here to exact justice and you realize it was never here?"

Bast's eyes are wide, but the smile that follows warms his heart. Before he can register her excitement, his skin starts to crack. His shadows spill from his body, but he no longer has any control over them. They devour the walls, the ceiling, the floor and everything around them. Bast is almost consumed by them, save the light she procures to reveal herself amidst his outburst of power. The shadows escape faster than he can bottle them up, and he knows there's nothing he can do to stop it. They weave and twine themselves throughout the house. He's certain that if any mortals happen to be passing by, they're witnessing a shadowy hurricane eat away at the Monroe house. *The clean-up from this will be…*

But he never finishes the thought. His skin rips and tears, and he howls in pain as he slumps to the floor. Bast rushes over to him. He's aware that she's calling to him, crying for him to get up. She utters spells and light spills all around him, but her magic can't touch him.

Agony grips him as he writhes on the floor. His paws twist and he yelps. Closing his eyes, he's not ashamed as tears fall and splash around him and his breath comes in ragged pants. Bast screams in horror. Before long, he sees stars.

If this is how I end… so be it. Calmness floods him. The pain no longer bothers him, even as he knows his form is being destroyed.

When the pain ceases, he expects he'll open his eyes in the wide expanse of the Neylka. What he doesn't expect is to wake up with his head cradled in his hands.

Hands.

The world goes black.

---

*H*is breathing has evened out by the time he opens his eyes. Thick blankets are tucked around his neck and shoulders. The warmth is comforting, unlike his unrelenting flames. The gentle clunk of a ceramic bowl on the table next to him draws his attention. He looks toward the sound and sees Bast, whose human form is far more beautiful than anything Terrence is prepared to behold.

"I thought you might want something to eat," she whispers. Her eyes betray a rainbow of emotions: confusion, care, joy, and apprehension top the list.

Groaning, Terrence tries to lift himself awkwardly. His limbs don't cooperate as they normally do. For one, they feel… *longer*. With a ragged gasp, he looks down and blinks. Hesitantly, he flexes a *hand*. A pale but familiar hand.

He can't stop weeping. The rage, grief, shame, and relief at seeing his limbs again in so many centuries threatens to sweep away his senses. When Bast traps him in a hug, he doesn't push her away. Her warmth comforts him. Burying his face in her shoulder, he lets himself go.

Several minutes pass without words. When he finally pulls away, he sees that Bast has joined him in his grief, though in silence. She dabs at her eyes.

"Thank you," he croaks. "For being here with me."

A smile peeks from behind her lips, though tears still run freely down her cheeks. "You're welcome," she says, her voice hoarse. "I don't believe I've ever seen you like this," she confesses. "I don't think I ever expected to, either."

"What, you never thought I'd lift my curse?"

"No," she laughs. "I was coming to terms with my Lafura being stuck as a shadow his whole eternity."

Terrence knows he's blushing when she uses that term, but he doesn't care. His heart is full. *All I had to do was recognize that I can't exact justice through revenge? What kind of stupid— You know what? Never mind.*

"I think it would be wise to stop there, as well. Perhaps we can raise our concerns later." Bast winks at him.

Instead of being shocked that she can hear his thoughts, he tentatively asks, "Do—do you have a mirror?"

Bast grins. "I thought you'd never ask!"

Beside his bowl of soup sits a hand mirror. She plucks it from the table and hands it to him, pride evident in the way she offers it. He's never seen her look so puffed up and giddy in his existence. *I should like to see more of this happiness in you.*

She hides a sheepish smile behind her hand, but her eyes never leave his as he brings the mirror up to his face.

A man stares back at him in the reflection—his dark brown eyes are almost black and his nose aquiline in shape. His strong jawline is framed by blond stubble, which he assumes would match his hair. *I suppose baldness follows over into Tyrladan?*

But hair is the last thing he cares about right now. He wants to get up and feel everything—his feet on the cool wooden floor and his hands against the walls and the table and everything he can think of. Even the most mundane things seem magical to him, like being born again.

The ache in his bones starts to flare up when he shifts beneath the covers. He manages to prop himself up farther, but is stopped by Bast's gentle hand.

"You need to rest. Arthur has been taken care of." Her fangs gleam in the light. She's one of the few Selben who chooses to keep them in every form. Fierceness becomes her.

Terrence slides back down beneath the covers as she hands him a bowl of soup. He takes a few sips before prodding with his next questions. "Taken care of?" He raises an eyebrow. "I was the one who was ordered to deal justice, if you'll recall." He hands her the bowl, content to wait until later to eat more. More than anything, he wants to sleep.

"Yes," Bast answers slyly. "I'm aware. I simply elected to free you from doing everything alone. What's the harm in accepting help? You ordered the kill and had a very mature moment—which was more than what I hoped for." Lowering her head, she grows quiet. "My actions could've prolonged your punishment... My eagerness got in the way of seeing what the broader message was."

The tears slipping down her cheeks fill him with rage. He leans over, ignoring the raw pain in his newly formed muscle tissue—*being human again hurts*—and swipes them away. He tucks his fingers beneath her chin and tilts her head to face him. Her silver eyes are misty, but she does her best to hide her tears.

"Listen to me, Bast. Every bit of my punishment was rubbish. You can't hold yourself accountable for 'holding me back' when you didn't know what the cure was. They finally chose to set me free of rules and restrictions to test me, which is a farce. I'm defending a goddess' honor, and they chose to set that up as the make-or-break point?" He shakes his head gently. "You can't hold yourself accountable for such dreadful schemes. You came to support me. That's what matters."

She grips his hands, her fingers running over his smooth skin with fascination and urgency. "I still can't believe you're whole again."

He warms under her touch, but he's too sore to get out of the blankets and hug her. Instead, he pulls her into him. She crawls in next to him and, for a few moments, they lay curled up with each other.

"How are you feeling? This is a big change for you," Bast guesses. "Does it hurt? Does having hands and legs hurt when you've only had paws for so long?"

Terrence shrugs and does his best to mask the pain. "It does, but it's bearable if it means I get to be whole again. I suppose I'll become used to everything again as I continue in this form." He smiles, flexing his fingers and reveling in the feeling of the cool t-shirt and soft pajama pants he wears. He believes he could stay in this moment forever, relishing in the simple act of existing. But there's something he must know…

"When you say taken care of… Did you place Arthur in Kohlu?"

Bast chirps, "Yes! I escorted him there shortly after you changed. I made sure you were comfortable and took several liberties in tormenting him before letting him go."

Terrence pulls back. "Did you learn nothing? I had such a strong, poetic moment back there and you *still* chose to try and seek justice?"

Bast laughs. "Frankly, I don't care much for Siralto and Tryta's design. I think it sucks. So why not do what *I* think is right? It was the perfect opportunity, and besides that, it was sanctioned, so I broke no laws. I risked no punishment *and* I got to make a child murderer pay. Who wouldn't jump at the chance?"

With a wince, Terrence looks away.

"I wasn't talking about you, Terrence. You had your moment—you realized what you were supposed to learn from your punishment. If Arthur was the key to that realization, then it's the only thing I'm grateful to him for."

Terrence grins, still in awe of his luck. "Do you think I can venture into Tyrladan now? I'd like to see it again and see where you've been residing."

Bast runs a finger along one of her more intricate hair cuffs, picking at the swirls and lines. He still doesn't know what the cuffs symbolize, so he makes a mental note to ask her about it later, if she's up for explaining.

"We can explore later," she offers. "We still have Father Simmons to deal with, remember? And he will require more harsh punishments."

Panic settles in Terrence's gut. *Where's the acorn?*

Sensing his discomfort, Bast reaches over to the table, scoots the bowl of soup aside, and reveals the acorn. She plucks it from its spot and places it in his waiting hand. It feels cool to the touch now and he wonders if it might be made of some kind of ice magic, rather than crystals as it appears. *That would be fitting for an agent of Death…*

He closes his fist around it and it disappears within his skin. It's strange seeing flesh and not shadows. On command, they come swirling to the surface and engulf his arm in darkness.

"I guess that part will never change. Maybe I'll always carry shadows with me."

"Terrence, love, you don't just carry them. You *are* shadow incarnate. That's what your magic represents—it's who you are. Death has his stars. I have my many shapes and strength and persuasive powers. You… you have shadows."

"Persuasive powers?" Terrence stares at Bast. "Is that your unique marker?" It occurs to Terrence that he's not seen her do anything particularly unique up to this point, beyond the most basic spells and actions.

"I make deals, Terrence. My eyes may look silver, but my tongue is my most precious currency." She winks.

Terrence blushes, realizing how that might be otherwise interpreted.

"I can easily convince people to do almost anything I want, unless they have strong resolve. Also, I generate power in contractual arrangements. Words are binding; I use deals to siphon powers from others," she continues, ignoring how flustered she's made him.

"So… you… are you admitting to me that you steal souls?"

"Perhaps," she answers mysteriously, examining her nails the same way she looks at her claws. "I'm also drawn to utilizing water in certain ways. I draw power from the raging seas and the babbling streams. You know what? It's probably better if I show you sometime rather than trying to explain it all."

"Remind me not to make you mad," Terrence teases, his awe for her ever-growing. "So, what do we do about Father Simmons?"

Bast hums, then looks up at him before pecking his cheek. "I think, right now, we need to let you rest. Finish your soup and get more sleep. You may think you have me fooled, but I know you're in much more pain than you'll admit. Changing bodies is no easy feat. Believe me, it took a long time for me to get used to it, and you've been stuck in one form for a very long time. I can't imagine how much worse that feels. I'll scrounge up some more blankets and we'll enjoy our spoils for another day or two. That'll give you time to relax."

Terrence nods, though he wishes she was wrong about how much longer he'll need to rest. His stomach chooses that moment to growl. "Hey, Bast?"

"Yes?"

"Could you get me some cereal while you're up? No milk, though."

Bast's face twists up. "I see your appetite hasn't changed. What kind of cereal?"

He laughs. "The one with the most sugar!"

Bast winks at him before striding out of the room, leaving him content to sip his soup and think about all the things that led him here. But most of all, he's thrilled as he picks up his free hand and uses it to stir the soup. Ordinarily he'd use magic, but he knows today where magic really lies.

Right here, in this moment.

UNICORN

Clarisse

As far as she's concerned, nothing Death could have revealed was more surprising or frightening than learning Leyun was not *real*. That she died a long time ago, and everything Clarisse thought she knew about her up until now was fake.

"Death, how do you, of all people, not realize that she was *dead*? Is the Neylka piloting a corpse around to try and capture me? What does this mean?" Clarisse paces about the library, her toes creating friction with the carpet. Had she worn socks, she'd be a lightning rod.

"Clarisse, please," Death groans. He steps in front of her and intercepts her latest lap of anxious pacing. Shaking her shoulders, he motions for her to look up at him.

Despite how terrified she is, all she wants to do right now is reach up and kiss him. The stern look on his face tells her she won't be having much luck with that right now. *But maybe later…*

"Would you pay attention?"

"Sorry! I'm stressed and I don't know what to think and my mind wanders and…" She finally takes a breath. "I'm afraid. I'm afraid and you're all I have, Death. There's a crazy being masquerading as someone else, chasing me through the Afterlife, and we don't even know where or what it is! Why? What's the purpose? Why is it afraid of sharing its identity with us?" Thoroughly stressed, she wants to slump to the floor and cry.

"Clarisse, it's imperative to approach this logically. For one, how do we know this book is a credible source? I find it odd that it arrives in the library right after you had an encounter with Leyun in your memories. Perhaps there's something else going on. She may not be able to reach you in here, but she *can* influence the magic around you to try and alter your perspective. I, for one, think this is a trap." He crosses his arms. "I may not usher souls from the Afterlife to their final end, but I would know of her passing."

"But have you seen her personally?" Clarisse raises an eyebrow. "I feel like I'm the only one who sees her. How do I know my own memories aren't driving me insane?"

"Then why would you remember her specifically? Clarisse... think with me for a moment. I don't want you getting ahead of yourself. I know this is frightening and rightfully so, but we must approach this with caution."

Clarisse focuses on taking deep breaths, finding it easier with each passing moment as she considers Death's perspective. Her gaze swings downward and she notices with a start that her hands are glowing. The warmth passing through her skin borders on uncomfortable. If she doesn't stop her spiral, she will engulf the room in flames as Terrence did to her house. To her surprise, Kreyuhl is still asleep, his small snores breaking the silence.

"Okay, so what do you propose?"

"We try and find Leyun. We have to. We must learn what happened to her if we go with the theory that this book is a credible source. Accurate information here and there does not mean the whole body of this literature is vetted," he sniffs. "What amateur thinks they know more of death and dying than I do? I *am* Death. *I* would be better suited to penning an authoritative tome on the subject."

Clarisse finds his persistent desire to be proper and authoritative amusing. "You're such a nerd."

"Call me what you will, but I insist that we start looking for this creature and take her on directly. If we find her or recent traces of her, then we'll know this book is a decoy. If we don't locate her, then we'll know we've been duped by a Leyun lookalike."

Shuffling her feet, dread starts to eat at her. "How do we get started? How do we know where to look?"

Death pats her head. "My dear, we don't even have to leave the house. I'll send some of my stars out as tracers to hunt her down. Any time she contacts you, we'll know because my stars will use that as another web to catch where the energy originates."

Her eyes are wide as she marvels, "How can you do that?"

Smiling, Death leans into her. "I'll show you."

Splaying out his hands, he summons a few of his stars. His are fascinating. They're much more orderly than hers are, just like their master. He swirls his fingers to break up their ranks and orders them into a line.

"Rohk'Leyun," he whispers.

One by one, they march out the door. He only sends about ten, their numbers indistinct as they race and twirl, their lights almost blurring together.

Clarisse motions to them. "What did you say to them? I thought I heard Leyun's name."

"I told them to follow her. *Rohk* means follow or chase, depending on the context," he explains.

"I see. Do you have to speak that command aloud, or can you say it in your head?"

Laughing, Death leans in and surprises her with a small peck on the lips. "No, love, we don't do magic the way your media likes to portray it. I merely gave them a verbal command because it was easiest to announce my intention. But you're free to give your stars commands in whatever fashion you think they'll understand best. It's important to be clear in your orders, especially in the beginning. Until your magic knows you, without specifics it can go a little haywire."

Cringing, Death shivers. Clarisse wonders what it looks like when magic doesn't listen. Her stars have always been cooperative. She can't imagine a scenario where they would let their independence override her commands.

"So... what do we do now?"

Shrugging, Death gestures to the wall of books. "We could keep reading?"

"Death, I still want to know why my stars picked the book out on their own. How did they know it was there? Are they conspiring against me?" Her heart thuds. *Magic wouldn't go that far, would it? Would insubordination come in the form of straight betrayal?* She feels her stars start to chitter, and a twinge of anger trickles through. *They don't like being accused of something like that, I take it.*

One of her stars zooms from her hand without being summoned. It attacks her face, much like an angry butterfly. It doesn't hurt, but the intention stings. She's almost certain she hears it swearing at her in Mansalo. As funny as the situation would be on a normal day, she's embarrassed to admit ever doubting her stars.

"I'm sorry," she whispers loud enough for them to hear. "I just don't know what I'm supposed to gather from this. If Leyun is dead, how is she chasing me? And how is she in that book anyway, if Death didn't write it?"

Her stars don't answer, undoubtedly further punishment for questioning them.

"Darling, I know it's difficult to grasp this, but I think they were showing you so you're aware that there is… something… going on regarding Leyun and her efforts to track you down. Until you learn to decipher their language more intimately, you'll have to do some guesswork and your own investigation. For now, we'll wait to see what my stars have to say and work on interpreting yours, okay?"

Clarisse nods. From beneath the windowsill, Kreyuhl groans. She approaches and places his head in her lap, then strokes his strange face as he wakes. His eyes are glassier than usual, but they're wide awake when he notices Clarisse's touch. He reaches up and sniffs her hand, then chirps with satisfaction when he realizes she's safe. Seconds later, he returns to his slumber.

"He really took the brunt of my magic use this last time, didn't he?"

Death stoops beside her. His hand reaches out and hovers over Kreyuhl's face. Clarisse says nothing as he begins to stroke Kreyuhl like a shy child meeting a dog for the first time. Keryuhl's chest rumbles and his eyes flutter open, but he doesn't move away. Instead, his eyes fix onto Death and something like agreement passes between them. Clarisse is glad that, after all this time, they've found a way to bond.

"Clarisse, he's your familiar. You will draw on him as he will sometimes draw on you, once you're strong enough. You're a team. You'll figure out a balance."

A few moments of warm silence pass between them. Clarisse sighs, letting a few of her stars flicker between her fingers as she tries to follow their patterns for signs, symbols, or anything that would tell her why they pointed to the book. She hopes they won't remain angry with her for long.

I'm sorry, my friends. You've been with me this long; I don't know why I ever thought you were capable of selling me out.

A few of her stars chitter, nestling between her fingers and growing warmer to the touch. Their yellow hue reveals their happiness, and Clarisse is glad to have them back on her side. She wonders how she can possess such an infinite number of them. Every day, their numbers continue to swell. *Am I like outer space?*

Death raises an eyebrow and chuckles. "No, my dear, I believe that's more my department. You're something else. You're far more precious than outer space."

"You brought balance to Earth when you were created. You managed to solve the issue of Earth being so screwed up. Without you, there is no reason to live life fully and no reprieve from the way it was made. Isn't that the point?"

Clarisse isn't sure when she began to understand his role so well, but she's sure it's from her reading. *There's no way my magic would know that... I have no memories of Death coming to haunt me. Maybe it's our bond.*

Death's lip quirks, but before he can say anything, he freezes. In his hand, a few more stars start to appear. They emit strange noises. She watches as Death stares at them, lost in deep conversation. Abruptly, he stands and closes the curtains at a nearby window.

"What's going on?"

"The stars found what they believe to be Leyun," he whispers.

Ice washes down Clarisse's spine and she feels tears prick at her eyes. *I'm not ready to face her again.*

Death peers through the curtain, and his muscles flex with an agile readiness that frightens her. He looks more predator than friend right now. If she was anyone else, she would accept her fate.

"Are you worried she might be watching?"

Death nods. "I want to take every precaution. You will not leave this library except for emergencies, understood? Until further notice, I want you in here. I want you safe in this space where she can't reach you." He reaches out to help her stand.

"How did your stars find her so fast? I thought she was dead?"

Death shrugs. "We still have to verify the source. It could be that they've found a corpse, but until her head is on a stake, I won't believe anything."

Stammering, Clarisse leans against the nearest bookshelf and tries to catch her breath. "I just don't understand why it's so imperative that I be 'whole' in the Neylka's eyes. What does Leyun stand to gain from this, anyway? Why does it matter to her?"

Death sighs. "It's the same way I'm compelled to do my job. She perceives you as… incomplete. Leyun was the horrible result of a failed attempt at recycling that no one understood, so it stands to reason that she would sympathize and follow these dogged orders to bring you in. In a way, she thinks she's sparing you the pain she's going through."

Clarisse trembles. "But why would I want to be recycled and never discover who I was? I don't want to forget I existed at all. I want to be with you!"

"Clarisse, you *are* with me. And again, you can't be forced there, save by the hands of very powerful gods, none of whom have a known stake in this claim."

Grumbling, Clarisse tries her best to see the reason behind his words, but the fear of being killed in such an ultimate fashion lingers in her mind. She turns to the shelves and does her best to sort through titles and find one that might distract her—even if it's not with knowledge. A good story book would be optimal right now to assuage her fears.

"Listen, it's going to be alright. I need to find Leyun, or whatever evidence my stars have managed to bring to me, and I need you to stay here with Kreyuhl. And I mean it — you must stay in the library, or I'll curse you in ways you never could've imagined. You're *mine* and I intend to keep it that way. No one will have you but me — not even the Neylka. The creature that chases you will have to learn that the hard way."

Clarisse reaches out to him, but he's out the door in a flash. Looking down at Kreyuhl, she's relieved to find that he's fully awake now. She doesn't think she could manage to stay calm if she was completely alone.

Frowning, she grabs a book and starts paging through it. This one, again, is in Mansalo and she's too tired to summon her stars to read again. A few of them tumble out regardless. They hum and buzz to strange tunes and dance around her head. She's certain she looks like a celestial lunatic to any passersby. Kreyuhl seems unbothered, though his attention is locked on the stars.

Kreyuhl, do you know what my stars are saying?

"They are offering you warnings. I'm not sure what is going on, but they pulled that book for a reason. I'm still getting caught up with your memories, so bear with me. Seeing Leyun exhausted me more than I could've imagined."

Clarisse can't stomach the dread that builds within her. She feels a retching spree on the rise and she's nowhere near a toilet to rid herself of the sick. Locked away in this library, she'd be sullying her books, which isn't on the table, even if she can't decipher the words in all of them.

"Your stars do not believe Leyun is truly dead, but there is something wrong with her. Her story should be over, but she still walks. That only happens through dark, dark magic, Clarisse. She should have been recycled a long time ago. The nature of her ability to remain… is frightening."

Clarisse wraps her arms around her body and shivers. The room is still cold from Death's presence. She walks over to Kreyuhl and snuggles against him for warmth. He doesn't protest as she nestles into his alabaster fur.

"You're alright, Clarisse. I'll protect you. Even so, I wonder how close she is. I know Death ordered us to stay here, but if for some reason we see her, I will whisk you away immediately, do you understand? You are to hop up onto my back and we'll take off. I'll carry you somewhere that I know is safe."

Is anywhere safe, Kreyuhl?

"There are places. They may not be safe from other things, but they will be safe from her. Remember, your powers have yet to serve as weapons, but they

are capable of striking down many a foe. I need you to connect with them more. Stop doubting what you've been given. You can create, but you can also destroy. Anyone who can set fire to a rose bed from several hundred yards away only hours after reaching Tyrladan is a force with which to be reckoned. You need to embrace that."

Just then, the stairs creak from outside the door. Clarisse is on her feet, frozen in place. Kreyuhl stands at the ready.

Death?

She hopes on all that is good and holy that her Reaper has returned for her, but she doesn't feel him near and he doesn't respond. Strange, lilting strains of music drift down the hall, echoing into the library. It strikes a nerve with Clarisse and sends a familiar urge of curiosity through her. It's not music for dancing, but the notes speak to her from deep within her soul. Its haunting melody makes her eyes glaze over and she starts to walk toward the door.

"No, Clarisse, you must stay here!" Kreyuhl warns. *"Whatever that is, it wants to lure you out of your sanctuary. If it manages to reach us, let me be the judge of whether it is a threat. I'll break through this window if need be, but I will not let you blindly go to face this danger."*

Kreyuhl steps in front of the door and blocks the frame with his bulky body. Despite the trepidation in her body, she wishes nothing more than to shove him aside so she can listen closer to the beautiful music. She's convinced it will help her unlock the secrets of her power. It's an illogical thought, but the desire increases with every note.

Kreyuhl… what if whatever is down there knows something about me I don't?

Her deeper instincts tell her to flee, but her heart tugs her toward the source. Kreyuhl doesn't budge, shoving her away from the door every time she tries to break past him.

"I'm sorry, Clarisse, but this is for your own good. You're being influenced by the creature lurking on the other side of this door. Death would never forgive me if I let you get hurt. Besides that, I'd never forgive myself. So stay where you are and plug your ears."

Clarisse blinks, feeling sluggish and removed from her emotions. Unnerved, she slumps to the floor and tries to concentrate on breathing. Glancing over, she sees a book whose title is unfamiliar to her. Instead of stopping to read the script, she flips through the pages hungrily, searching for words she might know and pictures to provide context, anything to keep her mind off the disturbing music.

The volume swells and she crams her hands over her ears, desperate to close off the temptation to run downstairs into the grasp of whatever strange, terrible creature awaits. *Leyun has never made music... but could it be her? Did the stars find her down there and she followed them back here?*

Shuddering, she slides her finger up and down the image of Kreyuhl she finds in the book—the place, not her familiar. The garden of the Selyento is embossed in beautiful foil that glimmers in the light of the library. Her stars emblazon the lines to busy her mind and keep her safe from the temptations swirling about.

"Stay strong, Clarisse. You can do this. I won't let you get hurt, I promise. I will do everything in my power to protect you."

A few moments pass before Clarisse realizes the music has stopped. She rubs her left shoulder, aware of the goosebumps creeping up her arms and down her back. The library feels like it's been dipped in a bucket of ice.

"Is there a blanket in here, Kreyuhl?"

He blinks, but he doesn't budge. His resistance to move gives her pause; trepidation creeps along the strings of their familiar bond. As the temperature continues to plummet, Clarisse realizes just how alarming the change is.

"Kreyuhl... I think I need you to break that window."

"You don't have to tell me twice."

Kreyuhl springs into action and charges toward Clarisse with his mouth wide. Snagging her shirt and flinging her up onto his back, he holds still just long enough for her to get a good grip. She twines her fingers in the sparse mane along his lengthy neck.

He glances back at her. *"Are you secure?"*

She nods and clenches her legs to get the best grip she can. It's not enough to make her feel balanced and she really wishes she'd taken up horseback riding on Earth. Not that her parents would have been able to afford it, but it's a skill she desperately needs. Right now, though, she knows they must get through that window, and fast.

She opens her palms and summons her magic. Focusing her energy on the window for a few seconds, the window cracks.

"Come on, Clarisse, I'll assist you."

Heat rises in her palms and permeates through her veins as Kreyuhl lends her more of his magic. Clarisse hopes he's rested enough and has recharged from earlier. While it's getting easier to wield magic, every spell drains her body.

When she hears the glass shatter, she cheers with glee. But her happiness is cut short when she turns to see, just before they jump, the eyes of a feral-looking unicorn.

Well, I guess she's not dead, after all.

She doesn't even have time to scream as Leyun lunges into the library, her jaw stretched wide. Kreyuhl takes off, the air beneath them taking forever to swallow them up and return them to the ground. When they land, he takes off and Clarisse holds on for dear life.

I hope Death finds us soon!

"I do, too, but we can't wait around for him to show up."

The suns, still high overhead, feel ominous. Their blinding light seems to be more of a beacon to help Leyun find her than a source of relief from the dark.

When she turns her head to look behind them, she screams. Leyun is so close to them that with one snap, she could pull Clarisse from Kreyuhl's back. Without thinking, Clarisse summons a weapon—a bow and arrow. It's clumsy in her hands but, woven from her stars, she knows the weapon will strike true. She pulls the arrow back and aims. Just as she's about to release it, Kreyuhl stumbles. Her body flies off his back and she hurtles onto the grass, scraping her skin as she rolls and tumbles down a steep hill.

Thundering hooves get louder, and she knows Leyun is frightfully close. When Clarisse finally rolls to a stop, she weeps and begs the creature to leave her alone.

"Please," she sobs, "I don't want to be erased!"

"Who said I'm going to erase you?" Leyun hisses.

The unicorn looms over her, taking careful note of Clarisse's wounds as her golden blood spills onto the ground. Her wounds heal fast, but her heart continues to pound. She fears it might explode if pushed any more.

"You're coming with me. It's not safe here."

Startled, Clarisse gasps. "What?"

Leyun doesn't bother to offer an explanation. She lunges and swings Clarisse's body onto her back without further discussion. Her arms are locked around Leyun's neck by some strong magic Clarisse is unable to break. Helpless and terrified, the creature drags her away and gallops off into the unknown.

PRAISES BE

Terrence

Standing outside the church, Terrence takes a breath. The steeple looms large. He clenches his fists, feeling refreshed and revived in his new body. He rolls the acorn around and around in his palm, the cool, crystalline exterior leaving imprints on his skin in the shape of its more jagged edges.

"How are you feeling?" Bast sidles up beside him, donned in her human body to mirror his newly found freedom.

Rolling his shoulders, Terrence waits to hear a satisfying click in his bones before turning to smile at her. "I'm feeling perfect, Bast. I feel well equipped to do my job for once, even if I'm not officially employed any longer."

Laughing, Bast holds his hands. "Take a deep breath and savor it. You're going to go in there and together, we're going to wrangle this trickster back into Kohlu. Afterward, you'll be free to go and redefine yourself in whatever way you wish."

Terrence thinks for a moment, trying to ponder what life might be like now that he's free. One more soul and he's able to just… *go?*

"Should I return to Tyrladan?"

"I think you should," Bast smirks. "You can help me guard the rivers of Yehta and figure out what you want to do. We can see where you might've belonged had you gone there first. I'm sure there's a place waiting for you."

"But not Altiya," Terrence grimaces. "Does anyone ever make it there, anyway?"

"It's the city of the gods, Terrence. No mortals live there."

Shaking his head, Terrence thinks of several reasons to justify his status as belonging there. *I've served for centuries and learned to control powers never before seen in a mortal — a true mortal.* With another shake, he returns his thoughts to the task at hand.

"How should I go about activating this acorn? I sense the dark power within it, but I'm not sure when it will decide to show itself... Am I missing something that you might know about?"

Off in the trees, he hears the shrill cry of several crows, their murderous ranks openly eager to see what might become of Father Simmons once Bast and Terrence break through the church's doors. Bast holds her hand out and Terrence reluctantly places the acorn in her palm, fearful it might detonate at any moment. His darkness stands at the ready, willing to do anything to keep her safe from any foul magic that might be radiating from it.

"It seems to know its purpose," Bast notes as she inspects it. "Are you sure you don't remember who gave this to you? It must have been an agent of the Selyento... but whom?"

Terrence shakes his head. The memory is unclear. He remembers a bright light, but the god or goddess who gave him this weapon eludes him.

"They just appeared. They gave me the acorn and disappeared. They didn't want to be remembered." Bast frowns, her face screwed up in worry. Terrence smiles. "You and I both know this is warranted behavior. They gave me my body back. This is the right path, Bast. Why else would they give me the go ahead?"

Shaking her head, Bast looks up at him. Terrence revels in the fact that he is, hilariously, taller than Bast. He's not yet shut up about it, but the glint in her eyes dares him to bring it up in a moment like this, her balled fists all too eager to find pay dirt in his face.

"It's not that... I just worry about you being exposed to this thing for as long as you have. Is it safe for us to be in its blast radius when it goes off? It feels… explosive."

Rolling his eyes, Terrence tries to bury his own reservations and dread somewhere deep in the pit of his soul. *She must be wrong.* But Bast is almost never wrong. Swallowing, he turns back to face the door.

"There's no sense in waiting anymore, Bast. If that's what's to become of me, at least I'll go out in one piece. But please, take this as an opportunity to get yourself to safety. I don't want you getting hurt if this thing is truly toxic to more than just its intended target."

Bast reaches out and shoves him, anger evident in her beautiful features. "As if I would leave you? You fool, I've been waiting since the first time we met to see you come into your own, and I will be with you until there is nothing left of either of us."

Terrence's heart swells and his eyes fill with tears. There are so many things he would like to say to her. Instead, he leans down and plants a quiet kiss on her lips. Her eyes widen as he pulls back, but he quickly turns and shoves open the door. He refuses to dwell on the heat rising in his chest. *If we survive this, I'll never let her go.*

The doors creak as they swing wide. The lights are not on, despite dusk creeping in with the early Winter evening. A cold wind slashes through the entryway, cutting Terrence through to the bone. He shivers and tugs the wool coat he stole from Arthur's closet closer. It's much too tight, but it was all he had without risking using too much magic so soon after his most recent change. His fingers ache to release his darkness into the cathedral.

Patience, Terrence.

He feels Bast behind him, her presence the only comfort in such a peculiar position. Clearing his throat, he stands up straighter as Father Simmons comes out to greet them. Terrence notes that Father Simmons' eyes have changed. They glow a bright, neon green. *Like his greed.*

"What a lovely couple you two make," Father Simmons croons, his hair stark white in the rays of light that break through the windowpanes. Terrence swears the man has aged by a hundred years in just the few days that he's been dealing with the Monroes. *How much magic has this man been wielding in such a short period of time? Does he know what he is? What he's capable of? Or has he known the whole time?*

Terrence turns his attention back to the fallen priest. "Thank you. My wife and I are visiting churches nearby to see which one we should join. Could you tell us what you believe? We heard you speak of someone called the Great Light, and the way this being is presented… well, it resonated with us." The lie curls off Terrence's tongue with ease. He stifles the smile that wants to break out with his pride.

"My husband was most impressed with some of your recorded lectures," Bast adds. "We've been… inspired. Would you mind giving us a tour and tell us what you believe?"

Father Simmons' eyes grow brighter. "You two don't fool me… *Terrence*," he snaps, his voice sharp like a knife's blade.

Now, Terrence allows himself to smile. "Ah, Simmons, I see you've finally awakened. Have you finally come into your own? This place reeks of new magic. Tell me, when did you figure out who you are and what you're capable of? I must say, I'm most impressed."

Bast huddles closer to him, her fists shaking from clenching them so tightly. He reaches over and grabs one, forcing her to place her hand in his. He feels her shaking cease, and the warmth from her fingers give him the strength he needs to continue.

"It is a burden, I must confess, knowing that I've been a *god* all these years. Deceiving the people, finding ways to lure people in and have them give me their coin. Everything about my plans has always gone exactly as I spelled them out. But your little friend, Clarisse, was my crowning masterpiece. She was the key to discovering who I was. Even in her death, she has shown me so much. Pay off the right people and settle the right bribes, and no one will ever truly hold you accountable for anything." Simmons smiles. "And now I'm too powerful for even the likes of *you* to take me down. A shadow— though I see you've found a new body—is no match for a *god*."

Bast laughs. It's strained and somewhat maniacal. If Terrence felt like he was in any way her target, he would turn and scream, then flee the building to escape her wrath.

"You think that because you possess some magic that you're somehow *divine?*" Bast scoffs. "Divine power is so much more than the ability to deceive beyond mortal measure. You are a *half breed*, you stinking oaf!" Bast spits. "You are an abomination against Tyrladan."

"Really? An abomination?" When Father Simmons smiles, his teeth glint in the murky light like some wild vampire.

"Yes, you are," Terrence answers, darkness seeping from his voice. It curls along the floor, setting small fires to the deep red carpet. He wonders if he'll etch out whatever stains of Clarisse's blood are left.

Just the thought of how she suffered at this man's hands drives him to the brink of madness. Darkness continues to spill from him, painting the walls and ceiling and descending them into darkness. Terrence laughs as Father Simmons stumbles back, his eyes wide with terror as he tries to put his hands out to steady himself.

"Just what the hell are you?" Father Simmons demands. "How *dare* you try and unseat a god!"

To his surprise, Father Simmons creates two lashing coils of light, bright green to match his eyes. He snaps them like whips, and one of them lashes Terrence's leg. It opens a gash and Terrence's blood spills onto the carpet.

He hears Bast gasp, but he's not going to stop now. Instead, he lets the pain rush through his veins and propel him forward. *The acorn be damned.*

Charging forward, he slams into Father Simmons and barrels him to the floor. They roll around as Terrence tries to sink sharp, dark claws into the priest's face, tearing through his soft flesh and sending more blood spilling to the floor.

"How's *that* for a god?" Terrence taunts. "You bleed red just like the rest of us mortal souls, you coward!"

Snarling, Father Simmons places a blinding, green light onto Terrence's face that burns like a hot iron. Terrence swallows a scream as his body absorbs the heat, his own fires swallowing it whole.

"You damned fool!" Terrence bellows. "You think your puny fire can harm me? I am *made* of the dark fires of Kohlu! That's *Hell*, in case you were wondering!"

Joy floods Terrence's chest and he bounces back to his feet. He places one over Father Simmons and presses down, breaking his nose with a sickening crunch. Father Simmons screams.

"Why didn't you just skip town like every other coward?" Terrence asks. His curiosity has not been sated. This foolish man will not find reprieve from him until all his questions are answered. *I will make him suffer for his sins as he made Clarisse suffer.*

"Why would I need to run?" Father Simmons spits as blood pours from his broken face. "I knew what I was — *powerful*. I knew I could continue to dupe the people here instead of having to pick up and move to the next town. Why give up what I have here when I can just keep burning the next brat child to make a spectacle? I can convince them I am God incarnate! Only *I* hold the keys to their salvation!"

Father Simmons' eyes roll back in his head as he cackles. He splays his hands and shoots more dark power right at Terrence. Huffing, Terrence catches the bolts and rebounds them from his palms. The energy arcs back and nearly streaks straight into their master's chest. Father Simmons manages to dodge at the last second.

Pity, Terrence thinks.

"You really think you're a god?" Bast demands.

Terrence turns to find that she's the perfect vision of who she was during the times of Ancient Egypt. Her inky, leonine head sits perfectly affixed to a strong body. Golden adornments cover her, drenching her in the exquisite royalty she emanates naturally.

"You will bow to me, Simmons. I will show you what *true* power looks like!" Bast hisses.

One flick of her hands sends Simmons flying. The gust of wind that passes by him on the way to its intended target sends the hairs on Terrence's neck, which are standing at attention. The raw power emanating from her answers with finality the questions he had earlier about her powers.

She's a force of nature.

A monsoon builds within the cathedral, swirling and raging with desire to consume its latest prey. "What kind of god feasts on the fears of children?" The eerie tone in Bast's voice makes Terrence wonder if the acorn is really needed. "What kind of god finds pleasure in tricking the simplest, most vile of mortals? Anyone could trick someone like Arthur or Deborah. How pathetic that you see that as an *accomplishment.*"

Lightning strikes, searing Simmons' right arm and sending his body into violent convulsions as the electricity pulses through him.

Terrence's shadows jump to attention to grasp Simmons' body, and dark thorns pierce the evil priest's skin. His blood spills onto the floor in thick red rivers, but his body keeps writhing as he gasps for air.

"You can't kill me!" he sputters, his teeth now stained red. "I'm immortal! I shall prevail and sacrifice the next child in your names. Bast and Terrence, yes?"

Bast's storms grow darker, and the silver in her eyes burns white-hot with rage. Electricity crackles through her veins and pulsing waves rise from her feet, carrying their jolting power forward. Terrence stumbles to get out of the way. Just because he can survive such a blow doesn't mean it won't hurt. In his desperate attempt to move aside, he stumbles and the acorn slips from his shadows, tumbling out onto the floor.

Bast hisses and takes a quick step back to give it a wide berth. Terrence rushes over to join her; the storm pauses as quickly as it was summoned.

"What?" Father Simmons spits. "You're both afraid of a nut?" He laughs and shakes his fists, and then he does the unthinkable—he closes his hands around it and crushes it between his fingers.

Terrence's heart drops through his chest like a bomb. Scrambling, he fumbles to grab Bast's hands and ushers her out of the church. The pure dark magic escaping the crushed remains of the crystal acorn scream so loud, his eardrums threaten to burst. He's almost certain he feels blood rush down his earlobes from the shattered remains of his brain inside his skull.

He turns as they reach the door to see the horrors spewing from the small weapon of mass destruction. From within it, shadows darker than his own spew forth, straight from Kohlu as they rush to the surface to swallow Simmons whole.

They weave and grab at the man's limbs and start to pull. As much as Terrence can stomach most gore, the sight makes him blanch. He turns away and steers Bast to safety as the whole church is engulfed in the dark, void-like flames that only Hell can muster.

Safety almost eludes them… almost. Only at the safety of the tree line do they turn to look back. They crash to the ground together, panting.

"You're telling me that acorn was a portal to frigging KOHLU?"

Terrence gasps, his question robbing him of what little air he has left. "That's a bit of overkill, I'd say! You and I had it under control!"

Bast shakes her head, her eyes wide. "Something's horribly wrong. Who is Clarisse? Why would that kind of punishment be sanctioned?"

Terrence shakes his head. "She carried stars with her like weapons. They spoke to her, Bast. How did I not realize she was something more? I really *was* blind. Whoever she was, the gods are *angry* that she was tormented. I've never seen them be so… calculated."

"And you're sure you don't remember who gave that to you?"

Terrence squints, racking his brain in the hopes of conjuring the answer that so eludes him. "Can't you look through my memories? That's one of your gifts, right? You said you did it with Clarisse."

Rolling her eyes, they both take a moment to look back and watch the church melt, bending in on itself. The metal groans and splinters beneath the weight of the toxic air. The framing screams when the building collapses, destroying whatever evidence might be left inside of what happened to Father Simmons. His soul, Terrence hopes, is being dragged into Kohlu at this very moment. Overkill is one thing, but the satisfaction of that man's ultimate destruction still sits sweetly on his chest.

"Look at me, Terrence."

Terrence turns back to Bast and she places a palm on his forehead. His vision goes white as his memories start to play back for her. He's helpless as she sifts through them one by one as though they're a cheap, low-budget flick to watch at the cinema on a weekend.

The clearing comes into crisp focus in his mind. The acorn is freshly placed in the dirt, its shell unmarred. He knows now that Hell is contained within its crystalline walls. He blinks as Bast continues to peruse his memories, the events playing out as clearly as they did the day he first received the acorn.

Bast's face contorts into one of terror as his eyes look up in his memory, straight into the face of a unicorn.

"That's right," he whispers. "The unicorn!"

Bast screams and rushes back in the direction of the church, her legs a blur against the horizon as she tries to reach it. "No! No! What was Leyun plotting? Why would she do this? Is this some kind of cruel trick?" She runs her fingers through her hair, knocking a few cuffs loose as fear and rage overtake her. Terrence rushes up beside her and rests his hands on her shoulders. Bast whirls around and buries herself in his chest. "What did we just do? What ammunitions did we just give that terrible creature?" Bast sobs against him, her voice muffled. "How… how did I miss this? Leyun has been hunting Clarisse."

Terrence's body goes stiff. "That creature is hunting our Clarisse?"

Bast looks up at him, her eyes shining with tears. "We must tell Death. We have to tell him right now if there's any chance of saving her."

"Why is Leyun hunting her?"

"To place her back in the Neylka. To recycle her properly this time," Bast chokes. "But that's not what I want for her. She deserves freedom, just as you and I have gotten to enjoy. She deserves to remember who she is, not have that robbed of her before she's had a chance to live!" Bast balls up her fists and clenches her teeth. "If I could fight the Neylka I would."

Choking on her fury, she tries to find peace by steadying her breathing. Terrence watches her close her eyes and tilt her head to the sky.

"I don't have time to ground myself fully. We have to hurry." She turns tear-filled eyes to him. "How averse are you to seeing your former boss so soon? You don't have to go with me if you don't want. Truthfully, there's not much I can do besides deliver the message. I'm helpless to defeat Leyun," Bast confesses. "Her magic is so raw and powerful. The most I can do is help Clarisse evade her, if it's not too late."

Terrence steps forward and cups Bast's chin in his hand. "I will not let you handle this alone, Bast. I will go with you. Death be damned, you are my Lafura, and I am indebted to you for helping me today. Father Simmons was no small feat, and clearly, Leyun wanted some justice done for her, even if it was in her own savage way."

Bast's eyes gleam. "I'm not prepared to forgive the beast until I see her turn to save Clarisse."

Terrence nods. "Of course. I was only saying… the enemy of your enemy is your friend and what not. At least in practice… for specific circumstances." Terrence holds out his hands, hoping Bast doesn't take his rationale the wrong way.

She rolls her eyes and motions for him to follow.

As she opens a doorway to Tyrladan, he swallows the dread building in his throat. He's not ready to face Death, but he's ready to take on life anew with Bast. If that means facing off with the head Reaper, he's more than equipped.

REBORN

Clarisse

Opening her eyes, Clarisse realizes she's been asleep on Leyun's back for quite some time. Her body aches from the odd position astride the unicorn's back. Bone-deep exhaustion and Leyun's magic kept her pinned for the strange ride, lulling her to sleep. Taking a deep breath, she tries to remain calm, knowing the creature dragging her along can't force her to end her existence as she knows it. *I have the power over that choice, not her.*

Turning back, she sees that Kreyuhl is still chasing dutifully after her. To her surprise, his face is not awash with fear as her own heart is. He seems almost calm.

"Something isn't right, Clarisse," he speaks into her head. *"Leyun and I spoke while you slept. She's not taking us to the Neylka for the reasons you think."*

Accepting his words proves difficult with sleep still clouding her mind. Blinking, she tries again to understand what she just heard. The nervousness from earlier boils to the surface to overpower her raw fear. This is a different kind of trepidation—one that snakes its way through your core and eats you alive from the inside slowly, like a roast turning on a spit over the fire.

Sweat breaks out along her hairline and goosebumps ripple along her skin. "Leyun," Clarisse croaks, "where are we going? And how did you manage to dupe Kreyuhl into thinking you're here to help?"

Slowing to a trot, Leyun's bouncing frame sends Clarisse hurtling from her back and onto the ground. She slides through the dirt face first; the long, tall blades of grass that stand at attention from somewhere in Yehta slice her face. Clarisse knows by the three suns that they haven't reached the Neylka. Groaning as she stands, she wonders why Leyun hasn't taken her there and why she released her with no argument.

Leyun trots back to face her. *"I'm not letting you go. I'm stopping so I can explain myself. Let me ask you, other than that one tiny bite I took, what have I come to talk to you about each time I've visited you? Have I ever said anything about taking you to be recycled? Kreyuhl and I spoke, and he said you believe I'm only chasing you to carry you to the Neylka to end your existence as it presently stands. Is that correct?"*

Shaking, Clarisse nods. Leyun's eyes are like violent, silver daggers. She fears she might be stabbed just from the anger simmering within them.

Leyun straightens, this time speaking out loud instead of inside Clarisse's mind. "Who told you this? Or did you just assume it to be true? I want you to think for a moment—*who* told you I was after you to drag you to the Neylka like it's a common recycling bin?"

Clarisse chews her lip and tries to remember where she first learned that Leyun was hunting her. A block of ice settles in her stomach as she remembers, for the first time in ages, that it was Fal who first told her Leyun was hunting her.

"Does this have something to do with the unsettling feeling I had about Fal the last time I met with her? About... about... how I felt she was hiding something?"

"Clarisse, Fal is in league with your former husband. *They* want you recycled. Not me. And for some ungodly reason, they think I would drag you into the Neylka to have you erased. Fal can't read your path. To her, you are an abomination and have no place here in the Afterlife. She can't trace you, which means she has no power over you. And your husband... Well, you already know things didn't end well with him."

Shivering, Clarisse feels like her chest might explode from the rage and terror coursing through her. *Do I believe Leyun? Is she trying to trick me?*

"How do I know you're telling the truth? And why wouldn't my husband want me to come back? Why does it matter to him what I do?"

Leyun's unsettling eyes shine in the light of the three suns. "I don't know about your husband's plan; I just know Fal is in league with him. I am unsure of his motivations, but I sense great darkness. Clarisse, there are things you still don't know. Things that have yet to be revealed. Until such a time, unfortunately you're just going to have to trust me. There's no way I'm letting you slip away from me now. Not when we're this close."

Clarisse's mind starts to clear as irritation sets in. "Close to what? I'm tired of people not explaining things to me. I'm tired of being overwhelmed and not remembering who I am and having people just assume that I can catch on and carry on like it's nothing!" Clarisse is yelling, but she's not about to stop. Hot tears pour down her cheeks, but she doesn't wipe them away.

Kreyuhl sidles closer and nestles his head in her hair. His soothing magic wraps around her soul and squeezes tight. *"Breathe, Clarisse. I'm here with you. I won't let anyone hurt you. Just hear her out, okay? You don't have to understand everything right now."*

But I'm tired of being in the dark, Kreyuhl. I want to understand. Why can't I remember? Why is my memory so messed up? Why do I struggle to understand the most basic things or use my magic without being so tired all the time?

"Because you're not whole, Clarisse. You never were," Leyun sighs. *"I know this because I'm not whole, either. You're my missing half."*

How can you say that? Clarisse's fists shake. *How can you claim that you're the missing part of me and expect me to believe it? What? Are you saying not all of me came back out at once? How long have you lived without me? Why didn't you find me sooner?*

Clarisse chokes at this thought. *If I'm somehow a part of you, why didn't you come to rescue me? Why don't you know about my memories? Why aren't you tied to Death like I am? Is he your Lafura, too? Does he know?*

Sighing, Leyun approaches her. Without thinking, Clarisse takes a step back before tumbling to the ground. Kreyuhl's tail darts out to break her fall. Leyun leans forward and tips her horn to Clarisse's hand before she can rip herself away. As if summoned, Clarisse's stars stream out of her skin.

"*Magic!*" they whisper. "*Our magic.*"

Stars erupt from Leyun's body to shower the sky with blinding, bright yellow lights. Clarisse squints, afraid to face the brilliance of her own magic. Warmth spreads through Clarisse's veins, invading every crevice of her being. Memories begin to flood through her, passing through her skin and tracing her body like a map, full of all the answers she's ever needed. While some secrets remain, for the first time, she feels… *charged.*

I am a being of light.

Closing her eyes, she lets the power course through her. She wonders if Death can feel her tug at their bond. She doesn't feel anything in return, but she's hopeful all the same.

I want him to feel how strong I am.

Memories of a blank, white expanse haunt her—memories that are not hers, but hers all the same. Years and years of galloping with no direction and nowhere to go. All come flooding back.

I am Leyun.

"*Reborn.*"

Clarisse screams and her body convulses as the lights glow brighter. As her memories meld with Leyun's, the creature emits an agonizing shriek as she's consumed by the memories of being beaten, burned, and whipped for possessing magic. Years of being rejected and outcast and overlooked arc between the two, leaving raw devastation in their wake.

"*I am you.*"

And I am you.

It passes as quickly as it began, and a serene ocean of security laps through her blood and calls Clarisse back to Yehta.

"*And so you've been recycled,*" Kreyuhl croons.

A jolt of realization passes through Clarisse. *This entire ordeal was intended to make me whole again?*

When she looks up, Leyun is gone. Looking down at her palms, she sees that the mark Leyun left is brighter now—it glimmers in the sunlight as dusk begins to settle in the crook of the horizon. A blazing pain sears her forehead. Conjuring a mirror, she notes a bright white star where a horn might sit is emblazoned on her forehead.

Perhaps Leyun is the picture of my soul, as Death's is the wolf? Yes... this seems right.

Clarisse stretches out, letting her limbs lengthen and her shape change. When she looks back in the mirror, she is faced with the magical beast that so haunted her. The image leaves her breathless. She shakes a mane that burns golden in the light. A whispering breath passes through her.

"So... Fal wished to have me erased? Instead, I have been made whole." Clarisse chuckles. "Pity the fool who thought they could stamp me out or make me forget. And pity my poor husband, who still can't be rid of me."

Something about this thought doesn't seem right. Something lingers at the edge of her memory, but it's not enough to hold her up anymore. Instead, she smiles. Turning to Kreyuhl, she laughs. "I suppose we're more alike than you thought, my friend."

Kreyuhl chirps, happiness evident in his tone.

Surprised, she asks, *So you knew this whole time?"*

"My magic was not enough on its own to help you remember who you were. That's not correct for a familiar; nor is it normal for a familiar to forget so much. But I am glad to report that now, I remember quite a bit more. You are a goddess of the stars and light. Henceforth, your name is Leyun. You have been reborn. You may never remember all of who you once were, but who you are now *is what matters. And now, you may fully wield your magic. I can already feel the power pulsating from you. It is ready to recognize what you are. Who* you *are."*

Leyun is pleased to hear Kreyuhl speak this way. He sounds more... together.

Did I really order that justice be taken out for myself? The memory of Terrence taking the acorn makes her chuckle.

"You dealt Father Simmons the chains that pulled him into Hell."

Leyun lets a few fresh tears fall. *Does that mean I won?*

Kreyuhl gives a pleased hiss. *"In fact... you did, Clarisse – I mean, Leyun. You won."*

Will Death be mad at me?

"No, I don't think he will." Kreyuhl sighs. *"I do think you need to return to him, though. I sense a disturbance to which we must attend."*

She cocks her head to the side, startled by the mane that trickles into her eyes. Being a unicorn will take some getting used to. *Disturbance?* An unsettling feeling of dread passes through her connection with Kreyuhl and she pauses. *"Does this have to do with Fal? Does she think she's successfully sent me off to my doom?"*

Kreyuhl nods. *"If you don't return to your Lafura soon, he has the grounds and means to erase her. Murdering someone's Lafura is considered high treason, and he is a stickler for justice... in Tyrladan, at least. The laws are his here, as much as they are Fal's. We might want to stop the impending doom that will settle over the Afterlife before it spirals out of control."*

As much as Leyun wants to allow Death to seek his revenge, she knows it wouldn't be wise.

"Do you remember the way we came?" Leyun asks. *"I was asleep for most of the ride."*

Kreyuhl blinks. *"Follow me. And be quick. We don't have much time."*

Leyun sets aside her worries and focuses on charging ahead as Kreyuhl takes off for her corner of Yehta. She hopes they make it in time.

Besides, she thinks, *I have to tell him I'm whole again. I won.*

THE END

The Tales of the Selyento
continues with:

The Game of Gods and Stars

THE CURRENT MANSALO CODEX

Grammar Rules

No conjugation for verbs—context alone determines how a verb is used.

‘ attached to a phrase indicates an understood you. (Either in command or regular conversation).

Qualities of possession (their, your, etc.) should be conjoined with the objects they possess.

A

    Ahklena: To redo/to relive. (Magical) The process of reliving your life after you have died (or during).
    Ahleh: Return
    Ahlura: Magic
    Aleh Awlo: South West
    Alti: Mountain
    Altiya: Heaven/Elysium

Adan: Live/life (command, action, being, etc.)
Arke: Happy

B

Barulatye: Book
BarulatyeSelben: Book of the Gods
Ben: Soul
Bendala: Binding of souls
Bur: East

C

Chella: Open/to open

D

Dya: Dream
DyaChella: To revisit a dream, either yours or someone else's (context dependent)

F

Fleckerleke: Harsh swear word–interpret it as you will
Fal: Fate
Falme: Fate string

K

Kohlu: Tartarus
Kreyuhl: The Passing Point/Place (The garden of the Selyento)

L

Lafura: Soul Mate (of the chosen variety)
Lafuran: Soul mates (plural)
Li: Water

Lia: Rain

Lo: Language/to be of something

M

Mansa: War

Ma: You

Mar: Your

Me: String

Marlo: Day

N

Na: Death (the concept, not the creature)

Narlasha: Special instrument in Tyrladan. Strings made of light that change with the time of day. Not playable at night. Brightness and tone of the strings rise and fall with the setting sun or sun(s), depending on where it is played in Tyrladan.

Neylka: Nothing (the nothingness between the worlds in the Afterlife)

P

Penda: North

R

Ralun: Minor Mansalo god of darkness (accomplice to Terrence)

Rashia: Squirrel

S

Sel: Music

Selben: Gods

Selbena: God

Selbeno: Goddess

Selyento: Tree of music Sira: Fire

Siralto: Goddess of Light

T

Thma: Gift
Toines: (Comparable to dollars—currency)
Tye: Paper
Tyrladan: Afterlife
Tryta: Darkness (the God)

U

Uht: Place

V

Velyasa: Window/portal

Y

Ya: To
Yehta: Limbo/purgatory

ACKNOWLEDGMENTS

I would like to express my sincere thanks to my editor, Stacy Sanford, for helping make this story tight and clean and the work I so desperately wanted it to be! I would also like to thank my cover artist, Lily Dormishev, for making this beautiful book shine. I would also like to thank my mother, my grandmother, my Popop, my Nana, and my grandfather, to whom this book is dedicated. I only wish he'd lived long enough to see Clarisse's story continue. I would also like to thank my friends, Rachel and Journey, for being my sounding board through these difficult times. Last but not least, I would like to thank my lovely Cheryl for being the most wonderful "literary agent" a girl could hope for and, most importantly, such a wonderful friend. I want my readers to know that, above all, it really does take a village; who you surround yourself with absolutely can make all the difference.

AUTHOR'S NOTE

Thank you again for taking the time to read *Beyond the Stars*. The story is far from over and will continue in book 3, The Game of Gods and Stars! If you want to be updated first for when it will be released, special sneak peaks, and fun short stories in the meantime, sign up for my mailing list and follow me on social media!

You can find all the links to these things by visiting:
www.linktr.ee/ErisMarriottAuthor

Lastly, if you would be so kind as to leave a review of what you thought, whether it be on Amazon, Goodreads, or whatever your preferred platform, that would be greatly appreciated! Reviews really help authors like me have our work be seen, as well as what we can do to improve!

---

www.erismarriottauthor.com
facebook.com/ErisMarriottAuthor
instagram.com/erismarriott

www.ingramcontent.com/pod-product-compliance
Lightning Source LLC
Chambersburg PA
CBHW030928210726
48290CB00007B/2117